"So I should try to get a hot blonde doctor in her early thirties?"

Her lips parted in surprise. He hadn't intended to describe her, at least not consciously. "Sorry," he said, clearing his throat. "I didn't mean..."

"Me?"

He forced himself to meet her eyes. "I believe this is what you call a Freudian slip."

Color rose to her cheeks at his rueful confession. The blush did nothing to detract from her beauty.

"I'm sure you wouldn't want to—"

"Definitely not."

They were agreed then. She'd rather jump off a bridge than pretend to be his wife, and he shouldn't have implied that she'd be perfect for the role, because she wasn't remotely qualified. He'd like to have her in his bed, but that was a different thing and also not happening. Nothing was happening.

Nothing whatsoever.

INFILTRATION RESCUE

Susan Cliff

HARLEQUIN
ROMANTIC
SUSPENSE

HARLEQUIN®
ROMANTIC SUSPENSE™

Recycling programs
for this product may
not exist in your area.

ISBN-13: 978-1-335-62655-4

Infiltration Rescue

Copyright © 2020 by Susan Cliff

This edition published by arrangement with Harlequin Books S.A.

For questions and comments about the quality of this book,
please contact us at CustomerService@Harlequin.com.

Harlequin Enterprises ULC
22 Adelaide St. West, 40th Floor
Toronto, Ontario M5H 4E3, Canada
www.Harlequin.com

Printed in U.S.A.

Susan Cliff is a longtime romance reader, part-time writer and full-time California girl. She loves to daydream about exciting adventures in exotic locales. Her books feature heartfelt romance, gripping suspense and true-to-life characters. Get swept away with Susan Cliff!

Books by Susan Cliff

Harlequin Romantic Suspense

Witness on the Run
Infiltration Rescue

Team Twelve

Navy SEAL Rescue
Stranded with the Navy SEAL

Chapter 1

Avery Samuels rested her forehead against the steering wheel and groaned.

It had been a hell of a day. A fifteen-year-old boy had come to school with a handgun. His actions had resulted in a campus lockdown, followed by an evacuation of students and staff. As the district psychologist, Avery was trained to handle intense situations, and to counsel students in the aftermath of traumatic events. She'd listened to frantic teens and parents while the young offender got dragged away in handcuffs. There would be more fallout tomorrow, but at least the incident hadn't ended in bloodshed.

Trying to think positively, she gathered her belongings from the passenger seat. Rain pattered against the corrugated aluminum rooftop of the carport. It made a pleasant melody that neither lifted her spirits nor pummeled them further. Perhaps a cup of tea would do the trick. A cup of tea, some hot soup, cozy slippers. She felt a pang of sorrow for Smoke, who wouldn't be there to greet her at the doorway. Her phone chimed inside her purse, reminding her of a text she'd ignored earlier. She'd been too busy to read it, much less respond. Retrieving the device, she checked the screen.

A man named Agent Diaz is on his way to see you. Please talk to him.

Avery frowned at the message from her aunt Ruth, who wasn't really her aunt. She'd taken Avery in at thirteen and raised her like a daughter. They weren't related by blood, but they were still close.

Avery put her phone back in her purse and exited the vehicle. She'd call Ruth as soon as she got out of the rain. She couldn't imagine why Ruth wanted her to speak to an insurance agent—on a stormy evening, no less, after regular business hours. Avery didn't like strangers coming to her home. Ruth knew that better than anyone.

Avery held her jacket over her head and made a mad dash from the carport to her upper-floor apartment. As she climbed the steps, she became aware of two figures on the landing. She didn't see them until she'd almost reached her door. She'd been distracted by the challenge of navigating wet stairs in high heels, her vision obscured by rain, and the edges of her jacket. There also wasn't much daylight left, at dusk.

She froze at the sound of a male voice. He gave an ordinary greeting, nonthreatening, but she hadn't expected anyone to be standing there. His physical presence added to her unease. He was a dark shadow of a man, tall and broad-shouldered. Although she couldn't see his face in the gloom, she knew he was a stranger. She faltered on the next step and lost her footing. She might have tumbled over the railing if the man hadn't reached out to steady her. He grasped her elbow, quick as lightning. He'd probably saved her from a fall, but she didn't thank him for the courtesy. She was too stunned by his speed and strength. His unyielding grip manacled her forearm, holding her prisoner.

The contact triggered something inside her, something twisted and tortured and long-buried. Adrenaline surged in her bloodstream. She forgot about Ruth and the insurance issue. She forgot about the stressful day at work, and her plans for a quiet evening. Her thoughts raced to her worst-nightmare scenario:

They'd found her. After all these years, they'd found her.

In her mind's eye, she saw flashes of her childhood home. She remembered the rituals, the punishments. The horrors she'd escaped from. They couldn't take her back there. Not without a fight. She reset her feet on the slippery landing, bracing for a struggle. She'd protect her freedom with whatever means necessary.

Instead of hauling her away, the man released her arm. "Sorry," he said in an even tone. "I didn't mean to startle you."

He had a faint Spanish accent. It was quite pleasant, really. Avery's jacket slid from her slack hand, but she managed to hang on to her purse and briefcase. She glanced from the shadow-man to his less intimidating companion. A trim woman in her fifties stood at his elbow. They were both wearing raincoats over business attire.

These people weren't from the cult. They were *insurance agents*.

Avery wilted against the railing, weak with relief. Laughter bubbled from her lips. She was still in a state of panic, her pulse pounding in her ears. She just needed a moment to collect herself. The deluge continued, unabated. The man studied her with interest. Rain plastered her hair to her head as she stared back at him. He looked like a professional. Even so, he didn't fit her mental picture of an insurance salesman. He was too alert, too imposing. There was nothing jovial or benign about his expression.

The woman at his side flashed a badge on her waistband. "I'm Special Agent Richards. This is Special Agent Diaz. We're with the Federal Bureau of Investigation."

Avery blinked a few times as she digested the information. They were *FBI* agents. No wonder they were here after hours, standing in the rain with somber faces. She was afraid to ask what they wanted. Her tension resurged, making her shiver.

Special Agent Diaz spoke next. "Are you Avery Samuels?"

"Yes."

"We have some questions for you."

Special Agent Richards tilted her head toward the door. "Inside, if you don't mind."

Prompted into motion, Avery retrieved her jacket and fumbled for her keys. She entered the security code as soon as she stepped inside. They ventured in after her. She set her belongings on the entry table, feeling self-conscious. She must look like a drowned rat with her wet hair and smudged makeup. At least her apartment was presentable. She kept it tidy, even though she rarely entertained visitors. When she gestured at the coatrack, they hung up their dripping jackets next to hers.

"What's this about?" she asked, swallowing hard.

"It's about The Haven," Diaz replied.

Although she'd suspected as much, hearing the words spoken out loud had a chilling effect. She balled her hands into fists, uncertain. She never talked about the cult. She wasn't in contact with anyone from the commune. She'd left that life behind, but the fear had stayed with her. A part of her had always known her past would catch up to her. She just hadn't expected it to arrive on her doorstep in the middle of a storm.

She smoothed her dripping hair and tried to stay calm. Aunt Ruth wanted her to talk to these people. Playing dumb wasn't Avery's strong suit, and lying to the FBI was a crime, so she gestured toward the living room. She would listen to their questions. When they found out how little she knew, they'd leave.

"Have a seat," she said.

Special Agent Diaz waited for Avery and his partner to precede him. Avery sat down in her favorite reading chair. Richards got settled on the couch. Diaz took the space next to her, directly across from Avery.

She folded her hands in her lap. A multicolored blanket she'd knitted herself was draped over the side of the chair. She wished she could hide underneath it. Instead of dragging the cozy fabric over her trembling form, she focused on Special Agent Diaz.

He was nice to look at, if you liked rawboned men with big hands. She imagined most women did. He was ruggedly attractive, with hardened features that hinted at outdoor pursuits. His hair was dark and close-cropped, his collar damp. If his accent wasn't enough to stir interest, the rest of him would do it. She was too nervous to examine his physique in detail, but she got the impression of a lean build. She guessed he was in his late thirties, younger than Richards by at least a decade. Richards was probably his superior, but she didn't take the lead. The older woman seemed to be waiting for him to speak.

Diaz cleared his throat before he began. "I'm working with the Department of Homeland Security on a domestic terrorism investigation. There was an attack on FBI personnel by an underground militia known as the White Army. It's a white nationalist group with religious ties. We believe they were organized by the leader of The Haven."

Avery couldn't hide her trepidation. This was worse than she'd thought. The cult leader wasn't just preying on the innocent women and children under his wing. He was targeting law enforcement outside the commune. The FBI wouldn't turn a blind eye on a terrorist attack. "What do you want from me?"

"We need information," he said, leaning forward. "We know almost nothing about the cult or its practices. We've only recently learned of its existence."

"Why do you think I can help you?"

"You're the only former member we've been able to locate."

"Who told you I was a member?"

"Weren't you?"

Avery turned her attention to Richards. "Are you his boss?"

"I'm a liaison from the Portland office," Richards said. "Investigators from out of state are required to coordinate with local law enforcement before they conduct interviews. He also thought you might feel more comfortable with a female agent present."

Diaz didn't deny the claim. His instincts were correct; Avery wouldn't have let him inside her apartment if he'd come alone. She was wary of strangers, especially male strangers. Richards's age and supervisory attitude helped. She had the air of an experienced matriarch who didn't miss anything.

"How did you find me?" she asked him.

"I searched for adolescent wards of the state in this area. Your file mentioned a possible religious upbringing and unknown parentage. It's unusual."

"It's also sealed."

"I got a court order," Diaz said.

Avery could connect the dots from there. He'd read her file and gone to Ruth for more information. Avery had changed her name after she'd reached adulthood, so he wouldn't have been able to track her down without speaking to her "aunt" first. Ruth was the only one who could tell him about Avery's strange origins. Ruth had trusted Diaz enough to share Avery's most closely guarded secret.

Avery, however, did not trust him. She had a lot to lose by getting involved as a witness. She didn't want to testify in court or become a target for a right-wing militia. And what relevant information could she offer at this point? She hadn't been near the commune in twenty years. She didn't even know its exact location.

"I was a child when I left," she said. "My memories are…incomplete."

Diaz's gaze searched hers. "According to the sheriff's report, you were thirteen. Old enough to survive in the woods on your own for several weeks. You must have walked a hundred miles, barefoot."

She rose abruptly, her stomach queasy. She didn't want to relive those days. She had no idea how far she'd walked, or how long she'd been living like an animal in the wilderness. Sleeping in the dirt. Eating bugs. "I need to make some tea."

He settled back against the couch, unperturbed. "Take all the time you need."

Richards started scrolling through her phone. It occurred to Avery that she should call someone to check their credentials. She couldn't tell if they were legit by looking at them. Confirming their identities seemed wise before she agreed to share personal details. She crossed the room and dug her phone out of her purse. The screen showed another text message notification. It was Ruth again, asking if Avery was okay.

She wasn't okay. She was on the verge of a meltdown. She had to tell two strangers about her disturbing childhood, because Ruth had directed them to her. Avery felt obligated to assist the investigation. Turning them away would be cowardly, and it went against her code of ethics. Maybe she could help disband the cult, and free its members from their psychological prison. Innocent lives were at stake.

She always encouraged the young people she worked with to talk about traumatic events. She asked them to share their feelings and allow themselves to be vulnerable. It was a healthy part of the grieving process. But this physician had never been able to heal herself.

After she put the teapot on the stove, and turned up the heat on the thermostat, she placed a call to the local FBI field office. She had to wait several minutes to speak with a real person. The staff member asked for badge numbers, which Richards and Diaz recited dutifully. They didn't seem fazed by Avery's diligence. The man on the phone identified both agents as genuine. As proof, he sent Avery a temporary text message with photo IDs attached. Avery studied an official picture of Diaz in a dark suit, holding his badge up. His first name was Nicolas. He looked younger, but not lighter of spirit. The photo stayed on her screen for about thirty seconds before it disappeared.

The teapot whistled, letting off steam. She fixed a tray with three mugs. Richards accepted a cup. Diaz declined. A manila folder had been placed on the surface of the table, along with a pen. Avery had to sign an agreement to be interviewed. She was assured that her statement would be kept confidential.

Diaz had an app on his phone to record their conversation. He also took out a writing pad to take notes by hand. He started by identifying himself, Special Agent Richards and Avery. She reached for the wool blanket and wrapped it around her body. Her fingers shook with apprehension.

"Do you have any questions before we begin?" Diaz asked.

"Yes. How did you know I walked a hundred miles?"

He removed a printed map from the folder. "According to our intelligence, the commune is off the grid in an undeveloped area of Northern California." There was a mark on the spot. Diaz moved his fingertip north. "You turned up here, in Lorella, Oregon."

Avery examined the distance. She hadn't flown over those mountains. She'd hiked along trails and back roads when she could. When she couldn't, she'd trekked through forests with thorny underbrush. "I had shoes."

"Pardon?"

"I had shoes," she said, moistening her lips. "I wore them until they fell apart. I wasn't barefoot until the end."

He lifted his gaze from the map. "Is that why you stopped in Lorella?"

She hadn't stopped so much as she'd been caught raiding Ruth's garden, but she didn't say that. The memory made her stomach queasy. She'd gotten sick on summer squash and couldn't move. Ruth had found her curled up in a sunflower patch, half-conscious.

"There are a dozen small towns between the commune and Oregon," he said. "You didn't seek help in any of them."

"I wanted to leave California."

"Why?"

"I thought Oregon was a different country, and that I'd be safe if I crossed the border." It was an embarrassing admission, revealing the extreme isolation and ignorance she'd been kept in. Neither Diaz nor Richards appeared surprised by it.

Diaz rifled through the papers under the map. He had several color photographs of varying quality. The man in the first picture caused Avery's blood to run cold. "Do you know who this is?"

She took another sip of tea before answering. The cult leader had more gray in his hair and beard, but she'd recognize him anywhere. She still had nightmares of being his child bride. "It's Father Jeff."

"What can you tell us about him?"

"He's the leader of The Haven. The people worship him like a god."

Diaz showed her another photo. "And this?"

Avery studied the bespectacled young man with black hair and serious eyes. He looked like the Father Jeff she'd known twenty years ago. Jeff had two sons around Avery's age, by two different wives. Sister wives. "It looks like one of Jeff's sons. Jonah."

The next photo depicted a member of Jeff's militia. He was wearing an army jacket, holding an AR-15. His belligerent scowl triggered Avery's memory. "That's Jeremiah," she said. "I went to school with him."

"But not Jonah?"

"Jonah had private lessons, separate from the rest of the children. Father Jeff said he was gifted."

"Jeremiah wasn't?"

"No. He had behavior problems. Always in trouble."

"Did he get punished?"

She returned the photo to the stack. Although punishments for disobedience had been severe in the commune, she didn't recall Jeremiah being forced to kneel in the corner or hit with a switch. As the leader's first-born son, he was given free rein. Avery had once spent an evening locked in the storm cellar for shoving Jeremiah after he'd pulled on her braids. The experience had taught her to endure his abuse without complaint.

It was a sad lesson, one of many in her childhood, but it had a silver lining. The resentment she'd carried over the incident had given fuel to her rebellion. Without Jeremiah's bullying, and those hours in the dark, tomb-like space, she wouldn't have drummed up the courage to escape. The cellar story was unpleasant, and indicative of the emotional torment she'd been subjected to. Even so, it paled in comparison with the events surrounding her mother's death. She didn't know if she was capable of recounting that tale.

"Ms. Samuels?" Diaz prompted.

"I don't remember him being punished," she said. "He was a year older, and we weren't in the same classes. Boys and girls were separated."

"How was the community structured outside of school?"

She set her tea aside, thinking. "It was highly gendered. Ruled by male elders. Women were expected to stay home and care for children. Some girls were chosen as brides as soon as they turned fourteen. Others were allowed to wait."

"Did they marry boys their age?"

"No, they didn't. Boys had to work in a trade for fourteen years before they became eligible for marriage. The youngest husbands were twenty-eight. After fourteen more years, they could ask for a second wife, but not everyone earned this honor. It was reserved for Father Jeff's most loyal followers."

"How many wives did he have?"

"Three, when I left."

"At thirteen."

"Yes."

"Were you chosen as a bride?"

"I might have been, if I'd stayed."

"Is that what prompted your decision to leave?"

She glanced at Richards, moistening her lips.

Diaz interpreted her reluctance clearly. "Would you rather continue without me? I can leave the room."

"No," Avery said. He was a good interviewer, and the warmer personality of the two. Her reticence had little to do with him, though she found it difficult to meet his eyes. They were too intense, too arresting. She also didn't want to continue, period. She wouldn't feel comfortable talking about this to anyone. "I ran away for two reasons. First, because I didn't want to get married at fourteen. Father Jeff had already told my stepfather that I'd become a bride on my birthday, to whomever he selected as my husband."

"What did your stepfather say?"

"Nothing. He was okay with it, but my mother cried when she found out. She thought I was too young. She begged him to ask Father Jeff to wait another year."

"Did he?"

"No."

"She accepted his decision?"

"No, she didn't," Avery admitted. "She talked about running away as soon as the weather cleared. Then she got pregnant, after a series of miscarriages. She wasn't in any position to leave with me, and I wouldn't go on my own."

"What specific events led to your escape?" Diaz asked.

"My mom went into labor that summer, a month before her due date. The midwife came to help. I knew something was wrong, but I wasn't allowed in the room. I could hear her screaming." She exhaled a ragged breath, blinking rapidly. "Sorry."

"Don't be," he said. "Take your time."

After a short pause, she continued. "My stepfather slapped me for getting hysterical. He told me to pray for her, so I did. I prayed for hours." She omitted the visit by Father Jeff, who'd attempted to console her in the creepiest manner possible. "When they finally let me see her, it was too late."

Neither Richards nor Diaz expressed any condolences. Avery appreciated their silence while she regained her composure. Talking about her mother's death hadn't torn her apart as much as she'd expected, but she had a lot of practice holding her emotions at bay. She pushed past the pain in her chest and forced the words out. "I asked to be alone with her to say goodbye. Then I climbed out the window and started running. I thought I'd be killed if I got caught, but I didn't care. Death seemed better than staying in the commune and marrying an old man. So I jumped the fence and ran into the woods, as far as I could. I didn't have any food or water. I didn't even have a jacket. I almost gave up the first night."

"What kept you going?"

"Grief, I guess. Fear." Tears flooded her eyes, finally. Proof that she had real emotions. "Also, I was lost. I couldn't have found my way back if I wanted to."

Diaz offered her his handkerchief. It was an ordinary gray pocket square, nothing fancy. Richards's brow furrowed with disapproval, as if she thought he was overdoing the chivalry. Avery didn't agree. Touched by the gesture, she accepted the square of fabric.

"Was there a road?"

"There was a dirt road, only accessible by SUVs. I stayed far away from it because I could hear them looking for me. I headed east, toward the sunrise. Then I followed a creek alongside the highway. If I saw a person, I'd hide."

"What did you drink?"

"I stole a jug from a construction site and filled it up wherever I could." She didn't say what she'd eaten, because she couldn't bear to think about it. "By the time I got to Oregon, I was starving. I raided Ruth's garden one afternoon. I didn't even wait until dark."

"She gave us a picture of you," Diaz said, reaching into the file folder.

Avery hadn't seen the photo before. She was in a hospital bed, eyes closed, with an IV in her thin arm. She looked wild and emaciated. Her hair was tangled with debris, her face dirty. Although she didn't recognize herself in the photo, she felt exposed by it all the same. She felt like an oddity to be studied by scientists. A feral creature. No wonder Ruth had taken her in. She'd always had a soft spot for wounded animals.

Avery turned the picture facedown and slid it across

the table. Now it was impossible to meet Diaz's eyes. She didn't know why she felt so ashamed. It wasn't her fault that she'd been a victim of childhood trauma. She vastly preferred being on the other side of the couch, doing the psychoanalyzing.

Diaz tucked away the photo without comment. Maybe he admired her courage, but what she saw in the image wasn't that. It was weakness and vulnerability. She couldn't confront the visual evidence of her worst experience, even if it had resulted in a triumph of sorts. She'd escaped the cult, against all odds. But she'd also left her heart behind.

"Are we finished?" she asked in a light tone.

"Not quite," Diaz said.

She furrowed a hand through her still-damp hair. "I'm sorry, but it's been a long day, and I have some work to catch up on."

A muscle in his jaw flexed, drawing her attention to the fine grains of stubble there. "I wish I could offer to come back at a more convenient time. Unfortunately, I have to return to Sacramento tomorrow morning to attend a colleague's funeral."

Avery felt a stab of sympathy. "My condolences."

Diaz inclined his head in acknowledgment.

"Was he killed in the line of duty?"

"Yes. He was shot by a member of Silva's militia."

Her stomach fluttered with unease. No wonder Diaz was on a tear to locate cult members and ferret out information. He had a fallen comrade to avenge, and a narrow window of opportunity to complete this interview.

Diaz leaned forward to press his advantage. "This investigation is of grave importance, Ms. Samuels. I'd ap-

preciate your cooperation. I have a lot of questions, and
you might be the only person who knows the answers."

"I've already told you everything I remember."

"I don't believe that."

Her lips parted in surprise. He'd been polite and
friendly, thus far. She'd expected him to listen to her
story, make the appropriate noises and go away. It hadn't
occurred to her that he'd accuse her of withholding information.

She rose to her feet abruptly. "I haven't eaten all day."

Diaz glanced at Richards, who whipped out her
phone. "I'll order pizza. Why don't we take a break
and regroup?"

Avery didn't argue, though she had no desire to dine
with them. She realized she still had Diaz's handkerchief crushed in her hand. She tossed it on the coffee
table and strode down the hall, into the bathroom. She
stared at her reflection in the mirror, trying to summon
a cool, confident expression.

Instead she saw the wild, desperate girl from the
photo, her gaunt features superimposed over Avery's.

Chapter 2

Nick tucked away his pocket square and rose to his feet.

He rotated his head, trying to relieve some tension. He'd caught the red-eye to Portland this morning, and he'd spent most of the day in the passenger seat of Richards's government-issued sedan. Although he was no stranger to long hours in cramped spaces, he was wound up pretty tight right now. He needed an extended session in the gym, a stiff drink and some sweaty, anonymous sex to take the edge off.

That last part was wishful thinking. He'd settle for a full night's sleep. Actually, he'd prefer it, because he was exhausted. He knew he'd been working too much when going to bed early appealed to him more than getting lucky, even after a long drought.

Richards ordered a couple of pizzas while Samuels was in the bathroom. Nick's visit with Ruth Garrison in Lorella had felt like a huge break. He'd almost given up on finding a former Haven member to interview. Now that he had one in his sights, he couldn't afford to lose her, and his instincts told him he was on the verge.

Richards gave him an assessing glance as she set her phone aside. She was an experienced agent and a smart liaison. She'd let him take the lead all day, supervising rather than participating, and he liked that. He hadn't needed her assistance—until now. He gestured for her to join him in the corner of the room for a quick conference.

"Was I too harsh?" he asked quietly.

"No. You were fine."

"I think she's holding back."

"Let her."

He crossed his arms over his chest. "What do you mean, let her?"

"If she's not comfortable with personal questions, don't ask them. You don't need her to recount every painful experience."

Nick wanted to know if someone had abused her, so he could prosecute the sick bastard. He wanted to take down Silva, his militia and the entire community of backwoods, brainwashed child molesters.

Richards put a hand on his forearm. "Slow down and focus on what you can get, which is general information about the commune and its members. Try treating her like a consultant, instead of a victim."

Nick massaged the nape of his neck, nodding his agreement. Richards seemed confident in her assessment, and he believed in female intuition. Most FBI agents were men, and not all of them had the communication skills to be successful interviewers. The job required listening to subtext and interpreting body language. Women were often better at that. They could evaluate emotional responses and read facial expressions with greater accuracy. Nick still wasn't sure where he'd gone wrong with Avery Samuels. She hadn't been eager to talk about her past, obviously. Then the hospital photo had upset her. He'd thought the image would spark her memories, not shut them down.

Getting personal wasn't working. Richards had that right.

He also had to admit he'd been rattled by the pretty psychologist from the start. When he'd grasped her elbow to prevent her from falling on the stairs, and she'd gazed up at him with trepidation, he'd been thunderstruck.

He didn't understand his reaction. Her beauty hit him like a punch in the gut, but he'd seen beautiful women before. She was a blue-eyed blonde, pale-skinned and stylishly dressed, with a smattering of freckles across her nose. He didn't favor blondes in particular. He liked nice curves, and she had those, but he'd hardly noticed her figure. He was too captivated by her rain-splattered face.

Good looks alone weren't enough to send him into a stupor, so he figured there was something else at play. He'd felt a magnetic pull that went deeper than surface attraction. Which was odd, because she'd clearly been repelled by him, at first glance. He'd noted her stance. She'd been ready to fight him.

Richards had introduced them while he pulled himself together. It had taken several minutes to regulate his heartbeat. He'd tried not to stare, because it wasn't professional to ogle an interviewee. It certainly wouldn't win her trust or put her at ease.

Samuels returned to the living room now, her expression subdued. She'd put on a soft cardigan and black-framed reading glasses. She'd also exchanged her fashionable heels for a pair of fuzzy slippers. She looked adorable, if a bit miffed by his parting insinuation that she wasn't telling him the whole story.

"I ordered a large pepperoni and a large veggie," Richards said.

"Sounds good," Samuels replied, avoiding Nick's gaze. She seemed reluctant to sit down with him again.

Treat her like a consultant.

Nick picked up his file folder from the coffee table. He had aerial photos of the commune inside his briefcase, but he needed more space to display them. He approached the kitchen table. "Do you mind if I work here?"

"No."

"Feel free to get caught up on whatever you need to do," he said. "We can reconvene after the pizza's delivered."

Nick got busy arranging his images. She sat down at a computer desk and started typing. Richards gave him a nod of encouragement. He was on the right track. He couldn't force Ms. Samuels to answer his questions, but he could give her some breathing room. He hoped she'd cooperate, because she was his only source of information. He wished he had several days to work on her, instead of one night.

The pizza came while he organized his photos and jotted down a new list of questions. Samuels offered him a glass of *agua mineral*, which he accepted. The pizza boxes had been placed on the kitchen counter. He grabbed a paper plate and inhaled a couple of slices where he stood. Samuels's apartment was cozy and spotless. It looked like an Instagram layout, with perfectly coordinated furniture and warm accent colors. There were several framed photos hanging on the wall. One of Ruth in the garden. Two of a fluffy tabby that he hadn't seen any evidence of. A fourth of Samuels standing on a beach with a stunning dark-skinned woman. They were both smiling. It said Best Friends across the top.

There were no men in the pictures. No men in her life?

Samuels noticed him snooping, so he gestured toward the wall. "You have a cat?"

"Smoke died last month. Old age."

"Sorry to hear that," he said, and meant it. Nick hadn't expressed condolences about her mother's death, but he'd been in interview mode, and the incident was twenty years in the past. He'd also sensed that she didn't want to get too emotional. He could relate. He glanced around the apartment again, contemplative. There was an emptiness to it, despite the pleasant decor. Perhaps the cat had filled the space.

Samuels moved toward the dining table. She wanted to get this over with.

Nick was ready. He finished his last bite of pizza, wiped his mouth with a napkin and tossed his paper plate in the trash. They gathered in the kitchen area, which felt more casual than the living room. He took a seat across from Samuels and set his phone to Record while Richards lurked in the periphery.

"I'm interested in the daily operations of the commune," he said. "Can you identify any of these buildings, and tell me what they're used for?"

Samuels had no problem with this task. She pointed out the church, school and cafeteria. It was set up like a summer camp, with family cabins and communal areas. There was a playground, sports field and acres of farmland.

So far, so good.

"This building wasn't there before," she said, indicating Silva's compound. Her nails were short and painted with midnight-blue polish that accentuated her pale skin. The style struck him as sexy and modern, if a bit witchy.

"That's where Silva lives."

She flinched at the mention of the cult leader. "It looks like a fortress."

"Yes."

Frowning, she moved her fingertip to a cluster of cabins in the center of the commune. "He used to live here, near the church."

He wondered which cabin she'd lived in. "According to our intel, Jeff Silva stays in a separate compound with his wives and children. He visits The Haven, but he's not involved in its daily operations. He's become fixated on building his militia, and hatching terrorist plots, while Jonah manages the commune."

If she found the arrangement odd, she didn't comment. "What are you going to do with this information?"

He leaned back in his chair, weighing his response.

"If you had enough evidence to make an arrest, you wouldn't be here," she pointed out. "How does studying the commune help your investigation?"

"We tried getting to Silva by approaching him as an ally to his antigovernment cause. That ended in the death of an experienced undercover agent."

"A colleague of yours?"

"I knew him, yes."

"So now you're considering, what? Trying to infiltrate the cult?"

It was exactly what he intended, but he couldn't talk about the details. Also, he had no idea how he'd accomplish the task, or if he could get clearance for another undercover operation. "I'm just collecting intel," he said, keeping it vague. "The Haven doesn't have a website. They don't use technology. They're completely isolated. Which is why I need to collaborate with someone who's been inside."

She seemed to like this word, *collaborate*. It played to her strengths as a problem-solver. He didn't have photos of any individual members, other than Jeff and his sons. He asked her for the names of Silva's top followers. She recited at least a dozen before drawing a blank.

"Do you remember who did the farming?" he asked.

"The young men, mostly. They worked in the fields every summer."

"Who was in charge of the crops?"

"Brother Michael," she said, after a moment. "He was the head farmer."

Nick examined the fields again. Upon closer inspection, the crops didn't appear healthy or well-maintained. That could be a serious issue for a community that lived on food they grew themselves. He wrote down the name and circled it, pleased with their progress. Richards's advice had been spot-on.

"Where were you born?" Samuels asked him.

"Venezuela." Nick glanced up from his notebook. "Why?"

"I thought I heard an accent."

His brows rose in surprise. Most people didn't notice his accent, which was almost indiscernible these days. It tended to show up when he was exhausted, tongue-tied…or in the throes of passion. He couldn't remember the last time a woman had commented on it. "You have a good ear."

She studied him with interest. "How long have you lived here?"

"Twenty-five years."

"You came with your parents?"

"No."

She didn't press for the backstory, so he kept it to himself. He wasn't here for a personal analysis, though he wouldn't say no to a session on her couch. In his fantasy scenario, she didn't ask intrusive questions. They didn't talk at all.

He frowned at the direction of his thoughts. Imagining Ms. Samuels in a compromising position wasn't appropriate. She was examining his mouth, as if still pondering his accent. Her gaze lowered to his right hand, lightly gripping a pencil. When she moistened her lips, his pulse jumped with excitement.

Santa Maria.

He set aside his notebook, his neck hot. He needed to get a hold of himself. Actually, he needed to get out of here. According to his phone, two hours had elapsed since they'd had pizza. It was late, and he was losing focus.

"Can I email you the rest of my questions?" he asked. "I have to wrap this up."

"Sure," she said, seeming relieved. There were dark circles under her eyes. She looked like she needed a good night's sleep as much as he did, not a hot time in bed. He felt a stab of guilt for letting his imagination run wild.

He scrawled down her personal email and gathered his photos. The interview had gone well, despite the rough spots. He'd gained a wealth of information. He was reluctant to leave because there was so much more to learn. They'd barely scraped the surface. Instead of dwelling on what he was missing, he organized his files and put them away. Samuels stood by the door to see them out. They exchanged a polite handshake. Then he grabbed his jacket and stepped into the rainy night.

Richards walked toward her car, which was parked on the street nearby. He lifted his face to the sky and let the moisture cool his overheated skin. His neck muscles were still sore, his eyes grainy with fatigue. But he felt revitalized, rather than drained. He felt electric.

"You want me to take an Uber?" he asked, following Richards.

"Where's your hotel?"

He consulted his phone. "It's a mile from the field office."

"I'll drop you off. It's no trouble."

Shrugging, he climbed in the passenger seat. "Thanks for your help today."

"Just doing my job," she said.

"How did you know that would work? Treating her like a consultant?"

"I interviewed a detective once who'd been the victim of a home invasion robbery. It was difficult to get a detailed statement from him. He couldn't stand being on the other side of an investigation."

Nick mulled that over in silence. Some victims refused to talk, for a variety of reasons. Others were eager to make a statement. They wanted to be heard. They wanted justice. Samuels spent her days listening to troubled kids, helping them overcome trauma. She clearly preferred that to telling her own story.

"Are you thinking about going under?" Richards asked.

"Yes."

"How will you get in?"

"I don't know," he said. "They don't actively recruit, and my SAC might refuse to green-light another undercover op, considering how the other ended. But I'd like to submit a proposal and see what happens."

"Have you done that kind of work before?"

"Only short assignments. Nothing deep."

She was quiet for a moment. "You should be careful about approaching Samuels for a follow-up."

"Why is that?"

"She liked you."

He tried to look casually disinterested, while his heart was pumping out of his chest. "You think so?"

"Yes, and it could be a problem, especially if her feelings are reciprocated." She gave Nick a sideways glance that said she knew damned well this was the case. "You don't want to muddy the waters by getting involved with a contact."

He didn't bother saying that he couldn't get involved with Samuels from a distance. There were many ways to engage in sexual misconduct online. "Thanks for the advice," he said, meaning *mind your own business*.

She smiled at his glib response. "You're funny, Diaz. How close were you to the colleague you lost?"

"He was like a brother to me."

"Is this a revenge mission?"

Nick moved his gaze to the rain-slick street, blurred red from brake lights. Then he gave an answer straight from the FBI handbook: "The best revenge is justice."

Chapter 3

Avery thought of Special Agent Diaz often after their first meeting.

Over the course of the interview she'd gone from wishing he'd never found her to hoping he'd come back for another visit. Maybe the stress of the day and her heightened emotions had triggered a hormonal response, making him seem intensely attractive. As the evening wore on, she'd relaxed enough to study him in greater detail. She found herself glancing at his ring finger, which was bare. She liked his face, with its strong features and hawkish nose. She liked his voice, his accent, his watchful eyes.

Even his emails were kind of hot. He wrote a brief thank-you note about an hour after he left her apartment. She'd been sitting at her computer, too keyed up to sleep. When her email notification dinged, she'd felt a jolt of anticipation.

Of course, the note had been strictly professional. "I look forward to our next communication," he wrote, which didn't mean anything, but her cheeks had flushed with pleasure as if it was a flowery line from a love poem. She hadn't answered the email that evening. She had no reason to get excited. She didn't want to talk about the cult, no matter how sexy he was. This wasn't going anywhere fun. There would be no intimate exchanges, no harmless flirting, no sexting.

Definitely no sexting.

Diaz wasn't an appropriate candidate for a crush. He lived in another state. He probably adhered to a strict code of conduct prohibiting him from dating anyone he met on the job. He was out of reach, off-limits and unsafe. He worked in a dangerous profession. He'd scared the hell out of her on her doorstep and pressed her for uncomfortable information. She didn't know why she was so interested in him. She wasn't the best at self-evaluation, but even she could admit her reaction was strange. He represented a link to The Haven, the source of her worst nightmares and most painful memories. She should be giving him the cold shoulder, not getting all hot and bothered over him.

After a long deliberation, she replied to his email the following afternoon. She waited for his response with bated breath. He sent a list of follow-up questions a day later, as an attachment, with the request for as much detail as she could remember. He thanked her in advance for her time. Some of her giddiness dimmed as she read the list, which was extensive. His questions weren't overly personal, but they also weren't simple. They involved social structure and family connections. They required a deep dive into a subject she'd rather avoid, and a past she'd rather forget. She closed the document with a shudder. She made a mental note to deal with it over the weekend.

Saturday dawned bright and gorgeous, drawing Avery out of her apartment. She had plans to meet Ruth at the Spring Tulip Festival. They went every year with Ruth's nephew, Chuck, and his adorable family. Avery had bought a new dress for the occasion.

She found Chuck and Laura at the festival entrance, loaded up with kid gear. Strollers, diaper bags, sippy cups. They were the parental equivalent of doomsday preppers, ready for any small disaster. Chuck had one toddler in his arms and the other hanging off his ankle. Avery smiled at him and hugged Laura.

"They're getting so big," Avery said, gesturing toward the older boy, Tyson. "When are you going to have another?"

"Never," Laura said, and they both laughed.

Chuck gave Avery a dutiful peck on the cheek. "You look great."

"So do you."

He was the closest thing she had to a brother, and she enjoyed his company, but they didn't see each other often. She told herself he was busy with his family, and that was true. It was also true that Avery enjoyed her solitude. She attended these get-togethers because Ruth invited her. She didn't feel like she belonged, not really. She was a late arrival to the Garrison clan, and a bit of an odd duck. Chuck used to say she'd hatched from an egg in Ruth's garden. He knew only part of the story.

Avery spotted Aunt Ruth, who was in line buying the festival tickets, and waved. They went through the front gate and down the midway together. It was a warm day, borderline muggy from the recent rains. After a stroll among the flower fields and vendor stalls,

Chuck offered to buy everyone an ice cream. They found a picnic table in the shade to enjoy their cones. Laura took a seat next to Avery. Together, they watched the people in the crowd pass by. An attractive young couple caught Avery's eye. The woman had a baby in a carrier strapped to her chest and another child in a stroller, which she was attempting to navigate over bumpy ground. Meanwhile, the man she was with chatted on his cell phone, unencumbered.

Laura made a gun shape with her thumb and forefinger, shooting the gross offender. "What a jerk."

"Does Chuck ever do that?" Avery asked.

"Not in public. At home, he pretends not to see the dirty dishes." She switched focus to a second man in the crowd. "TDB alert," she said. "Tall, dark and bearded."

Avery chuckled in approval, licking her ice cream.

"Are you dating anyone?" Laura asked. The inevitable question.

"No."

Laura shook her head in disappointment. "You're supposed to tell me about your single-girl escapades so I can get a vicarious thrill."

Avery smiled gamely. "Sorry. I've been swamped at work."

"Next time," Laura said, elbowing her. "Or I'm going to let Chuck set you up with one of his college friends again."

Avery groaned in protest. Chuck meant well, but she didn't want him picking her dates. The last guy he'd selected had been a coffee shop barista who still lived with his parents. They hadn't hit it off.

Ruth broke in with a suggestion for Laura. "Why don't you take a walk with Chuck? I'll watch the little ones."

Laura leaped to her feet eagerly. Chuck put his arm around her shoulders, and she leaned toward him to whisper something as they strolled away. He threw back his head and laughed. Watching them, Avery felt a pang of something she couldn't quite name. It wasn't envy, because she didn't want what Chuck had. It was the feeling of being an outsider, looking in.

Her melancholy thoughts were interrupted by Tyson coming at her with sticky hands. Avery grabbed a paper napkin and attempted to clean him up. He turned into a limp noodle, boneless on the ground. Ruth clapped at the performance. Then she scooped Tyson into her arms and kissed his chubby cheek.

"You didn't say much about Agent Diaz," Ruth said.

"There wasn't much to say."

Ruth arched a brow of disbelief.

"Why would you tell him where I grew up?"

"He already knew."

"He suspected. That's not the same as knowing."

"Well, he acted pretty sure, and he was easy on the eyes. Maybe you noticed?"

"I noticed."

"You should thank me for sending a man that handsome your way."

"You sent him to interview me, not ask me out."

Ruth shrugged, as if Avery was splitting hairs. Avery sighed in irritation. She wished Ruth hadn't been so eager to cooperate with Agent Diaz. His visit had thrown Avery for a loop, and the fact that he was good-looking didn't soften the blow. If anything, it made the knife twist a little deeper. She couldn't stop thinking about him.

She didn't need help finding a man, however. She was fine with being single. Not everyone wanted to get married and have babies, like Chuck. She'd rather focus on her career. It had taken her longer to finish school because of the gaps in her education, so she'd been a full-time psychologist for only two years. She was still getting established in her field. She also wasn't ready to give up her independence. She might never be ready. The family model she'd grown up with had soured her on holy unions.

Tyson demanded to see the farm animals, so they walked over to the pens to indulge him. Ruth held hands with both children, cooing over the curly-tailed piglets while Avery stood nearby, her mind in turmoil.

Ruth bought each of the boys a handful of feed for lambs. Jake, who was only two, seemed wary of the nibbling mouths. Instead of holding out his palm, he threw his pellets in the face of a bleating mama.

Avery laughed at his impulsive choice. At the same time, tears she didn't understand pricked her eyes. Then Jake started crying, because his pellets were gone, and they all went back to the shade to cool off. Ruth scrubbed their little hands with wet wipes again and gave them a bag of crackers she found in the stroller.

"You never talk about it," Ruth said, picking up the pieces of their conversation. "Chuck doesn't know the details. He doesn't know why you…"

"What?"

"Avoid him."

"I don't avoid him," Avery said, dismayed. "I'm right here."

"You've been distant. More so since the kids came."

Avery had a hard time digesting this criticism. She wanted to say that Chuck wasn't her real cousin, but she could make the same claim about Ruth. They were the only family she had. "Did he say something?"

"No."

Relief coursed through her, because she cared about Chuck's opinion. Blood relation or not, she loved him. "I'll do better."

Ruth's blue eyes softened with sympathy. "I didn't mention it to make you feel bad."

"Why did you mention it?"

"Because it's all related. Your refusal to discuss your childhood, your withdrawal from family gatherings, your avoidance of men and relationships. You can't just bury the past and pretend it doesn't affect you."

Avery tucked a strand of hair behind her ear. "Who's the psychologist, you or me?"

Ruth smiled at the joke. They both were.

"I talked to Diaz, you know. I told him about my mother."

"Good."

"He sent me a list of follow-up questions."

"Oh?"

"I'll answer him." At some point.

"What's he going to do, raid the place?"

"He won't say. I think he wants to arrest Silva."

"Well, I'm glad you're cooperating with him. Maybe he can help you get some closure. For the infant."

Avery flinched at the suggestion. This was the most off-limits part of the discussion, the darkest of dark secrets. She didn't talk about her childhood for a reason. She couldn't speak of the little life she'd left behind. Since it was born premature, she'd always assumed the baby had died. Not knowing for sure ate away at her, but she refused to contemplate the possibilities.

"I should go," she said.

"Avery," Ruth scolded mildly.

"What?"

"I just want you to be happy."

"I am happy."

"You haven't settled down with anyone."

"I'm a free spirit."

Ruth gave her a skeptical look. "Is that so?"

"Yes. I learned from the best."

Ruth laughed at this, unoffended. She collected lovers with the carefree ease of a hippie at a drum circle. But she wasn't afraid to risk her heart, like Avery. She'd been married to the love of her life, who'd died young.

"I don't need a man to complete me."

"No, you don't."

For some reason, Ruth's good humor and placid agreements bothered Avery more than her well-intended prodding. Tears pricked her eyes once again. She said goodbye to the boys, hugged Ruth and left. She practically ran out to the parking lot. The hitch in her chest didn't ease as she drove home.

It lingered late into the evening, like a storm cloud hanging over her head. She tried going to bed early, but sleep eluded her. She threw off the blankets and returned to her laptop. Maybe she needed to exorcize her demons before she could rest easy. She opened a blank document and filled the page with the information Diaz had requested.

Some of the details eluded her. She remembered very little about sermon styles and religious practices. She was better with people. Names, ages, relationships. She sketched a crude map of the commune and listed every household she could think of. Every man, woman and child. A glaring omission stood out in her own family tree. Instead of "unknown infant," or "stillborn baby," she typed a question mark.

She sent the attachment before she could second-guess her decision. Then she stood abruptly, her stomach twisted in knots. She curled up on the couch in the dark, hugging the knit blanket around her shoulders, and waited.

His response came an hour later. It wasn't the careful thank-you he'd sent last time, but a quick note with a simple request: Will you accept a video call? I want to share some photos I can't send via email.

She opened the app for live chat with trepidation. The prospect of seeing his face again shivered down her spine. She considered changing out of her pajamas and putting on makeup, but it seemed silly to bother with her appearance at bedtime. This was a conversation, not a date. Also, she'd rather get it over with quickly. She clicked the icon and found an invite from N.Diaz. Within seconds, she was staring at his handsome visage on her computer screen. Her own image appeared in the upper left corner. Even in the dim light of her living room, she could see her puffy eyes and mussed hair.

She touched the disarray, self-conscious.

"Did I wake you?" he asked, his brow furrowed. "I apologize."

God, his voice. Even without the accent, it was sexy. Low and clipped, like a hot professor's. He chose his words carefully. She wondered if he made love with the same textbook precision, or if he went off script.

"I couldn't sleep," she said, dropping her hand. Her breast jiggled at the sudden movement, which reminded her that she wasn't wearing a bra beneath her T-shirt. The fabric was soft and thin from many washings.

His gaze darkened, but didn't dip. "We can do this another time."

She released the breath she'd been holding. "No."

"I have a couple of new satellite images from the

commune," he said, reaching for something off-screen. His attire was as casual as hers, a white cotton tee that clung to the muscles of his chest.

"Before I get into that, I wanted to thank you for everything you've done so far. The information you sent was incredibly thorough. Almost encyclopedic."

She accepted the compliment with an uneasy nod. It wasn't unusual for memories to be more complete in some areas than others, but most people couldn't recall the amount of detail she'd provided. She remembered her troubled childhood quite well. The next time she claimed otherwise, he wouldn't believe her.

Damn it. She shouldn't have been so accommodating.

He leaned forward. "I'm going to level with you, Ms. Samuels. I need a consultant, someone I can contact with various questions over the next few weeks. The FBI can pay you for your expertise."

She made a noncommittal sound. She didn't want to be a paid consultant.

"You don't have to answer now," he said, and held up a printed photograph of The Haven's burial grounds. "This is the cemetery."

"Right."

"There appears to be a new arrival."

She squinted at the grainy image. There were several dozen simple white crosses in a grassy clearing. One of the crosses was adorned with fresh daisies. The accompanying mound indicated a recent burial. "Okay."

He set the photo aside and held up a second one that depicted overgrown fields. "I have no idea who's buried there, but I thought of the head farmer you mentioned. If he passed away, it doesn't seem as if anyone has taken over his job."

"That is strange," she said. "He always started planting in the spring."

"Did everyone in the community help him?"

"No. The women worked in the vegetable garden, and picked fruit. Most of the farming duties fell to the young men. Brother Michael had a crew of teenaged boys every spring and summer."

"There are a lot of young men in the militia. The compound is surrounded by armed guards."

Twenty years ago, there hadn't been a militia—or a compound, for that matter. "Father Jeff always stressed the importance of growing our own food and making everything we needed. He wanted the community to be completely self-sufficient."

"Maybe his priorities have changed."

"Maybe."

"Did he ever make doomsday predictions?"

"Not that I recall. He said that modern society was destroying itself, but we were safe as long as we stayed pure."

"Pure?"

"Away from the influence of outsiders."

"Anyone outside the cult?"

"Especially the government."

"Was he a proponent of racial purity, as well as spiritual?"

"He might have been," she admitted. Although she couldn't remember any specifics, she had a vivid memory of Father Jeff stroking her pale hair. "He definitely preferred blondes. Blond children. Blonde wives."

Diaz absorbed this information without comment.

Avery drew in a shaky breath, glad for the reprieve. She didn't want to delve any deeper into Silva's prejudices and preferences. She couldn't bear to think about what might have happened if she'd stayed.

"Was there a suicide pact among members?" Nick asked.

A chill traveled along her spine. She hadn't expected this question. He was talking about drinking the Kool-Aid, Jim Jones style. "No. Never."

"Are you sure? You were thirteen when you left."

"My mother would have told me."

"Could he be considering it?"

"Mass suicide? That's an extreme leap."

"So is domestic terrorism. These are escalating behaviors."

She couldn't argue with his logic. The Father Jeff she'd known as a child was a master manipulator, capable of crushing violence. He might not hesitate to sacrifice his parishioners, even his own family, for some horrific glory.

"I'm concerned that we're running out of time," Diaz said. "I want to take action."

"What did you have in mind?"

"Silva makes a considerable income from book sales and event appearances," Diaz said, searching her gaze. "I'm going to his next event. I'll claim to be a loyal follower, as well as a botanist. If the commune is in need of a head farmer, I can fill the spot."

Avery gaped at him in disbelief. He thought he could just introduce himself, and get in? "They won't take you."

"Why not?"

She gestured to his face on the screen, speechless.

"I'm not white enough," he interpreted.

"That's not it. Cult members don't trust outsiders

of any kind. You're a single man, and you're too handsome."

His brows drew together. "How is that a problem?"

"Because you're the competition, in a place where
teenaged girls are forced to marry much older men.
The unlucky ones become second or third wives to elders. The leaders won't want someone like you around,
tempting their women."

He raked a hand through his hair. "What if I was
married? Would they recruit a couple?"

"I don't know. They accepted my mother as a pregnant teen, but she was beautiful and obviously fertile."

"Okay," he said, nodding. "I'll take that into con-
sideration."

She had a bad feeling about his plan, but she didn't
try to talk him out of it. She was too freaked out. Everything he'd said so far rattled her, and they hadn't
even discussed her most-feared subject.

"The assignment is classified, and I can't say much
more without a collaboration agreement between us.
Will you consider the consultant job?"

"I'd rather not."

"Ms. Samuels—"

"You can call me Avery."

"Avery," he repeated in a lower tone. With a hint of
an accent.

Heat rose to her cheeks at the sound of her name
on his lips. It felt like a caress, a rough thumb dragged
over the hollow of her throat. She wondered if he was
doing it on purpose. He had to be aware that women
found him attractive, Avery included. He knew how to
press an advantage.

"Let's talk about the list of names you gave me."

She let out a shaky breath. "Okay."

"There are no surnames."

"The Haven doesn't use them."

"Your mother's name was Sarah?"

"Yes."

"And you? What was your birth name?"

"Hannah."

"There was a question mark under your mother's name."

She fell silent, wishing like hell she hadn't included it.

"Did the child she was carrying survive?"

"It couldn't have."

"Are you sure?"

Tears blurred her vision, because she *wasn't* sure. She hadn't seen the infant's body. Trauma had sliced up her memories into shards of pain, fractured and incomplete. Had the midwife slipped away with a bundle in her arms? Instead of inquiring about her sibling, Avery had fled. She'd used death and chaos to her advantage. She'd left and never looked back.

A heavy wave of guilt washed over her. "I have to go."

Diaz didn't argue. "Thanks for taking my call."

She closed her laptop, buried her head in her hands and wept.

Chapter 4

Nick spent the next several weeks prepping for the event in Las Vegas.

It would be his first contact with the target, a critical moment that could lead to the most challenging assignment of his career. He had to make this happen. He had to avenge Davidson and restore himself.

The good news was that he'd convinced Avery to be his consultant. It had been a challenge to bring her on board. During their first video call he'd pressed too hard, and she'd shut down. In his defense, she'd opened up the conversation by leaving that damned question mark on her list. What was he supposed to do, ignore a possible bombshell? Not likely. It was his job to dig for information. Although she hadn't given him a direct answer, her panicked reaction spoke volumes. She didn't know if she had a sibling or not. She didn't know if she'd left her only surviving family member behind.

Nick could sympathize with this horror on a personal level. He'd been in the dark about his own parents for almost ten years. He'd returned to Venezuela as an adult and learned the truth about what happened to them. Visiting their graves had been a sad experience, but at least he had closure. She didn't.

He'd had to push Avery a little, because he needed to engage her emotions. If she cared about the people in the commune…that benefited Nick. He wanted to move on this, before Silva went into hiding, launched another attack or started culling his flock.

Nick couldn't rule out a mass suicide attempt. He'd mentioned the possibility in his proposal, because the threat of a tragedy might help him get a green light. He'd do whatever it took to get close to Silva.

No regrets.

Well, maybe one. He regretted communicating with Avery Samuels on video in the middle of the night, because he'd been plagued with longing ever since. He probably shouldn't have responded to an after-hours email to begin with. He hadn't been thinking beyond the investigation, which he was admittedly obsessed with. Requesting a video call had seemed innocent enough. He needed to show her photos, and he wasn't allowed to send classified files through text or email. She'd clicked on his invite. Within seconds, he was staring at her sleepy eyes and bedroom hair, mesmerized.

Yeah. That was a mistake.

Richards had warned him to be careful about approaching her, and he hadn't been careful. He'd been impulsive, and she'd been…in her pajamas. Soft and vulnerable. Bare-legged, he imagined. He wanted to know everything about her. What she did for fun.

Whom she dated. Why she was so afraid of male strangers. What she was wearing underneath that T-shirt.

He shouldn't have noticed the way the fabric clung to her breasts, or anything else about her appearance. He couldn't act on his attraction, even if it was mutual. She wouldn't hook up with him. She wanted to comply with the investigation and move on with her life.

The following afternoon he'd emailed again, using his most professional tone. He'd suggested she consult with him regarding general information about the cult, not her personal family history. For compensation, he'd offered to pay an hourly fee. It wasn't extravagant, but it was the best he could get from the Finance Department.

Two days later, she'd accepted. Which was damned lucky, because she was a priceless resource. He couldn't afford to alienate her. He also couldn't afford to get too attached. He wasn't the kind of man who jeopardized cases with romantic entanglements. There were no more late-night video chats.

The consulting contract helped to maintain the boundaries between them. It seemed to put her at ease, as well. She wasn't being interrogated. She was getting paid to advise him about Silva's practices and methodology. Nick squelched his curiosity about her childhood trauma and gave her space. When she wasn't talking about herself, she was a fountain of knowledge. He couldn't have asked for a better collaborator.

Now all of their hard work was paying off, because Nick was about to come face-to-face with his nemesis in Las Vegas.

This was a big break, because Silva rarely left the safety of his compound. When he did, the details were always shrouded in secrecy. He spoke to small gatherings of religious extremists. Although his name wasn't on any of the promotion materials, the rumors of Silva's attendance at an upcoming convention had been leaked online. Nick had heard the news in the "alt-w" circles he frequented. Alt-worship was an internet term for alternative spiritual beliefs, which included everything from old-school witchcraft to modern-day Mansonites. There were some twisted people and sick ideas in this armpit of the dark web, but Nick had seen the worst side of humanity before.

He'd created a user profile to navigate the space and interact with some of Silva's admirers. The next step was developing an undercover persona, based on his online profile. Nick would assume this identity to approach Silva.

He'd made arrangements to collaborate with Avery on Mondays and Thursdays from 7:00 to 8:00 p.m. Their sessions were the highlight of his week. He was looking forward to her feedback tonight more than ever. It was his final opportunity to brainstorm before he met Silva. Also, he liked seeing her face.

She answered the video call promptly, as usual. She looked beautiful, as usual. On Mondays she wore workout clothes because she did yoga. This was Thursday, which meant business casual. Her pin-striped blouse was unbuttoned to her collarbone, her hair pulled back. Glasses were perched on her pert nose.

"What's up?" she asked.

"I got him."

"How?"

"He's attending an exclusive event in Vegas on Saturday. I bought a ticket."

She seemed more startled than impressed. "You're going to meet Jeff Silva in Vegas?"

"I'm flying out tomorrow."

"Congratulations," she said, her tone begrudging. "Do you think you're ready?"

"You tell me."

She had the files he'd sent, which included a social media footprint of his undercover identity. He watched her click through the pages. "Nicholas L. Dean," she read. "Former botanist at DuPont Industries. Born in Madrid, grew up in California. Graduated from Seattle University. Married three years. Currently on sabbatical."

He knew the information by heart.

"What's the L stand for?"

"Lorenzo."

"Is that your real middle name?"

"I don't have a middle name. I have two surnames, Diaz from my father and DeLuca from my mother. She was Italian." He made the sign of the cross on reflex. God rest her vibrant, rabble-rousing soul.

"Nick Dean is Italian?"

"Half Italian, half English."

She didn't comment on the erasure of his Latin heritage. Silva might not have preached white supremacy in the old days, but he'd embraced this faction of modern online extremists. They had similar goals, to destroy progressive America. Nick could pass for half-Italian—he *was* half-Italian—and he wanted to get recruited. Pretending to be European seemed wise.

"Do you speak Italian?"

"Si, lo parlo."

She kept her gaze fixed on the profile, searching for flaws. "You're thirty-eight?"

"Yes."

"What do you know about botany?"

"More than they do."

"How?"

"My father is an agricultural scientist. I worked for him in college."

"I thought your parents were in Venezuela."

"I'm adopted," he said. "Let's focus on the profile."

"Okay," she said, agreeable. "Why are you on a sabbatical, Mr. Dean?"

"I had a health scare from using pesticides on the job. I'm recovering, but I won't work in commercial agriculture anymore. I want to live on a green farm, away from technology and corporate greed and dangerous toxins. I need clean air, and…spiritual guidance."

"Not good enough."

He didn't bristle at the criticism, because it was her job to give him honest feedback. "What's wrong with it?"

"Everyone's going green these days. Half the women in Portland are talking about toxins and doing cleanses. Ordinary people don't seek out cult membership after a minor health scare. You need more. You need an emotional reason."

She was right. He felt it. But emotions weren't his element. "It doesn't have to be a minor health scare."

"What if you've got a terminal illness, and you believe you'll be cured by faith?"

"If I'm sick, why would they recruit me?"

"You don't have to be sick, just terminal. You have a few years left. You can work. You're still strong, physically."

"But not mentally?"

"You need a believable weakness. If it's mental, all the better. Because you're very fit and they will consider you a threat."

He glanced down at his athletic physique. He stayed

in shape. He jogged and lifted weights. Maybe it would be easier to feign a disease of the mind, rather than the body. "I'll look into brain tumors."

"Great," she said brightly. "What about your wife?"

"I don't have one yet. They won't assign a partner until I'm closer to recruitment."

"You should think about how someone who loves you would react to your illness. It might be easier for you to imagine her emotions."

He nodded his understanding.

"She won't be under the same scrutiny as you. If she's young and pretty and demure, she'll be accepted."

"How young?"

"Younger than you, ideally. She'll be judged on her looks and her ability to have children."

"What about her job skills?"

"A medical background would help."

"So I should try to get a hot blonde doctor in her early thirties?"

Her lips parted in surprise. He hadn't intended to describe her, at least not consciously. He'd been thinking about Silva's penchant for blondes, which she'd mentioned weeks ago. "Sorry," he said, clearing his throat. "I didn't mean…"

"Me?"

He forced himself to meet her eyes. "I believe this is what you call a Freudian slip."

Color rose to her cheeks at his rueful confession. The blush did nothing to detract from her beauty. On the contrary, a flushing woman made his mind go places it shouldn't. He needed to move on before this conversation went any further off the rails.

"The agency wouldn't allow a civilian to do that kind of job," he said.

"Noted."

"I'm sure you wouldn't want to—"

"Definitely not."

They were agreed, then. She'd rather jump off a bridge than pretend to be his wife, and he shouldn't have implied that she'd be perfect for the role, because she wasn't remotely qualified. He'd like to have her in his bed, but that was a different thing, and also not happening. Nothing was happening.

Nothing whatsoever.

He couldn't stop fantasizing about her, and she seemed interested in him, but there would be no sexual affair. If the investigation progressed the way he hoped, he'd go undercover soon. He'd probably never speak to her again.

"Tell me about your colleague," she said. "The one you lost."

Although this topic wasn't much of an improvement from the last, it saved him from an awkward spiral of lust and regret. He struggled to find the right words to describe his best friend. "He was a good man. A good investigator."

"Was he your partner?"

"No, I don't have a partner. We teamed up a lot, though. He was the type of guy you could count on. Tough, dedicated, calm under pressure. He wasn't the best husband, but he was a top-notch agent."

"Why wasn't he a good husband?"

Nick tugged at his shirt collar. "He was unfaithful. His wife filed for divorce last year."

"Did they have kids?"

"Two boys," he said. He'd seen them at the funeral. "This job is hard on relationships. There's a lot of travel, time apart, hours spent on dark subject matter. You don't want to take it home with you. It makes you feel dirty. I imagine it creates a divide."

"You imagine?"

"Well, I've never been married."

"Why not?"

He just shrugged, evasive. He could say he hadn't found the right person, but he hadn't been looking. He enjoyed his freedom and avoided entanglements. Watching Chris's marriage crumble had reinforced Nick's preference for bachelorhood. He also didn't want the kind of love his birth parents had modeled: fiery, all-consuming, ill-fated.

"Have you ever lived with anyone?" she asked.

"Have you?"

"My cat."

He smiled at her answer. "Should we do an inkblot test?"

"I don't think we need to."

"You already have me pegged?"

"Commitment-phobe."

"Takes one to know one," he replied.

The timer on his phone indicated their hour was up. It always went too fast. This session had felt like a lightning round, perhaps because of his misstep. He couldn't tell if he'd offended her with the "hot blonde" comment. She'd said he was handsome, but that wasn't the same. He understood the power differential between them. It was up to him to maintain a high level of professionalism.

There was also something else between them, beyond power and attraction. There was a personal connection. He didn't want to feel it, but he did. He felt it hard.

"I have to ask you something," she said.

"Go ahead."

"What if you're walking into a trap?"

Her concern surprised him. Even though Silva was a dangerous man, Nick didn't anticipate trouble. This was a low-threat assignment. He wouldn't even be carrying a weapon. "That's highly unlikely, since we've never met before, and the conference hall is neutral turf."

"Just—be careful."

"I will."

The screen went blank as she ended the communication.

Nick exited the program and stared into space for a few minutes. He wasn't worried about the risk he was taking by approaching Silva. The real challenge would be psychological. He'd have to convince Silva he was a true believer. He'd have to kneel at his enemy's feet in worship. Nick didn't kneel well.

He shoved away from his desk and went for a strenuous jog, pushing his physical limits. It felt good to relieve some stress. He felt strong. He liked the brain tumor idea. He spent the rest of the evening researching details and practicing his pitch.

Then he worked on his outer appearance. According to Avery, he was too attractive. He studied his features with a critical eye. His hair was pretty good. Thick and healthy. Grunting, he took out his clippers and cropped it close to the skin. The severe cut, uneven in places, made him look slightly deranged. He smiled at his reflection, pleased with the effect. There were other things he could do to change his face, but he didn't want a complicated disguise. He searched his closet for an ill-fitting plaid shirt and a pair of loose trousers. His slip-on airplane shoes added to the dorky style. He donned an old Timex. It had belonged to his real father, who'd rarely worn the piece. Punctuality had been too pedestrian a concern for Ricardo Diaz.

The next day he arrived in Las Vegas. He cased the conference hall before the event to memorize the layout. Silva was supposed to speak that afternoon, but no specific time was given. Nick attended a morning workshop on the history of religious freedom. It was a mix of right-wing propaganda and misinformation.

At lunch he sat down with a group of "alt-w" members of various ages. Like him, they were here to see Silva. Nick didn't bother interacting with them. They were the weekend warriors of religious extremism. More spectators than participants. Nick had become familiar with this phenomenon during his stint in cybercrimes. There were thousands of bold and chilling statements made online without any action taken. Which was good, because the world hardly needed more violence. But it was difficult to sort through the chaff for legitimate threats.

"I heard Silva's not coming," one of the chaff said. He had a lip ring and a Slayer T-shirt, as if he also dabbled in Satanism. "It's just his son in the greenroom."

"He'd better show," another guy said. "I paid to see him."

There was a short discussion about Silva and the benefits of polygamy before the conversation switched to the latest government conspiracy against gun rights. Nick wandered off to scope out the greenroom. An unarmed security guard was stationed outside the door. He wasn't a member of Silva's militia. Just a basic rent-a-cop.

Nick slipped outside to a shaded terrace, his mind in turmoil. If Silva didn't show, Nick would have to adjust his approach. He hadn't prepared for this contingency.

On impulse, he used the Skype app to call Avery. She answered on the third ring. She was wearing a snug tank top and fire-red lipstick. The background noise indicated that she was in a bar or café. He wondered if she was on a date. She looked *hot*.

The surge of jealousy caught him off guard. He shouldn't be speaking to her in a public setting, on her personal cell phone, outside of their regular consulting hours. He was breaking three rules at once.

"Are you busy?" he asked, his voice low.

"I have a minute."

"Sorry to bother you," he said, glancing around to make sure he was alone. "I heard that Silva sent Jonah to this event in his place. What do you remember about him?"

"Not much."

"You never played together?"

"We played chess once, when he was ten or eleven. It was weird."

"How so?"

"Well, I kept trying to lose, because I thought he'd get mad if I won. But every time I made a mistake, he counteracted it with his own wrong move. He knew what I was doing, and he didn't like it."

"He wanted to play fair?"

"I think he wanted to be in control of the game."

"Was he a bully, like his brother?"

"Not at all. He wasn't physical. He stayed indoors and studied, even in the summer."

Nick heard another woman's voice, along with a waitress asking for their order. "Who are you with?"

"A friend."

The door opened at his back. Nick glanced over

his shoulder as Jonah Silva strolled out. "I have to let you go."

"Okay."

"I love you," he said, as if he was talking to his wife. Then he hung up and plastered a smile on his face. He didn't have time to wonder about Avery's social life, or process what she'd said about Jonah's personality. Ready or not, Nick had to act. He couldn't afford to let this opportunity go to waste.

"You're Jonah Silva," he said.

Jonah gave Nick an impatient glance. He was a striking young man with slick black hair and green eyes. He wore a nice black suit, not the homespun work clothes of his parishioners. And he gripped the railing as if he wanted to hurl himself over it.

Nick ignored his go-away signal and stepped forward for a handshake. Jonah wasn't so standoffish that he refused.

"I'm Nick Dean. It's an honor to meet you."

"Right."

"I didn't know you were making an appearance," Nick said, still pumping his arm. "I'm excited to hear you speak."

Jonah put his left hand on top of Nick's to slow the motion. "You are?"

Nick finally released Jonah's hand. It was the hand of a scholar, smooth and slender. "At your last event, you offered some insightful interpretations of your father's sermons. I read a copy of the transcript online." This was true, at least. Nick had scoured every piece of literature connected to The Haven. "Your words moved me."

Jonah Silva was not immune to flattery. "Thank you, Mr...."

"Dean. Nick Dean."

Jonah nodded, as if committing it to memory. He didn't say anything more, so Nick decided not to press his luck. He'd primed the well. If Jeff Silva didn't show, Nick would take aim at Jonah. Maybe this was a blessing in disguise. The younger man might be an easier mark. He wasn't as closely guarded as his father. Avery had hinted at a boy who preferred intellectual pursuits and wanted to control things. Nick wondered if Jonah had been under his famous father's thumb too long, itching to take over.

"I'll see you inside," Nick said, and left him standing there. Wanting more.

Chapter 5

Avery stared at her phone for a few seconds, lips parted in surprise.

Nick Diaz had cut his hair. And he'd said he loved her?

Her best friend, Corinne, gave her a curious glance as she ordered from the breakfast menu. Avery followed suit, a flush rising to her cheeks. After the waitress left their table, Corinne leaned forward to get the scoop. She'd just flown in from a family trip to the Caribbean. She looked effortlessly beautiful with her fluffy afro and golden-brown skin.

"Who was that?"

Avery wasn't supposed to talk about her consultant job, but Nick wasn't supposed to call her cell phone at random hours, either. Her Skype app was synced with her laptop, so he got right through.

"You're dating someone!"

"No," Avery said, setting her phone down. Corinne hadn't been able to overhear their conversation in the crowded café.

"Then why are you on Skype?"

"It was Nick Diaz."

Corinne's eyes widened in recognition. Avery had told her about his first visit. "*Special Agent* Nick Diaz?"

"Shh," Avery said, even though no one was paying attention to them. "It's classified."

"It's classified," Corinne repeated. "Mm-hmm."

Avery laughed at her expression.

"This is the guy you said was tall, dark and handsome."

"He's attractive," Avery said. "But we're not dating."

"You're doing something with him. I can tell. Give me that phone."

Avery handed it over, because there was no real evidence of their exchanges. There was a profile photo of Nick from his Skype account, just a basic headshot, which Corinne studied in detail before giving the phone back.

"It's nothing," Avery said.

"Your face is red."

"It's hot."

"*He's* hot."

Corinne knew some of the details of Avery's childhood. Avery had confided in her years ago without getting specific. "He's trying to get close to the people I grew up with. They're involved in serious crimes, apparently. He called to ask a question about someone, and I think they walked in while he was talking."

"Why do you think that?"

"He said 'I love you,' before he hung up."

Corinne flapped her palms on the table in excitement. "He's an undercover cop? You should definitely go out with him."

"He lives in California."

"Northern California?"

"You're missing the point, Corinne. He's a professional contact on a dangerous assignment. Not boyfriend material."

"He's boyfriend material," Corinne declared. "Or at least phone-sex material."

The waitress arrived with their food, momentarily interrupting the conversation. They both dug into their plates.

"Has he given you any signals? Other than saying 'I love you'?"

"That wasn't a signal."

"But you like him."

Avery took another bite of French toast, shrugging.

"What would you do if he showed up on your doorstep? You'd hit it, right?"

She couldn't lie to her best friend. "Yes."

Corinne smiled with satisfaction, as if it was all decided. For her, it wasn't outside the realm of possibility for a man to travel hundreds of miles in hopes of a hookup. She was a fashion model. Heads turned everywhere she went.

Avery distracted Corinne by asking about her trip, her family and her love life. They paid for lunch and took a stroll in a nearby park. It was another bright spring day, with flowers blossoming at every turn.

"How's Chuck?" Corinne asked.

"He's good," Avery said. "I saw him at the Tulip Festival."

"Does he have a dad bod now?"

"He's got more muscles."

"That's not what I meant."

"I know what you meant. Do you think I avoid him?" Corinne kept strolling, her hands in her pockets.

"My aunt Ruth said I've been distant since the kids came along."

"Oh."

"Well?"

"You know how people with kids are," Corinne said, waving a hand in the air. "They get all goo-goo gaga. I don't blame you."

Avery sat down on a nearby park bench. Corinne had basically reinforced Ruth's opinion. She agreed that Avery had withdrawn, but she didn't understand the reason. It wasn't because new parents were annoying. It was because babies made her uncomfortable. They reminded her of pain and loss.

Corinne took the seat beside her. "I should tell you something."

"What?"

"It's about Chuck."

Corinne and Chuck had dated the summer after high school. It was a brief fling. "Do I want to know?"

"I had an abortion."

Avery gaped at her in shock. "When?"

"Before I started college."

"It was his?"

"Yes."

"Did you tell him?"

"Yes."

"Why didn't you tell *me*?"

Corinne looked across the park, swallowing hard. "I was afraid you'd take his side. He wanted to keep the baby."

"I had no idea," Avery said, floored by the confession.

"I was also afraid you'd hate me. I didn't want to lose you, along with him and everything else."

"He broke up with you over this?"

"He was young."

"You were younger."

Corinne's eyes filled with tears. She brushed them away with a shaky hand.

"I could never hate you," Avery said.

"You don't think I'm terrible?"

"No." She put her arm around Corinne's shoulder. "I love you."

Corinne reached up for Avery's hand and held it there against her collarbone. They were quiet for a few moments, processing things. Avery couldn't believe her best friend had kept this secret for so long. More than ten years, and Avery had never had an inkling. What kind of psychologist was she, to be completely unaware of Corinne's anguish? What kind of friend wouldn't notice, for that matter?

"I should have told you," Corinne said finally, releasing her hand. "I'd decided to bury it. God, that's a poor choice of words."

"What changed your mind?"

"I don't know. You seemed upset about being distant from Chuck, and I felt guilty for giving you a flip answer. Then I thought, maybe *I* drove a wedge between you and him."

"No," Avery said, after a brief reflection. Chuck wasn't the type to harbor deep resentments. He might have been heartbroken after his fling with Corinne, but he'd moved on. "He's in a good place."

Corinne offered a weak smile. "He's not pining away for me?"

Avery smiled back at her. Men tended to become obsessed with Corinne, so it wasn't arrogance that made her wonder about Chuck. It was experience. "I don't think so. He seems pretty happy with his life."

"So why is Aunt Ruth on your case?"

Avery pulled her gaze away. "Oh, you know. The usual. She wants me to settle down. She thinks I'm afraid of men and relationships."

Corinne didn't let her off the hook. "You've never been in love."

Avery resisted the urge to point out Corinne's single status. It was apples and oranges. Corinne traveled all over the world for work, and she'd had multiple love affairs. "I was with Phillip for two years."

"Phillip was your psychologist."

"So it doesn't count?"

"It counts as a messed-up example of what not to do."

Avery couldn't argue there. Although she took partial responsibility for the mistake, he'd seduced her. It was wrong for him to date a patient. He'd stopped treating her after their first sexual encounter, but that didn't change the ethics violation. She'd ended things when she applied for her own license. She couldn't imagine viewing one of her students, or any other person in her care, as a possible love interest.

"I didn't mean you," Corinne said. "You're not messed up."

"My mother died in childbirth," Avery said. "Did I ever tell you that?"

"No."

"It wasn't a hippie commune. It was a religious cult. I ran away after she died, and I don't know if the baby survived."

"Jesus, Avery."

"Avery isn't even my real name."

It was Corinne's turn to put her arms around Avery. She cradled Avery's head against her chest to comfort her. Avery wanted to say that she *was* messed up, and she always would be. She'd always have a missing piece inside her, a dark mystery. The question mark she'd left on the list was part of her.

"You're not messed up," Corinne said again. "You're kind and beautiful and I love you."

Avery closed her eyes and tried to believe those words.

Chapter 6

Nick listened to Jonah's lecture with rapt attention.

He sat in the front row with one leg crossed over the other, his too-short khakis showing cheap black dress socks. He took notes and made eye contact. He didn't want to look obsessed, just intensely interested, with a dash of socially awkward.

He was glad he'd arrived early, because every seat was filled. There were at least a dozen attendees standing in the back. They'd come to see Jeff Silva, not his son, so Jonah had his work cut out for him. He was a good speaker, comfortable at the pulpit and invested in his topic. He believed what he was saying. He projected well and enunciated in a clear voice. The problem was his audience didn't care. Jeff was the prophet. He was the cult leader. He'd written a book of mystical mumbo-jumbo called *The Path*, which had sold enough copies to pay for his compound. He was the grand wizard of religious extremism. He had a secret commune and an unknown number of teenaged wives.

Jonah was a scholar type with a slight "children of the corn" vibe. He didn't have the charisma of a true guru. He wouldn't appeal to conspiracy theorists or the hypermasculine gun crowd. He wasn't outdoorsy enough for off-the-grid, antigovernment fanatics. With his slender build, tailored suit and handsome face, he could pass for a young lawyer or politician.

They didn't like him.

The feeling was probably mutual, but Jonah was smart enough to hide it. He gave a vague explanation for Jeff's absence and launched into a practiced introduction of his father's greatest feats, complete with high-definition slides.

The vintage photos of Jeff in the early days of the commune were excellent. He looked hale and hearty with his full beard and woodsy-Californian tan. There were pretty blondes in long skirts in the background.

Even Nick, who hated everything Jeff Silva stood for, found the scenes viscerally appealing. They hinted at a simpler life, and a masculine, back-to-nature aesthetic. Nick wasn't immune to that message. He could get into farming, fishing and building his own cabin. What he rejected were the religious beliefs, which included the subjugation of women. He was turned off by the idea of underage partners and multiple wives. He had nothing against polyamorous relationships, or any other sexual pairings, but the benefits of polygamy were lost on him. He wasn't interested in siring a horde of children.

Jonah didn't dwell on the illegal or immoral aspects of his father's flock. He offered a thoughtful, introspective analysis of Jeff Silva's spiritual writings. It was no small task, because the base material was shallow and trite. Most of the listeners weren't as engaged as Nick. A fair number of attendees walked out.

When Jonah was finished, Nick clapped with so much vigor that he dropped his pencil and notebook on the floor. He gathered the items and waited for the crowd to disperse. A couple of guys hung around to ask Jonah questions about Jeff. Then they were alone, except for the security guard at the door.

Nick had a dog-eared copy of *The Path*. He presented it to Jonah proudly. "Do you mind signing it for me?"

Jonah signed his name in an elegant scrawl.

"I enjoyed your lecture."

"Glad somebody did."

Nick glanced around the empty space, aware that Jonah hadn't received a warm response. "I don't mind missing your father. I wanted to see him, but I think this was a blessing in disguise."

Jonah gave him a puzzled look.

Nick clutched the book in his hands. "I've been studying the text for months," he said, which was true. "I wasn't able to grasp the deeper meaning of every passage. Your words cleared up so many questions for me. When you speak, it all makes sense."

Jonah smiled with pleasure. Jeff Silva's book didn't have a deeper meaning, as far as Nick could tell. The cult leader was no literary genius. He'd ridden an inexplicable wave of luck and timing as a young prophet. He had the shameless confidence and grandiosity of any high-functioning sociopath with narcissistic personality disorder. Jonah was intelligent and articulate, but doomed to stay in his father's shadow.

Nick knew he had to sell Jonah on his next pronouncement, so he went for broke. "I had a life-changing moment while I was listening to you. I don't know if it's fate, or a miracle, or something else beyond explanation. I just know that I want to join you and your father. I want to live the way you live."

Jonah stopped smiling and picked up his briefcase. "I'm glad you were inspired, Mr. Dean."

"Nick."

"My father and I attend events like this to lift spirits and encourage alternate religious pathways. We make connections with people and we accept donations, but we don't recruit new members."

Nick wasn't surprised by the brushoff. He didn't expect to get an exclusive invite on his first try. "Hear me out before you decide. I'm a botanist by trade. It's my dream to work on a communal farm among true believers, away from the toxins of society. I'm ready to supplicate myself, like you said."

"You can go off-grid without joining our sect."

"It's not about going off-grid. The path I choose is yours."

Jonah started walking away from the podium. "We don't initiate outsiders anymore. My father forbids it."

Nick followed him down the aisle. "Maybe you need some fresh blood."

"He doesn't think so."

"What about you?"

"What about me?"

"Do you have a say?"

Jonah paused, narrowing his eyes. Instead of answering that, he made a swift countermove. "Are you married, Mr. Dean?"

"Yes."

"Where's your wife?"

"At home."

"Have you discussed your plans with her?"

Nick massaged the nape of his neck. "Not yet."

"Do you intend to leave her behind?"

"No," Nick said, after a short pause. Avery had advised him to play a devoted husband. "I'll convince her to come with me."

Jonah wore a skeptical expression, as if he'd heard tales about modern women. Very few men were willing to leave the comforts of society to join a cult like theirs. Even fewer women would sign up for a life of toil and submission.

"I know I can convince her, because I've been struggling with a health issue, and I haven't told her my latest prognosis."

"Which is?"

"I've got a rare brain disease. It's terminal."

Jonah's brows rose. "My condolences."

"Doctors are quacks," Nick said, dismissing the bad news. "I can beat it. Physically, I'm still strong. I just need to live clean, stay active and pray. My wife will support me. We'll fight it together."

"The Haven doesn't have any medical facilities. We're faith healers."

"Perfect," Nick said. "I hate hospitals."

Jonah rested his briefcase against his thigh, contemplative. "I'd like to help you," he said, and he sounded sincere.

"I'll do anything," Nick said.

"You'll have to divest your assets and leave your home. Leave everything. That's what total supplication means. You'll have no communication with the outside world. No income, no property, no bank account. No cell phones. No connection to anyone but us."

"I understand."

"Go home and talk to your wife. If she's willing to take these steps, contact me. I'll consider your request."

Nick drew in a breath of excitement. He was making progress! He couldn't imagine what kind of idiot would give away every dime he'd saved, every possession he owned, for a chance to worship a madman and die in the woods. "This is amazing!"

Jonah nodded his agreement. "Amazing."

Nick wondered if Jonah wanted to rebel against his father more than he wanted to help a dying man get his final wish. It didn't matter to Nick, of course. He'd exploit either option. "How do I reach you?"

"Send me a message," Jonah said. "It's brotherjonah@gmail.com."

Of course it was.

"Thank you," Nick said, shaking his free hand. "Thank you so much."

"Sure."

"I'll need a few weeks to get everything settled."

"Good luck."

Jonah strode out the door with the security guard trailing behind him, and that was it. The arrangements had been made. Nick felt a surge of dark triumph. He was closer to getting inside the commune and taking Jeff Silva down. Closer to killing him, if he had to.

Nick hoped he would.

But he couldn't celebrate too soon. Maybe Jonah had no intention of keeping his promise for a meeting. Nick hadn't expected to win him over so easily. His goal for this weekend was to engage in a conversation with Silva, and establish a channel of communication. As far as Nick was concerned, he'd hit it out of the park. He'd made a real impression.

He couldn't wait to tell Avery the news. She'd been

a key factor in his success. Her advice was spot-on and her insight invaluable. He'd like to reach through his phone and kiss her. He'd like to do more than kiss her.

He walked to his hotel with a spring in his step. As soon as he entered his room, he called SAC McDonald for a debriefing. McDonald seemed impressed with his performance. He'd been reluctant to send Nick to Las Vegas. McDonald didn't want to risk more lives on special ops involving Silva. The FBI couldn't afford to do nothing, though. One of their agents had been murdered.

"Okay, Diaz," McDonald said. "You've got your green light."

Nick pumped his fist in the air. "Thank you, sir."

"We'll flesh out your identity and everything else in case they do a background check."

"I'm sure they will."

"The timeline is a problem."

"We have to move fast," Nick said. "It was an impulsive offer. I don't want to let the opportunity slip away."

"So I have to find you a young, attractive female agent with undercover experience who is available now, and willing to do a long-term, top-level assignment."

"Yes," Nick said.

"The list of qualified agents under thirty is going to be short."

"Go up to thirty-five."

"I'll see what I can do. Write me a detailed report of your interactions with Silva and turn it in tonight."

"Yes, sir."

"Good work," he said, and hung up.

Nick opened his laptop and logged in. He spent the next couple of hours writing his report. After he submitted the file, he checked his inbox. There was a message with a link to a professional profile for Special Agent Ellen Hawkins, a former army medic with undercover experience as a cyberdecoy for online predators. She was a pretty blonde cheerleader type. Young and green, at twenty-six.

Nick doubted he'd find a better match. He needed someone with nerves of steel, and most army veterans fit the bill. She'd be a team player. He responded with an affirmative. Then he shoved away from the hotel desk, sprawled across the bed and called Avery. She answered on the second ring. She was home now, curled up on her couch with a glass of wine. Her lipstick was bitten off, eye makeup slightly smudged.

"I hope you don't mind these extra calls," he said.

"I wouldn't answer if I did."

"Why don't you get a kitten?"

"A kitten?"

"To replace the cat you lost."

"Do I look lonely?"

"No," he said. She looked *cozy*. He could easily imagine a soft ball of fur in her lap, purring with pleasure. "It went well," he said, describing the afternoon's events. "I got the green light from my boss."

"Congratulations."

"I owe it all to you."

"I didn't do anything."

"Sure you did. You knew my story needed more. I wouldn't have gotten anywhere with Silva if I hadn't told him I was dying. He asked if I was married, too. Even what you said about the chess game gave me an edge."

"Now you have to find a partner."

"They already selected someone."

"A hot blonde doctor?"

Heat crept up his neck at her teasing tone. "Not a doctor. A former army medic."

She took a sip of wine. She seemed subdued, even sad.

"What's wrong?"

She sighed, shaking her head.

"Tell me."

"Off the record?"

"Come on. This isn't an interview."

"Is it a consultation?"

"No."

"What is it, then?"

It was unprofessional, inappropriate and ill-advised. "It's informal," he said, settling against the pillows.

"Why did you ask me who I was with today?"

He shouldn't tell her the truth. He should claim it was a confidentiality issue. "I thought you were on a date."

"And?"

"Were you?"

She laughed. "Would you be jealous if I was?"

"I can't answer that." Because *yes*, he would be. He wanted to be the only one with her, spending time on her couch. Him, or a fluffy kitten.

"I have a cousin," she said, changing the subject. "Not a real cousin. He's related to Ruth, and he's like a brother to me. He's married now with two little boys. Ruth says I've been distant since he started a family."

"Ah."

"I suppose I have been. I'm better with the kids at work. Patients."

"That's understandable."

"I feel bad about it. And I think you're to blame."

"Me? What did I do?"

"You… You caused all of this upheaval!" She gestured with her free hand to emphasize her distress. "You started it by asking Ruth about me and hunting me down and making me remember things I don't want to remember." Her brows drew together and her lips trembled. "I don't want to obsess about what I might have done differently, or who I left behind. I don't want my life turned upside down. I can't sleep at night, because of you. I'm torn between agonizing over the past and worrying about the future."

Nick wasn't sure how to respond to this heartfelt confession. He couldn't sleep, either, for different reasons. "If it's any consolation, I feel disrupted, too."

"How?"

"I don't do this. I don't…get close to people easily."

She fell silent for a moment, absorbing those words. He hoped they carried weight with her, because they were rare. He didn't engage in deep conversations with anyone. He didn't talk about his childhood, or reveal his innermost thoughts.

"I don't want you to go," she said finally.

"To The Haven?"

"What if they kill you?"

Once again, her concern caught him off guard. Not only was he unaccustomed to emotional entanglements, he also hadn't fielded a question like this before. He didn't tell his adoptive parents about dangerous assignments. It wasn't allowed, and he didn't want them to know. "I need to score an initiation meeting before I worry about getting killed."

"They could kill you at the initiation."

He smiled, raking a hand through his hair.

"It's not funny."

"I'm not going anywhere yet. When I do, I'll have

an arsenal of backup at my disposal. My team will take every precaution."

"That haircut is terrible, by the way."

"Thank you. I did it myself."

"I can tell."

"Do I look ugly?"

"Hardly."

Damn. She was good for his ego. "When this assignment is over… Can I call you?"

She inhaled a shaky breath. "What do you want to call me for, Nick?"

"To say all the things I can't say now."

"All right," she said softly.

The urge to continue this exchange until it became explicitly sexual was difficult to resist. He suspected she'd be open to his advances. She felt the same attraction he did, the same connection. The intimacy between them had already been established. She'd been drinking. She might do anything he asked.

"I should go," he ground out.

She smiled, as if she could see the arousal etched on his face. "Sweet dreams," she said, kissing her fingertips and touching the screen.

Then she was gone.

He tossed his phone aside with a low groan. He spent several moments with his fists clenched at his sides, his pulse pounding.

When he had his body under control, he rose from the bed. He considered hitting the hotel bar for a nightcap, and to scan the crowd. This was Las Vegas, the land of tawdry hookups. He wouldn't have any trouble finding a partner.

Even so, the desire for anonymous female company wasn't difficult to set aside. It was nothing compared with his very strong, very specific need for Avery. He couldn't afford to get spotted by someone in Silva's circle, either. He was playing a dutiful husband and religious zealot, not a lonely bachelor on the prowl.

He'd have to drink alone.

Decision made, he ordered room service and raided the minibar. He poured himself a neat whiskey and stared into the mirrored wall behind the liquor cabinet. His father's eyes stared back at him, dark and intense. Sometimes the resemblance bothered him. Tonight it didn't.

He might be his father's son, but he was his own man. He would be defined by triumph, not tragedy. Pride welled up within him, because he'd done it. He'd approached Silva, played his part and set the groundwork for initiation to the cult. The wheels were in motion. He was one step closer to reaching his goal.

He raised the glass to his reflection. *Salud.*

Chapter 7

Avery continued to consult with Nick as spring blossomed into summer.

His new partner, Special Agent Ellen Hawkins, had joined them on their first call after Las Vegas. She was a cute, athletic blonde with a no-nonsense attitude. Avery felt a pang of envy every time she imagined the pretty young woman playing Nick's wife. She wondered how far they would go in their roles, and how intimate their connection would be.

Hawkins's presence had a chilling effect on the sexual tension between Avery and Nick. Which was for the best, because their conversations had been veering into inappropriate territory. His interest in her was clear. She'd spent the rest of the weekend fantasizing about how the exchange might have progressed if he hadn't restrained himself. She was lucky he'd ended the call instead of issuing a tawdry request. She wouldn't have denied him.

She knew it wasn't healthy for her to obsess over a man she couldn't have. If she was psychoanalyzing, she'd say her fixation on him was another attempt to avoid real relationships. She could be dating someone suitable instead of daydreaming about Nick. He represented risk and danger, not stability. She couldn't afford to get attached.

Thanks to Ellen Hawkins, the professional tone between them had been reset. What happened in Vegas stayed in Vegas. There were no more sexy conversations, no more suggestive comments. They were all business.

Avery had been working with Hawkins to develop a persona that would suit her and the assignment. The more the role matched her true self, the easier it would be to inhabit. Avery had encouraged her to draw on personal experience to create the illusion of authenticity. She'd extended this advice to Nick, whose backstory included the loss of his parents in a plane crash. Avery assumed he'd invented this detail because it was close to the truth. The important part was emotional truth. Avery wasn't an expert in deception, but she understood human nature, and she knew the cult mentality. They were suspicious of outsiders. Everything Nick and Ellen said would be scrutinized.

The hours of collaboration paid off. After several weeks of waiting, Jonah Silva issued an invitation for Nick and his wife to meet him in Reno, Nevada. They were scheduled to begin the initiation process in mid-June.

Avery had mixed feelings about the victory. It signaled the end of her consultations with Nick, and the beginning of an even darker chapter. He was about to embark upon a dangerous mission, one that could have serious repercussions on Avery. He might ignite a firestorm by unearthing the cult's twisted practices and dirty secrets. He could also meet the same fate as his fallen comrade.

During the last week before summer vacation, Avery was too busy at work to worry about Nick. She had students to counsel, duties to perform and a thousand loose ends to tie. By Friday night, after a rousing graduation ceremony, she was dead on her feet. She went home with Chinese takeout and collapsed on the couch to binge-watch her favorite drama. Tomorrow, she had plans to adopt a kitten. The rest of her summer was wide open, except for some meetings and professional development opportunities. She would visit Ruth, and Chuck. In August, she'd vacation at the beach with Corinne.

Exhausted, she turned off her phone and climbed into bed. Nick and Ellen would meet Jonah this weekend. They'd either be invited into the flock, or not. There was nothing Avery could do to change this course of events. Nick's plan was in motion.

She tried not to think about it. She tried to think about kittens, and Malibu vacations. Her closest neighbor was having a party. It sounded like a family gathering, with upbeat music and frequent laughter. The rain that had been threatening all day arrived, pattering the rooftop. She'd never been more aware of her solitude.

She'd buried her head in the pillows, lost in sleep. The nightmares she'd anticipated hadn't come. Hours later, she woke with a start. She straightened in bed, listening for a disturbance. Now her neighbors were silent, and someone was knocking on her door.

She frowned at the strange noise. Who could be out there in the middle of the night? A drunken reveler at the wrong apartment? She grabbed her robe from the hook, her pulse pounding with trepidation. Instead of turning on a light, she crossed the living room in silent steps. She didn't intend to answer. She was almost afraid to look through the peephole. Before she reached the door, the knock came again, along with a man's voice.

"Avery? It's Nick."

Nick, at this hour? She glanced through the peephole. It was definitely him. She turned on the entryway light and unbolted the door. "What are you doing here?"

"Can I come in?"

She gestured for him to step inside. He was soaking wet in a dark pullover sweater and plaid slacks. He almost looked like a different person. He looked like Nick Dean, brain-diseased botanist. She handed him a clean towel from the kitchen. Instead of using it to wipe his face, he held it in a tight grip, his expression grave.

"Sorry to barge in on you. I've been trying to call all night."

"I turned off my phone."

He was carrying a brown leather briefcase, which he placed on a nearby chair. His eyes skimmed her robe-clad figure. It was blue chenille, more cozy than sexy, but she wasn't wearing much underneath. "Ellen had an accident."

"What?"

"She was out jogging and got hit by a car."

Avery clapped a hand over her mouth. "Oh my God. Is she okay?"

He nodded. "She has a broken ankle and bruised ribs. We're supposed to meet Jonah tomorrow, but she can't travel. It's over."

Avery understood why his team would have to cancel the whole operation. It was too late to replace Ellen. Jonah wouldn't accept any delays or excuses. He'd consider the accident a sign from God that the initiation wasn't meant to be.

Nick was devastated, clearly. He just stood there, his shoulders taut with tension. He must have taken a late flight to get here, which was odd. He could have waited until morning to call her. Instead he'd felt compelled to break the news in person. It dawned on Avery that he wouldn't have made this choice for professional reasons. He'd sought her out for personal ones. He hadn't traveled all night in a rainstorm to tell Avery about Ellen's accident.

He'd come to act on the attraction between them.

Her breath hitched in her chest. It was the sexiest, most romantic thing anyone had ever done for her.

He seemed uncertain about how to proceed, however. They were technically still colleagues. He probably wasn't supposed to bed the women he recruited as consultants. The forbidden aspect of his visit excited her further.

She stepped forward and took the towel from his wet hands. She dabbed his tense face with the fabric, then passed it over his short hair. A pulse throbbed at the base of his throat. Their eyes met and held.

"You should take off that sweater," she said.

He pulled the garment over his head, compliant. Although he didn't need her assistance, she gave it. She wanted to touch him. He was wearing a basic white T-shirt underneath the sweater. It was also damp, clinging to the muscles of his chest. Heat radiated from his skin, despite the chill. She knew he felt the same desire she did, the same need to act on their attraction. His gaze lowered to her lips. When she parted them in invitation, the dam broke. He buried his hands in her hair and crushed his mouth over hers.

Avery returned his kiss with an eagerness that bordered on desperation. She might have been embarrassed if his need hadn't matched hers. His mouth devoured hers in greedy strokes, as if he couldn't get enough. She drank him in with all her senses. His hands were cool but his body was hot, burning with a fever within. He tasted like mint and bourbon, and he smelled like rain. Their tongues met and tangled, making her moan. She slid her arms around his neck and pressed her breasts to his chest. His heart pounded in rhythm with hers.

He kissed her like a man who'd been planning this moment, fantasizing about it for weeks. He kissed her as if the joining of their mouths could erase his disappointment over the broken assignment, and release whatever demons he carried inside. He kissed her breathless and weak-kneed, his arousal swelling against her.

She gasped as he moved his hands from her hair and shoved them into her robe. He broke the kiss, panting. She was wearing a thin tank top and panties underneath. The sight of her sleeping attire seemed to send him over the edge.

With a low growl, he lifted her against him, palming her bottom with big hands. She didn't object, not even when he carried her to the couch and climbed on top of her. She was too busy reveling in sensation. His erection pulsed against her center, right where she wanted it. His mouth continued its sensual assault. His tongue plundered deep, again and again. She dug her nails into the nape of his neck and wrapped her bare legs around his waist. She'd never been so turned on in her life. There was something magic between them, something raw and electric. Her body was ready for anything. Her sex felt warm and achy, her nipples tight.

Her only thought was yes.

Yes, yes.

She might have actually said it out loud, because he

lifted his head to study her. She could feel the exciting length of his erection, emphasized by the delicious weight of his hard body. His gaze lowered to her breasts as her chest rose and fell with ragged breaths. He looked painfully aroused, almost tortured with desire.

She expected him to take off her panties and unbutton his slacks. She imagined being filled by him, digging her fingernails into his well-muscled back. Instead of giving them both the satisfaction, he straightened abruptly and disentangled himself from her. He closed her robe with a shudder of regret. Then he moved to the opposite end of the couch.

Avery rose to a sitting position, blinking in confusion. She didn't know how to interpret his withdrawal. Had he just rejected her?

"I didn't come for this," he said, his voice hoarse.

She tightened the belt on her robe. "Okay."

"I want you," he added, giving her a sidelong glance. "Obviously."

Her eyes dropped to the erection straining the front of his pants. He didn't try to conceal the evidence of his arousal. She'd already felt it, and to be honest…it was too big to hide. She dragged her gaze upward. His mouth twisted wryly.

"Why did you come?" she asked.

"I have a proposal for you."

Her stomach fluttered with unease. "What kind of proposal?"

"You can take Ellen's place."

She felt as if he'd doused in her cold water, and slapped her for emphasis. The blood drained from her face. "No."

"Hear me out."

She didn't want to hear him out. She wanted him to

make love to her, or leave her alone. She couldn't believe she'd misread him so completely. What a fool she'd been for imagining he'd traveled all this way just to be with her! This wasn't a romantic gesture. It wasn't even a clumsy seduction attempt. It was official business.

"You're the only one who can fill in on short notice," Nick said. "You know all the details in the profile. You can play the role as well as she can. Actually, you're a better match." He gestured to the air between them, indicating their sexual chemistry.

"I'm a better match because you'd like to sleep with me?"

"It's more than that. We have a thing."

"You have a thing," she said pointedly. "You're thinking with it."

"If I was, it would be inside you."

She jumped up from the couch in an attempt to escape from the erotic images those words painted. "I'm not an FBI agent, Nick. I have no undercover experience. I'm not qualified. You said yourself that they would never let a civilian play the role."

He stood with her. "Circumstances have changed."

"I can't do it," she insisted.

"I wouldn't ask if I didn't think you were capable. You're smart. You're resilient. You're an expert in human psychology. You're not the average civilian. You're the girl who walked a hundred miles."

"I'm the freak who ate bugs in the woods."

He smiled at this, undisturbed.

"They'll recognize me."

His eyes drifted down her curvy body. "I considered that, but I doubt it. You've changed a lot in twenty years."

She crossed her arms over her chest. That was true,

she supposed. She wasn't a scrawny waif anymore. Her hair was a darker shade of blond, her freckles had faded and she wore glasses. Three years of braces in high school had altered her appearance dramatically. The cult members probably wouldn't recognize the woman she'd become, but that didn't mean she wanted to return to her childhood nightmare.

Nick stepped forward and grasped her elbow gently. "I won't let them hurt you. I would have protected Ellen with my life. I'll do the same for you."

She shook her head in disbelief. "You can't guarantee my safety in a remote fortress guarded by a violent militia."

"No, I can't," he admitted. "But I can break cover and call for backup if I need to. There will be air support and all-terrain vehicles ready at a moment's notice. I'll have daily communication with my team. If something goes wrong, I'll contact them. I'll do whatever it takes to get you out."

Tears of anxiety filled her eyes. "What about you?"

"What about me?"

"Will you get out?"

He wrapped his arms around her trembling shoulders. "Of course I will. I'm just saying that your safety will be my top priority."

She held herself stiffly, not yielding to his embrace. Intuition warned her that he wasn't telling the whole truth. Her safety wasn't his top priority; this case was. She believed he would protect her with his life—but how much did his life mean to him? Not enough, she estimated. He was a risk-taker by nature. He had his heart set on justice. He was obsessed with taking down Silva and avenging the FBI. He would complete this assignment, or die trying.

Anguish tore through her as she considered the possibility. She couldn't bear to leave him behind, the way she'd left her mother. Nick was asking too much, and she'd already sacrificed enough. He'd disrupted her peaceful existence and invaded her dreams. Now he was dropping another bomb on her.

She pushed out of his arms, distraught.

He must have sensed that she wasn't going to capitulate, because his eyes hardened with resolve as he played his final card. "What if she's alive?"

"Who?"

"Your sister."

She pressed a palm to her quaking stomach. "I never said the baby was a girl."

He crossed the room to retrieve a photo from his briefcase. She studied the grainy image he presented. It was a pretty young woman standing behind a chain-link fence. Her pale blond hair was drawn into a single braid, the preferred style of married women in The Haven. She bore a strong resemblance to Avery's mother. She was tall and slender, with a rounded stomach that could mean only one thing: full-term pregnancy.

"Oh my God," Avery said, clutching the photo. She stared and stared at it, unable to tear her eyes away.

This was her sister. The baby had lived. And she was about to have a baby of her own.

"How did you get this?" she asked.

"It was taken last week. We had a drone near Silva's compound."

The implications were unmistakable. Her sister would be nineteen this year. She was already married.

To Father Jeff.

"Oh my God," she repeated. Horror filled her completely. She would never be able to unsee this picture, or stop imagining the awful details of her sister's daily existence. She would never feel whole again.

Nick stayed silent, letting her process the news.

"How did you know?"

"I didn't know for sure," he said. "I had a hunch after I saw the photo of her on Silva's property. There aren't that many teenagers in the commune, and she's the only blonde. Tech enhanced the image enough to do a facial scan for genetic similarities between the two of you. It's a likely match."

She set the picture on the kitchen table with shaking hands. A cold calm enveloped her. "I'm going to make tea."

Nick returned to the living room while she put the kettle on to heat. Tea was Ruth's cure-all. It had been a part of Avery's life at The Haven, as well. She remembered her mother brewing a cup for a variety of ailments and occasions. They'd grown tea in the garden before moving to her stepfather's home. Avery hadn't thought of that in a long time.

She didn't want to go back to the commune, but she would. She'd do it for her mother, and for the sister she'd never met. Her only surviving family member was suffering at the hands of a madman. Silva might be abusing her. He could even be hatching a suicide plot. She was pregnant and in need. How could Avery refuse to help?

Nick's mission would be dead in the water without her. It could take months or years to get another opportunity to infiltrate the commune. She understood how much time and energy he'd invested in this idea. He'd do anything to see it through, even recruit an unwilling partner. His tactics felt like emotional warfare. She'd opened up to him about her traumatic past, and he'd used it to his own advantage. He'd maneuvered her into an impossible position. Maybe he had no other choice, but she still resented him for doing it.

She glanced into the living room, where he lurked like a dark shadow. "What time is the meeting?"

"Today at noon."

"You can't drive to Reno by noon."

"There's an 8:00 a.m. flight out of Portland."

"You already booked it?"

He inclined his head in admission. He'd known she wouldn't say no to his proposal. Her cheeks heated at the memory of how eager she'd been to say yes to anything he desired on the couch a few minutes ago. She didn't think him noble for calling a halt to their sexual encounter. It wasn't professional ethics that had stopped him, or a belated attack of conscience. He'd done it because he wanted her to go undercover with him more than he wanted anything else. Sleeping with her wouldn't have helped him reach his goal.

She was grateful for his restraint, no matter what the reason. The betrayal would have cut even deeper if they'd been intimate.

The kettle's whistle brought her back to the stove. As she poured herself a cup, she straightened her shoulders with resolve. Nick wouldn't get another opportunity like the one he'd just passed up. There would be no more seductive overtures from her, no more fantasies about a romantic relationship between them. She would play his wife, but it would be a cold day in hell before she invited him to touch her again. The "thing" between them was over. He'd killed it by forcing her compliance.

She brought her tea to the living room without offering him a cup. It was 3:00 a.m. They had three hours to prepare for the meeting with Jonah. She wouldn't sabotage their chances to gain entry to the commune out of spite. She had to think about her sister, and protect herself. The best way to get through this was to treat it like a performance. She had to be convincing as Nick's dutiful, devoted spouse.

Ugh.

"We should go over the profiles," he said.

She turned on the lamp by the couch. It shined a spotlight on the space where they'd almost become lovers. She hadn't even thought about protection. She wondered if he had. She took a sip of tea, which didn't help calm her nerves.

He dug a notebook and pen out of his briefcase. "We'll change Ellen's birth year to yours."

"You don't think I can pass for twenty-six?"

"You can, but it's not necessary. How old are you?"

"Thirty-three."

"Well, now you're thirty-one. That fits better with my age anyway."

"Okay."

He quizzed her on the basic information in their profiles until he seemed satisfied with her level of recall. She answered all of his questions easily; she had a good memory for details. He hadn't shared any photos of Ellen with Jonah or posted them online, so Avery didn't have to worry about not looking the part. Ellen was a pediatric nurse, intensely private, with no social media footprint. She had a younger sister. She was estranged from her parents, both of whom had drug and alcohol problems. She'd met Nick through mutual friends.

"How do you feel?" Nick asked, searching her gaze.

"How do you think I feel?" she replied in a shrill voice. "I'm terrified. I'd rather die than go back there."

"What can I do to put you at ease?"

The first suggestion that came to mind involved

finishing what they'd started earlier. He'd probably consider it good prep for their roles, like a sexy team-building exercise. But that was never going to happen. "You can't put me at ease," she said. "I haven't been trained in spying or deception. I'm not cut out for a job like this."

"You don't have to worry about collecting information or spying on anyone. I'll take care of that on my own. You can let me do most of the talking, too. When you answer a question, try to stick to the script."

"The script doesn't fit."

"How do you mean?"

"Well, we haven't tried to start a family because we both wanted to wait. But I'm thirty-one, so…"

"They'll question it."

"Yes."

"All right. Let's say we were trying, but it didn't happen. Then I got sick, and we put it on the back burner."

She twisted her hands in her lap, still anxious.

"What else?"

"There's more to a marriage than important dates and manufactured memories. Every relationship has depths and nuances."

"We don't have time for depth or nuance. I'm brain damaged and you're beautiful. We'll make up the rest as we go."

"You think they'll accept me based on my looks alone?"

"Your looks and your medical background."

"Which I'll have to fake."

"You said yourself that I'll be under more scrutiny. I'm the one who needs to convince them I'm worth something."

"Who's going to the meeting, besides Jonah?"

"He didn't say."

"What about our sleeping arrangements?"

"What about them?"

"Will we be sharing a bed?"

"Only in the literal sense."

"I'd prefer my own space."

He nodded an acknowledgment. "We don't have to sleep together. I'll take the floor. That might be more comfortable for me, under the circumstances."

"Why would sleeping on the floor be more comfortable for you?"

He buried his head in his hands instead of answering. She realized he meant that he'd be tortured by temptation if he slept close to her, their bodies touching or almost touching. That "thing" between them would pain him all night.

"Oh," she said, flushing. Although she wasn't a vindictive person, she took a perverse pleasure in the thought of him suffering a little.

He massaged his eye sockets in a telltale gesture. He obviously hadn't slept. He looked kind of run-down and ragged, as if he'd been burning the candle at both ends, or trying to alter his appearance to seem less healthy.

"You should get some rest," she said.

He consulted his watch, a clunky Timex that a Seattle hipster might wear ironically. Nick Dean's outdated watch and unflattering clothes didn't change the man underneath. He still had a tall, well-muscled physique and excellent bone structure. The best disguise he could manage was "hot nerd."

She brought him a pillow and a blanket before she retreated to her bedroom. She set her alarm for five thirty, but she didn't sleep. She curled up in the dark and listened to the rain, holding the nightmares at bay.

Chapter 8

Nick woke at dawn, instantly alert.

Two hours of sleep wasn't enough, but it was better than none, and he rarely got eight hours on work nights. He'd recharged enough to function. Adrenaline would keep him pumped for the rest of the day.

He'd have to manage stress, rather than fatigue. He'd underplayed the danger of the mission to Avery because she was already freaked out. It was the most challenging assignment of his life, and her presence complicated everything. She had no experience in law enforcement. She wasn't even a willing partner. His behavior toward her had been inappropriate, to say the least. There was no way he'd get the green light from the department to go undercover with Avery instead of Ellen. He didn't have time to go through the proper channels. A request like this could take weeks to clear.

Which was why he hadn't asked.

Nick didn't make a habit of ignoring rules and procedures, but these were extreme circumstances. He was counting on his SAC to let it slide, just this once. McDonald wanted Silva as much as Nick did. Even if McDonald didn't approve of Nick's methods, he wouldn't interfere. He couldn't, because he didn't know what Nick was doing.

Ellen's accident had happened less than twelve hours ago. She'd called him from the hospital, and he'd gone straight there. He'd known in an instant that she couldn't travel to Reno. She couldn't even walk. The bruised ribs caused her pain with every breath.

Nick had considered contacting Jonah and telling him about the accident. He'd discarded the idea, because he doubted Jonah would be willing to reschedule their meeting. Jonah was too cagey, suspicious of the outside world. There would be no second chances at initiation. This was Nick's only shot to infiltrate the cult, and he felt it slipping through his fingers. Then Ellen had gripped his hand and suggested a replacement.

Nick was desperate enough to try anything, and asking Avery to fill in wasn't that much of a stretch. Ellen wanted the show to go on, with or without her. She promised not to contact anyone in the FBI until after the meeting with Jonah. Nick would attend as planned, with Avery instead of Ellen. By the time his team found out about the switch, it would be too late. Nick and Avery would either get initiated, or they wouldn't. End of story.

It was shady, it was risky, it was rogue… And it might just work. If he pulled it off, all of his rule bending would be forgiven. If he didn't, he'd get reprimanded, perhaps even demoted. He didn't expect the worst, because he was a stellar agent. He'd been with the FBI for thirteen years, he spoke three languages and he had an impeccable record. He probably wouldn't be fired unless he failed to protect Avery Samuels.

That was the worst-case scenario, however. He'd die before he let her get hurt. He'd guard her like a sentry.

He couldn't afford to cross the line with her again, either. He'd slipped up this morning. He'd been blindsided by the sight of her in the flesh, with sleep-mussed hair and bedroom eyes, wearing a striped robe that begged to be unwrapped like a Christmas present.

He hadn't planned on starting a make-out session the minute he walked through her door. When he felt her hands on his chest, he'd lost the ability to think. He'd been so close to throwing it all away just to have her. He was still kind of tempted, in fact. The taste of her, the feel of her underneath him…

Damn.

He wouldn't be forgetting that anytime soon. The chemistry he'd noticed from the first touch had turned combustible.

But a chill had fallen over her after he'd convinced her to come with him. She'd gone from clutching his hair and whispering yes in his ear to freezing him out. He understood her change of heart. She was terrified of what lay ahead. She hated him for dragging her into this. There would be no smoking-hot affair to distract him from the investigation.

He rose from the couch and folded the blanket she'd lent him, frowning. There might not be any kind of affair between them, ever. The missed opportunity bothered him more than it should have. He'd always put his career ambitions first, and relationships second, but there was something special about Avery. Something that made him wish he could win her back when this was all said and done.

Which was ridiculous, because he'd never believed they could make it work *before* he'd ruined his chances with her. There was too much intensity between them for a casual fling, for one thing. They were also colleagues, and they lived in different states. Long-distance affairs were complicated. Nick didn't do complicated.

He heard her emerge from the bedroom and walk down the hall. She was wearing that robe again, which covered her adequately but still managed to stir his imagination. Especially now that he'd seen what she had on underneath.

Don't think about it.

"Morning," he said.

"Morning," she mumbled, entering the kitchen. "Do you drink coffee?"

"Yes."

He found his sweater hanging on the back of a chair. It was still damp, and still ugly. He tugged the garment over his head and ducked into the bathroom. She had toothpaste and a plastic-wrapped toothbrush sitting on the sink. He used both, wondering idly if she kept supplies like this for men who slept over. Men who didn't get relegated to the couch, as he had been. Lucky bastards.

He washed his face and dried it with a towel, checking his appearance. He looked like Nick Dean. Dorky, slightly unkempt, bad haircut. He had some extra clothes and a shaving kit in his rental car.

When he returned to the kitchen, Avery was sipping coffee at the counter. He poured himself a cup.

"Thanks," he said, testing the brew. Perfect.

"Should I pack a bag?"

"Jonah said to come as you are. Just the clothes on your back."

Her expression didn't change at this news. For a novice, she was good at disguising her emotions.

"I have your ID," he said, searching through his briefcase for an envelope. He'd made the fake document last night at work. He'd transferred the photograph from her driver's license, so it looked like the original. The card was more evidence of his preplanning, which assumed her capitulation. She scanned it without comment.

The envelope held another surprise for her: two wedding rings. One was an antique with a silver band and a modest diamond. The other was newer, but less interesting. "I wasn't sure about the fit."

She tried on both and kept the antique. It wasn't an impressive piece. Nor was he the stuff dreams were made of, as far as husband material. He found his own ring, a simple gold band, and jammed it on his finger.

"Are you expected at work?"

"No. I'm off for the summer."

"You need a story for friends and family."

She narrowed her eyes. "You want me to lie to my family?"

"They'll notice if you disappear for a month. Won't they?"

"Yes," she admitted.

"Tell them you got invited on a last-minute trip. One of the volunteers canceled and you stepped in. It's somewhere remote, without cell service, but relatively safe and easy to visit. Where would you go, if you had a choice?"

"Costa Rica?"

"Sure."

She took her coffee to the chair in the living room, along with her cell phone, and composed a text message. He finished his cup and rinsed it in the sink. "We have to leave in thirty minutes."

She didn't glance up from her phone.

He grabbed his bag from the rental car and freshened up with a quick shave in the guest bathroom. Then he checked his texts for messages. Nothing from his SAC. So far, so good. He sent a thumbs-up to Special Agent Hawkins. She wished him good luck.

Avery came out of the bedroom in a soft floral dress with an oval neckline and a belted waist. It was demure, at knee-length, but stylish enough to turn heads. Her simple hair and makeup reminded him of a '40s pinup. She had a clutch purse and heels with little straps over the bridge of her foot.

She paused in the hallway, as if she expected him to criticize the look. He didn't. He was too busy admiring her moxie. And her legs.

Displays of fashion and female confidence wouldn't be allowed inside the commune. Ellen Dean wouldn't know that, but Avery Samuels did. Perhaps this outfit was an act of rebellion, and a bit of rubbing it in his face. He'd always liked women rubbing in his face. He appreciated a bold spirit, as well. His mother had been a spitfire.

He rose to his feet. "Ready?"

She tucked the ID and her glasses into her purse. He left everything but his wallet behind. They couldn't bring their cell phones or any other personal belongings. His briefcase, badge and credentials would stay in her apartment.

"Do you have a gun in there?" Avery asked.

"No. I left my service weapon at home."

She nodded, squaring her shoulders. Then they were off. He drove the short distance to the airport as the sun burst over the horizon. Her eyes glinted with misery, crystal blue in the morning light. He returned his rental car before they checked in. They had an hour to kill, so he offered to buy her breakfast.

"I'm not hungry," she said.

"Tea?"

She made a noncommittal sound. He ordered her a cranberry-orange scone and a cup of Earl Grey. She sipped her tea and nibbled at the scone while he ate two breakfast sandwiches. Then he finished her scone.

"Where do you put it?" she asked, studying his physique.

He patted his flat stomach. "In here."

She returned her gaze to the crowd, her cheeks pink. He couldn't guess what she was thinking. She'd hardly said two words to him all morning. That was a concern. Ellen Dean could be anxious, but she couldn't treat her husband like a stranger.

"Are you a nervous flier?" he asked.

"No. Are you?"

"Not at all. I like flying."

Her brow furrowed in confusion. "Your parents died in a plane crash."

"Oh. Right."

"I told you to base your profile on real life, to add authenticity."

"Well, they're dead. That's authentic."

"How did they die?"

"Flight 180 out of Genoa."

"For real."

He crumpled a paper napkin in his hand, watching a plane roll down the tarmac. He wasn't eager to rehash a personal tragedy, but he did want her to loosen up. Like him, she felt more comfortable in the listening role. "They were killed during a political uprising."

"In Venezuela?"

"Caracas."

"That's where you were born?"

"Yes."

"Who killed them?"

"I don't know. There were a lot of protests going on. Rioters were being shot in the streets, and opposition groups had been bombed. My parents were well-known activists. They disappeared one day and never came back."

"You never learned what happened?"

"The story I heard, as an adult, was that they were clubbed by union breakers. They attacked my dad because he was leading the strike. My mom tried to intervene. One of them shoved her back and my dad went crazy. They both fought hard, but they weren't armed. Survivors buried their bodies in a field nearby."

"Who told you that story?"

"A friend of my aunt's. I went back to visit about ten years ago."

"How old were you at the time they were killed?"

"Twelve."

"Did your aunt take you in?"

"She couldn't, because she had enough trouble feeding her own kids. She took me to an orphanage. One day an American couple came to visit. They wanted to adopt a younger boy, but he was sick, and I wasn't."

Her eyes softened. "That was lucky."

"Not for him."

She glanced at his hands. He'd twisted a napkin into a noose.

"Now you see why I didn't base the profile on real life," he said.

"What were they like?"

"My adoptive parents? They're great."

"Your birth parents."

He smoothed the noose into a flat square again. Oddly, this question pained him more than the others. He wanted to say they were reckless, irresponsible people with no redeeming qualities. They'd lived and died for their ideals, instead of him. "They were passionate," he said, clearing his throat. "They loved each other."

She smiled at this answer. "And you?"

"And me," he allowed, begrudgingly.

She didn't seem horrified by the story, but she had an unusual perspective. Her childhood was even sadder and weirder than his.

"Are we a pair of head cases or what?"

"Just you," she said, but her voice was light.

Nick's spirits lifted. If she could make a joke at a time like this, they were in good shape. He felt confident his risk would pay off. She was a fighter. She could handle the stress of the assignment. Everything was going to be okay. And if it wasn't, he'd take action. He'd get her out at the first sign of trouble.

They boarded the flight a few moments later. As soon as they touched down in Reno, he called Jonah on a cell phone that had been purchased for this occasion. He left a message, as instructed. Then they sat down in the noisy terminal and waited for a response.

Avery donned her black-framed glasses and glanced around anxiously, as if she assumed they were being watched. They were. Nick had two team members stationed in a vehicle outside the airport, ready to follow, and two more inside the terminal.

Nick had identified both agents in the crowd. They weren't easy to spot, and they'd been advised to stand at a distance. They might not have realized Avery wasn't Ellen yet. Their job was to keep an eye on the scene, and the two women looked similar from far away. They were blonde, attractive, average height. Not the same body type, but close enough. If they studied her, they probably wouldn't focus on the differences.

Jonah sent a text within the hour: Hyatt Airport Hotel.

It was less than a mile away. Nick had expected a more circumspect choice, considering the high level of paranoia among cult members. Maybe Jonah Silva wasn't the most cunning strategist. Why would he be? He'd lived a sheltered life.

Feeling confident, Nick left the airport with Avery. He was better at managing fear and stress than the average person. His ability to remain calm, or even thrive, in dangerous situations made him an excellent candidate for undercover work. There was a professional advantage to being emotionally detached.

After a short cab ride, they arrived at the hotel. They were followed by two agents in an unmarked car. Jonah wasn't in the hotel lobby, so they sat down to wait. Avery perched on the edge of her seat, clutching her purse. Nick thumbed through a rock climbing magazine. There was an article inside about the manly art of living off the grid.

He showed it to Avery, who was also pretending to read. She showed him an advertisement for tampons, in rebuttal. He appreciated her sense of humor, and her viewpoint. "Roughing it" was certainly easier for men than women.

Just before noon, they were approached by a tall, bearded gentleman in a homespun suit.

"Mr. and Mrs. Dean?"

"Yes," Nick replied, standing with Avery. "I'm Nick, and this is my wife, Ellen."

"I'm Brother Sage."

If Avery recognized him, she didn't show it. Brother Sage was at least forty, somber and distinguished-looking.

"Shall we?"

Nick and Avery followed him down the hall and out a back door, where a muddy SUV idled. Nick hadn't counted on going to a second location, but it didn't matter. Both his cell phone and watch had GPS. They climbed inside the vehicle with Sage. A woman in dark sunglasses sat behind the wheel. She put the pedal to the metal.

Brother Sage introduced her as Sister Imogen. This name sparked recognition in Avery, along with a fleeting expression of panic. After they said hello, Nick grasped her hand and gave it a squeeze of encouragement. She took a few deep breaths and seemed calm again. Nick studied Sister Imogen with interest. Her presence was a surprise, considering the role of women in the commune. She wore a severe gray dress, buttoned high. Twin braids were tucked into a neat bundle at the nape of her neck. Nick assumed she was unwed, based on the hairstyle. He wondered if she was related to Jonah.

The next location was a quiet hotel on the outskirts of the city. His team would have figured out Avery's identity by now. If McDonald wanted to intervene, they would get pulled over at some point. Nick had no control over that outcome, so he disregarded it. He needed to focus on playing his role and supporting Avery.

At midday, Reno was smoking hot. Brother Sage led them across a blistering parking lot and down a curving path, to a small conference room that overlooked a golf course. Reddish-brown cliffs loomed in the background. The space featured a large round table, bland carpet and functional air-conditioning. Windows on all sides filled the room with light and offered a 360-degree view of their surroundings. There would be no ambush here.

"I need to confiscate your cellular phones," Brother Sage said.

Nick handed his over easily. "Ellen doesn't have one."

"I gave it to my sister," Avery said.

Brother Sage didn't question the story, which was from the script. He disappeared into a separate room while Sister Imogen stayed behind. She was pretty, despite her plain attire and stiff posture. Nick estimated her age at twenty-five. He tried a disarming smile. She wasn't immune to it. Her hand rose to her hair in a flustered gesture.

Brother Sage returned a moment later with Brother Jonah, whose eyes skimmed right over Nick and lighted on Avery. His reaction was so easy to read it was almost comical. He hadn't expected Dean to have a knockout for a wife.

"Good to see you again," he said to Nick, shaking his hand quickly before moving on. "And you must be Ellen."

Avery flushed at his perusal, which was perfect. Jonah grasped both of her hands and gazed at her in godly wonder. He didn't appear to disapprove of her stylish clothes. He also didn't show any sign that he found her familiar. Nick released the breath he'd been holding. They'd cleared the first hurdle.

Jonah released Avery. "Have a seat, please."

Nick pulled out a chair for Avery and another for himself. The cult members took the opposite side of the table like an interview panel. This wasn't a simple meeting to get to know one another. They were auditioning for a lifetime position. Nick glanced at Avery. She was clutching her purse in a white-knuckled grip. She knew Jonah, even if he didn't know her. He looked like a slicker version of his father.

"Let me explain our process," Jonah said. "In the past, my father has accepted new members on rare occasions. *Very* rare occasions. Our numbers have remained steady over time, and that's the way we like it. We're private. Exclusive."

Nick and Avery nodded politely.

"Since I took over daily operations at The Haven, we haven't welcomed any outsiders. This is a very unusual, very special circumstance, and I wanted it to be fair. My father isn't here to share his infinite wisdom, so I brought my most trusted advisers, Brother Sage, our builder, and Sister Imogen, my secretary."

Sister Imogen puffed up like a proud partridge. Brother Sage didn't bat an eye.

"We'll ask questions until we're satisfied. Then we vote."

"All three of you get a vote?" Nick asked.

"All three," Jonah said, seeming pleased with his own progressivism. Perhaps he wanted to be thought of as an egalitarian, in direct contrast to his father. "It has to be unanimous. If one of us votes no, we leave you here. If we vote yes, the initiation begins."

Avery reached for Nick's hand and held it. A pulse fluttered at the base of her throat. This was a do-or-die moment, and she'd already said she'd rather die than go back to The Haven. He believed that, but he also believed she couldn't walk away from her sister. She had been in the dark about her sister's existence for twenty years.

"Are you ready to proceed?" Jonah asked.

"Yes," Nick answered.

"Yes," Avery said, after a pause.

"Very well. Let's begin."

Chapter 9

When Avery heard the name Imogen, her anxiety sky-rocketed.

Sister Imogen had gone by "Immy" as a child. She'd been younger than Avery by four or five years, but they'd grown up in the same household. Imogen's mother had been cowives with Avery's mother.

Despite this family connection, Imogen didn't appear to recognize her. Perhaps because Avery had been treated more like a babysitter than a true family member. The girl had been precocious and bossy, prone to tantrums. Like Jonah, she hadn't played with children her age. She'd skipped two grades. What Avery remembered most about Imogen wasn't her keen intelligence or her stubborn personality. It was her adoration for Jonah. She'd followed him around like a puppy, hanging on his every word.

Still did, apparently.

Imogen's hairstyle indicated her unmarried status, which was odd for a woman her age. Perhaps she was The Haven's only "spinster." Avery worried that Imogen's memory would be sparked by her presence at any moment. The other problem was simple female rivalry. Imogen worshipped Jonah, and Jonah...

Jonah was smiling at Ellen Dean. He seemed quite taken with her, while Imogen all but vibrated with disapproval.

Avery didn't know whom she was more rattled by, Imogen or Jonah. The young Silva resembled his father enough to give her the creeps. Father Jeff was taller and more imposing, with the quintessential scruffy beard of a guru. Jonah was clean-shaven and slender in a smart black suit. He had bold eyebrows and slicked-back hair. He reminded her of a life-size ventriloquist dummy. There was something insincere about him, behind the polished veneer. Was he Father Jeff's puppet, or did he speak for himself?

Nick squeezed Avery's hand to reassure her. Jonah might be a creepy puppet, and a criminal coconspirator, but he liked pretty women. He'd judged Mrs. Dean on her looks, just as Nick had predicted.

The first round of questions went to Nick.

"Brother Jonah mentioned that you have a serious illness," Sister Imogen began. "Can you tell us how you got sick?"

"Sure," Nick said, releasing Avery's hand. "I was diagnosed with Creutzfeldt-Jakob disease, better known as CJD. It's similar to Alzheimer's, so it affects memory and brain function. The doctors think it was caused by exposure to pesticides, which makes sense. I worked for ten years as a field botanist for a large agriculture company. They gave me a settlement to cover the medical bills."

"This is a fatal disease?"

"Yes. They say I have three years or less."

"How do you feel?"

"Okay," he hedged, glancing at Avery. "I struggle to remember things. Directions, dates. I get mixed up."

"Are you expecting to be cured?"

He frowned at the question. "I believe I can be cured, but I'm really looking for a place to breathe. Society is the disease. There's a moral pollution, along with the other kinds. We have to cleanse ourselves of that first."

His answers were well received by the panel. Sister Imogen gave the floor to Brother Sage, who didn't mince words.

"How can you be an asset to us if you're too sick to work?"

"I'm not too sick to work," Nick said mildly. "Physically, I'm fine. I might have a hard time collecting data, or writing research papers, but I can do manual labor. I want to get back into basic farming."

"We lost our head farmer," Jonah said.

Nick straightened at this announcement. "Really?"

"We need someone who knows how to rotate crops and tend land," Brother Sage said. "What would you grow for the commune?"

He gestured to the scorched earth outside. "In this climate?"

"No," Sage admitted, but didn't elaborate.

"I can't say what I'd grow because it depends on a lot of different factors, like the weather, the natural resources and the number of mouths to feed. Some crops are so labor-intensive, they're not worth the effort for a small group."

Again, his answers sounded reasonable. Maybe a little too reasonable, for a guy with a degenerative brain disease, but he was in the early stages. He had to present himself as healthy enough to be useful.

"What if you aren't cured by faith?" Jonah asked.

"I prefer to think positive," Nick said.

"That's admirable, but our way of healing isn't guaranteed. We've lost members to various accidents and illnesses. You have to consider the possibility that you will succumb to this disease."

Nick's face hardened with resolve. "I'm going to die if we don't join. That's guaranteed. I have nothing to lose."

"Tell me about your family."

"There isn't much to tell," Nick said. "I'm an only child, and my parents are dead."

Jonah turned his attention to Avery. "And you, Mrs. Dean?"

She gripped the armrests and tried not to panic. "Call me Ellen."

"Ellen," he repeated, studying her with interest. "Your husband is asking you to follow him into the unknown. What do you have to lose?"

"Just him," she said softly.

"You don't have any family?"

"I do, but we're not close."

"Why is that?"

She moistened her lips, nervous. Her throat was so dry, it was difficult to speak. Her brain supplied the information in the profile, but she wasn't sure how to deliver it authentically. She wasn't an actress. "My parents are drug users," she said. "They've struggled with addiction for many years. It's been difficult to stay in touch with them. For my own good, I had to put up some boundaries." She swallowed hard. "My little sister has gone down the same path, unfortunately. I've put her through rehab twice."

Jonah's brow furrowed. "Your family is a burden to you?"

Avery hesitated before answering. She'd invented this bit of emotional motivation herself in an attempt to explain Ellen Dean's willingness to leave society. But maybe it didn't reflect well on her. In The Haven, no one walked away. She reached for Nick's hand again, uncertain. He pressed his thumb to the center of her palm.

"It's not that they're a burden," she said. "I've just come to realize that I can't save them. I can save Nick."

Nick squeezed her hand in approval.

"If you join us, you won't have contact with anyone on the outside," Jonah said.

"Sometimes it's better to cut ties."

Jonah leaned back in his chair, neither agreeing nor disagreeing. He gestured for Brother Sage to take over.

"You're a pediatric nurse."

"Yes," she said, glad for the subject change. "I love children."

"Tell us about your nursing skills."

"I worked at a doctor's office for seven years, so I did a lot of basic care. First aid, vital signs, blood tests. The usual."

"We don't believe in modern medicine," Imogen said.

Avery smiled, because she'd anticipated this sort of comment. "That's not a problem. I've studied homeopathic methods and herbal remedies. Nature provides so much of what we need to heal and grow."

Brother Sage looked hopeful. "Do you have experience with childbirth?"

Her smile slipped. "No, but I can learn."

"Good," he said gruffly. "The midwife could use an assistant."

Imogen cut in again. "How old are you?"

"Thirty-one."

"Why don't you have children of your own?"

"We haven't been blessed yet," Nick said.

Imogen scanned Avery's colorful dress, her expression skeptical. "We have no luxuries at The Haven. No beauty products, no frivolous items, no material conceits. How can someone like you adjust to our way of life?"

Brother Sage nodded at this question. He didn't trust frivolous items, either.

"I don't need luxuries," Avery said. "I want what's best for Nick."

"Is there anything you want for yourself?" Jonah asked.

Avery swallowed hard. She realized that she hadn't won them over the way Nick had. He projected confidence and sincerity. He was very good at this job. She wasn't as convincing, and Sister Imogen's snide questions had raised doubts about her character. Ellen Dean was too pretty, too modern, too childless. It wasn't "natural."

Nick gave her an encouraging nod. Their fate was in her hands. Did she really want to impress this panel of religious zealots, and secure an invitation to backwoods hell? Or did she want to sabotage their chances and go home?

She thought of her sister—her real sister—and tears filled her eyes. "I want a baby," she said, her voice quavering with emotion. "No matter what happens to Nick. If God chooses to take my husband, at least I'll have his child."

Nick stared at her in awe. She flushed, hoping she hadn't overdone it. She needn't have worried. Jonah and Sage exchanged candid looks of approval. These were men who believed in being fruitful and multiplying.

Only Imogen appeared unmoved, which wasn't a surprise. She'd taken an instant dislike to Avery.

"I think we've heard enough," Jonah said. "Let's vote."

Avery drew in a shaky breath. They weren't even going to leave the room to discuss it. They were going to vote yes or no, right here and now. Nick smiled reassuringly. He thought they had this in the bag, despite Sister Imogen's cool reception. Maybe he didn't consider her a threat to their acceptance.

"Brother Sage?" Jonah prompted.

"Yes," he said, without inflection.

"Sister Imogen?"

Imogen placed her palms together and glanced heavenward, as if seeking guidance from above. She considered Nick's handsome face, deceptively guileless. Then she studied Jonah, whose eyes shone with quiet fervor. He controlled this process, no matter what he claimed. If Sister Imogen voted against the men, he would *not* be happy.

"Yes," she said, like a true devotee. Not of the cult, but of Jonah.

"Excellent," Jonah said. "I vote yes also. It's unanimous."

Nick jumped to his feet and shook hands with everyone. Then he drew Avery into his arms for a celebratory embrace. Dread and despair welled up inside her, warring with the physical thrill she felt as his hard body enveloped hers. As much as she resented him for dragging her into this, she wasn't immune to his touch.

"You won't regret this," he said in her ear. "I promise."

She didn't know if he was speaking as Nick Dean, or Nick Diaz. It didn't really matter. Their identities had been subsumed. Now they would be swallowed into the cult, and become cogs in the communal machine.

They left Reno in the SUV. Sister Imogen drove, with Jonah riding shotgun. Brother Sage sat in the back, next to Nick and Avery. After they crossed into California, they were given blindfolds. Avery donned hers without argument, though she knew they were hours from The Haven. Brother Sage tucked her glasses into his pocket. Nick put his arm around her. The long drive in utter darkness should have terrified her, but his warmth and strength felt comforting. She'd hardly slept the night before. The mind's ability to endure and compartmentalize never ceased to amaze her. She rested her head against his shoulder, drowsy.

The next thing she knew, she was jostled awake by a hard jolt. Nick had both arms locked around her protectively. The teeth-rattling movement continued as the SUV traveled over rough terrain. They were getting closer to the fortress in the woods.

An hour later, the vehicle pulled to a stop. Nick didn't move a muscle, but Avery reached for her blindfold.

"Keep your eyes covered," Jonah said.

She waited, pulse racing. "Are we there?"

"We've reached the end of the secular plane," Jonah said. "But the journey's not over. We walk from here."

The engine turned off and the doors opened with a musical ting. Although they were notorious for eschewing the evils of modern society, these cult members traveled in style. The late-model SUV had all the upgrades.

Avery was sitting closer to the door, so she got out first. She set her feet carefully on the rocky ground and took a tentative step forward. Nick followed, grasping her elbow.

Jonah spoke from a vague place in the near distance. "Part of the initiation process is a spiritual rebirth. You'll be born again as members of our family. You must come to us as babes, with no trappings from the old world."

Beside her, Nick cleared his throat. "Trappings?"

"Clothing, jewelry, shoes. You have to leave them behind."

"You want us to take off our clothes?"

"Every stitch."

Avery's stomach sank. She couldn't believe this was part of the initiation process.

"We have robes for you near the water. It's not far."

She stifled a moan of dismay. They had to strip naked and walk through the woods. Blindfolded.

"I'll go first," Nick said, as if this was some magnanimous offer. He probably didn't care who saw his private parts, and Avery doubted their companions would examine him closely. Imogen was too prudish to look, and the other two were men. She stood like a statue next to Nick, listening to his shoes drop and clothes rustle.

"Your wristwatch," Jonah said.

Nick wasn't bothered by nudity, but he drew the line at this. "It was my father's."

"We don't allow status items. The wedding rings have to go, too."

He must have complied, because she heard the metallic snick of his watch clasp. Then he reached for her trembling hand and worried the ring off her finger. It slipped loose, disappearing into the ether. Silence stretched between them.

She realized it was her turn to remove her clothes.

She had to show her loyalty and devotion to her husband, and her willingness to obey orders. She had to supplicate herself with this humiliating exercise.

"Do you want me to help you?" he asked quietly.

No, she didn't want him to help her. She wanted to slap him for bringing her into this. With stiff motions, she unfastened the straps on her high-heeled Mary Janes. They weren't practical for a trek through the woods, or air travel, for that matter, but they were damned cute and she was sorry to lose them. As she took off her dress, she became aware of Nick's body in front of her. He'd made a privacy shield between her and the others. Although she appreciated his attempt to protect her modesty, she assumed the men could still see her. She cringed as her dress fell to the ground. Her bra and panties went next. She was glad she'd worn basic lingerie, not sexy lace garters and silk hose.

When she was completely naked, she stayed in a half-crouched position behind Nick, one arm covering her breasts and a hand between her legs. She wasn't ashamed of her figure, but she didn't want to show it to strangers, and she hated feeling vulnerable. The blindfold added to her helplessness. She couldn't guess where Jonah was standing.

"Follow the sound of my voice," Jonah said.

She reached out tentatively and found Nick's bare shoulder. He tensed at her touch, like an animal poised to fight. She slid her hand down to the crook of his arm, shivering.

"Ready?" he murmured.

Avery wasn't capable of speech. Her lips were tightly compressed, her skin prickled from cold and embarrassment. She guessed it was late afternoon or early evening, based on the chill in the air. In the remote mountains of Northern California, nights were crisp, even in summer.

She wanted to run away, screaming. But when he stepped forward, she went with him. She was committed to his plan, for better or for worse. Being forced to walk naked through the woods was a fitting start to a horrifying ordeal, she supposed.

The earth was cool and damp beneath her feet. Sharp pebbles bit into her tender soles as they navigated the path. She didn't let go of Nick, who seemed confident and sure-footed. Jonah had launched into a solemn prayer.

Avery had never heard the initiation rites before, so she couldn't evaluate their authenticity. The words were similar to many of Father Jeff's sermons. It was part hippie mystic, part conservative Christian. The fact that these two ideologies were diametrically opposed to each other didn't matter where they were going. Cult membership was predicated on blind faith, not logic and reasoning. Also, the community was incredibly insulated. They didn't know they'd been indoctrinated. They accepted Father Jeff's teachings without question.

It was more difficult for Avery to understand his fan base outside the commune. Why would anyone choose to follow a guru whose beliefs were so twisted and misogynistic? Not to mention, lacking in coherence. She could write a second dissertation on the phenomenon. It was some kind of mass dementia, exacerbated by social media.

When she heard the sound of rushing water in the close distance, a childhood memory struck her. She'd been here before, to view a baptism. They'd called it a nature blessing. Parents brought their newborns to the blessing pool, which was located at the base of a modest waterfall. It wasn't far from the commune boundaries. There was a series of swimming holes along Holy Creek, if she remembered correctly, but only one was "blessed." Family and friends gathered around while Father Jeff performed the ceremony.

She couldn't recall whom she'd seen get baptized. Baby Imogen, perhaps.

Someone shoved a bundle of fabric into Avery's hands. Avery let go of Nick to grasp the roughhewn cloth and clutch it to her chest. A fine mist from the falls settled on her skin, which was already pebbled with goose bumps.

"You can remove your eye coverings and don the blessing robes," Jonah said.

Avery pulled off the blindfold. At sunset, the scene might have been called picturesque. Golden light filtered through the trees and rippled on the surface of the pool, which Jonah had waded into. He held a leather-embossed cult bible, open to a page with a ribbon bookmark. Brother Sage and Sister Imogen stood by his side. The twenty-foot waterfall offered a quaint backdrop, and gave everyone a misty halo. Thankfully, they were the only participants. Jonah hadn't invited an audience.

Avery was too uncomfortable to appreciate the natural beauty of the setting, or of the man standing next to her. She didn't check out Nick's tall, hard-muscled body, but she could guess how he looked. He exuded masculinity. Underneath those ill-fitting clothes, he was a man in his prime and it showed. She could see the proof in Sister Imogen's wide-eyed gaze.

Oh God. This was a disaster.

Avery fumbled with her robe as Nick donned his. It was a simple white garment made of muslin, with a neck opening like a poncho. When she was covered, she reached for Nick's hand again. His robe reached just below his knees. Hers ended at her feet. He didn't offer any empty platitudes or reassuring smiles. There was no way to ease the gravity of this moment. He seemed to be waiting for her to collect herself.

She took a deep breath and tried to ground her thoughts in physical reality. She could feel Nick's strong hand in hers. The pebbles beneath her toes. The rushing water beckoned. There was no turning back now. Straightening her shoulders, she nodded at Nick.

Together, they waded in.

Chapter 10

Nick couldn't have picked a better partner.

Avery was handling the pressure like a pro. He couldn't believe how well she was doing, considering her personal history. She'd passed the interview with flying colors. He'd figured she could get through it, but he hadn't expected her to be so poised. He'd seen genuine tears in her eyes when she'd claimed to want his baby. She'd known exactly what to say and when to say it. Jonah Silva had lapped up every word.

Before the meeting, Nick had thought he'd made a real connection with Jonah. Apparently not, because the young leader had forgotten him the moment he'd set eyes on "Ellen." After a light interrogation, Jonah had called the vote. It was clear he wanted to take them on as members. Or, just her. Either way, they were in.

The real test had started as soon as they exited the vehicle. Being forced to strip naked and walk through the woods, blindfolded, was an unsettling experience. He hadn't been thrilled about taking off his clothes, but losing his watch was a bigger problem. Nick hoped they didn't inspect the Timex, because it had been modified with a few FBI upgrades. The communication device and GPS unit were carefully disguised as ordinary components, but they could be discovered if someone tech-savvy took the pieces apart. Were there any tech-savvy members in The Haven? Nick didn't know.

Avery had been even more reluctant to disrobe than Nick, which was fine. These throwbacks didn't trust women who removed their clothes easily. Nick was glad she hadn't refused outright and told Jonah to go to hell.

Nick understood why they'd been ordered to strip. Jonah was paranoid about outsiders. He wanted to make sure the Deans weren't bringing in contraband, and he'd wanted them to feel powerless. Nick had to assume that Jonah wanted to see Avery naked, as well. He would relish the sight of a beautiful young woman doing his bidding. Nick had tried to ruin the show by shielding her from view, but his efforts might have been in vain. Jonah had seen her by the pool, regardless. He hadn't gaped at her like a kid in a candy shop, but he'd catalogued the goods. Nick had watched his eyes skim over her naked body before she donned her robe. Nick had forced himself to stay silent, his hands clenched into fists.

Nick wasn't sure how to categorize Jonah Silva. Nick considered everyone in the cult a perpetrator or a victim. Although Jonah didn't strike him as a victim, his actions so far were more creepy than criminal. The young leader presented himself as a milder sort of extremist. He didn't have a harem of teenaged wives. He didn't talk about watering the tree of liberty with the blood of patriots. That didn't mean he was a decent person, or an innocent bystander in his father's anti-government plots. Nick didn't really care what Jonah believed or didn't believe. If the aspiring guru laid a hand on Avery, Nick would make him pay. Until then, Nick would use every chess piece to his advantage. The fact that Jonah liked beautiful woman, including Avery, worked to Nick's advantage.

They survived the blessing ceremony, which was thankfully short. Both Nick and Avery were treated to a dunk of ice-cold water. Jonah read some mumbo-jumbo from his book. Then it was over, and they waded out of the pool.

Avery shivered beside him, her teeth chattering. The wet robe clung to her curves. Nick put his arm around her and pressed his lips to her damp hair. She didn't shove him away, but she tensed at his touch. She hated every moment of this, and it wasn't Jonah she blamed for putting her through the ordeal. It was Nick.

Sister Imogen handed them a pair of scratchy towels, her lips pursed with distaste. Nick gave his towel to Avery. She tucked one around her body and wore the other over her head like a shroud, hiding her pale face. They walked another half mile or so to the edge of the compound. It was surrounded by an ordinary chain-link fence, about eight feet high, with no razor wire or any additional barriers. The real deterrent was the armed guard standing sentry at the front gate. A pimple-faced boy with an army jacket and a rifle said hello to Jonah.

Then they were inside. Nick wanted to pump his fist in the air and shout celebratory curses in multiple languages. Instead, he got down on his hands and knees and kissed the ground. Then he hugged Jonah around the ankles. It didn't feel natural to take such a submissive position, but Nick had to go the extra mile. He blubbered his thanks in a hoarse voice. Jonah patted his head like he was a good dog.

Nick rose, wiping imaginary tears from his eyes. When he put his arm around Avery again, she wasn't quite as stiff. If he could soothe her embarrassment by humiliating himself, he would.

Jonah smiled at them indulgently. "I'll let Sister Imogen get you settled."

Brother Sage walked away with Jonah while Imogen stayed behind. Twilight had settled over the commune, but there was a lighted pathway in the distance.

"You have electricity," Nick commented.

"It's solar," Imogen said, leading them toward a row of rustic cabins. "These are our one-bedroom units, for couples or small families. Bathrooms and showers are there." She pointed to two structures on the opposite side of the path. It was like a campground, with separate facilities for men and women. Nick already knew all of this from the photos, but he was fascinated by the close-up view.

Imogen stopped at the last cabin. "Here you are. We've missed supper, but there should be some provisions inside. And clothes, though I'm not sure they'll fit." She frowned at Avery. "I'll have to bring shoes for both of you. What sizes?"

"Twelve," Nick said.

"Seven," Avery murmured.

Imogen nodded. "I'll send them over within the hour. We have a music recital tonight. Everyone attends."

"At what time?" Nick asked.

"Eight. You'll hear the bell."

Nick clasped one of her hands between his. "Thank you."

"You're welcome," she said to him, sounding genuine. With a sniff at Avery, she turned on her heel and left.

Nick opened the door and ushered Avery inside. The cabin had electricity, but little else. There was a work table, two ladder-back chairs and an old-fashioned wood-fired stove. The kitchen sink was the only hint of running water. In the bedroom, which had no door, there was a twin bed that wouldn't fit Nick by himself, let alone Nick and Avery together. A pile of clothes, folded neatly, sat on top of the blankets.

Nick touched a finger to his lips, although Avery hadn't said a word. He gestured for her to get dressed while he inspected the rest of the cabin. It appeared clean and bare. After she was finished dressing, he took his turn in the bedroom. There were homespun pants and a shirt for him, along with long-john underwear and socks. He searched every inch of the space as he donned the clothes. There were no listening devices or hidden cameras inside. An empty basket sat at the foot of the bed.

He emerged from the bedroom, noting that her clothes didn't fit as well as his. Her blouse was several sizes too small. She'd left it unbuttoned, revealing white muslin undergarments that were as old-fashioned as his. She crossed her arms over her chest, self-conscious. Nick wasn't sure she would accept his comfort, but he had to give it a try. He drew her into an embrace, which she endured as stoically as she'd endured everything else today.

"I'm sorry," he said.

"Are you?"

"I didn't know they'd make us strip."

"You said you'd protect me," she whispered.

"And I will," he said, releasing her. "No one will lay a hand on you."

"But they can look their fill?"

"That won't happen again."

She turned her face away. She didn't trust him.

He grasped her chin to bring her gaze back to his. "You're doing great. I loved what you said in the interview."

"You would."

Damn, she was beautiful. Her hair was damp, her skin flushed. Devoid of makeup, she looked younger and more touchable. Her unpainted mouth beckoned. He knew better than to dip his head for a taste. She wouldn't respond the way she had earlier, with fevered kissing and hands all over him. This morning's yes had turned into a permanent no. She didn't even want to sleep *next to him.*

And yet, he felt the same heat between them, the same temptation. The kisses they'd shared had been the hottest of his life. He could imagine how good they would be in bed together. Even so, he didn't plan to act on his attraction. He brushed a thumb over her cheek, swamped with regrets.

A thump outside the cabin interrupted the moment. She pulled away from him, seeming flustered. He opened the door to find a bundle wrapped in a burlap sack. The delivery boy scuttled away into the twilight. Nick brought the sack inside and upended it. There were two pairs of leather boots and wool socks, along with a different blouse for her and a belt for him. He donned the boots and belt while she changed her blouse. The boots for him were almost new. Hers were worn and scuffed. The second blouse was an improvement over the first, but only because she could button the front. It was faded gray, and so big it could fit two of her. Nick wondered if Sister Imogen had selected the unflattering attire on purpose. Avery sat down to put on the boots, her nose wrinkled with distaste.

"Someone doesn't like you," Nick ventured.

"I gathered that."

"Do you know why?"

She gaped at him. "You don't?"

"No."

Instead of saying it outright, she made a heart shape in the air and mouthed "Jonah." Nick puzzled out her implication. Imogen was in love with Jonah, but her feelings weren't reciprocated, and Jonah had been making eyes at "Ellen." Therefore, Sister Imogen was jealous of Ellen. That made sense. Nick was glad to have a perceptive partner to interpret these emotional undercurrents for him. Avery might not be enjoying this assignment, but she was doing a bang-up job.

There was a simple meal of bread and cheese at the table. A small collection of ceramic dishes were stacked on the counter next to the sink. Avery filled two mugs with water. Nick tore off a hunk of bread and paired it with a chunk of cheese. The bread had herbs in it and the cheese tasted fresh. He ate in ravenous bites.

"I'm going to ask for my watch back," he said, swallowing. "I need it to remember my routines."

"I need my glasses," she said. "Ask for those, too."

He grabbed more bread. "Okay."

"Do you think you'll have to get on your knees again?"

If the question was meant to make him feel less masculine, it worked. He wasn't proud of his actions as Nick Dean today. He'd allowed his wife to be ogled by strangers. Instead of objecting to the mistreatment, he'd thanked her ogler. Avery seemed to be suggesting that Nick was willing to do anything, including service another man sexually, for this assignment. He wasn't quite that dedicated. "The next time I get on my knees, it will be for you."

She flushed at the comment. "Don't hold your breath."

"I never do."

They finished their meal in silence. He probably shouldn't have baited her, but she'd fired the first shot. Also, a bit of verbal sparring wasn't the worst thing for a married couple. Disagreements indicated strong feelings. Passion, even. His parents had fought like cats and dogs, but they'd always made up afterward. Nick was struck by a vivid recollection of his mother throwing a teacup at his father, who'd ducked just in time. Porcelain had smashed on the wall behind his head.

Nick frowned at the memory, which he hadn't thought of in years. He didn't know why he was thinking of it now. He didn't need passion with Avery. There was no reason to act like a real married couple behind closed doors. He should be trying to help her stay calm, not ramping up the tension between them. Spats and sexual innuendo wouldn't put her at ease. Fantasizing about giving her pleasure wouldn't help him sleep at night, either. He was already aroused by the idea, his pulse throbbing with awareness.

He tore his gaze away from her, because he couldn't afford the distraction. He wasn't here to lust after his partner—or to catch feelings for her. He was here to take down Silva by any means possible.

After dinner he went outside to look around. He visited the men's restroom, checking out the facilities. There were shower stalls and basic facilities. Sinks with mirrors. Nick wondered if he'd get access to a shaving kit. Surely some of the men used razors. Old-fashioned straight razors. He touched the fine grains of stubble on his jaw, contemplative. A blade like that would have multiple uses.

A bell rang in the church tower, startling him. It was time to join the club. He found Avery waiting for him on the front step of the cabin. Other members were heading down the lighted footpath in the distance. When he grasped her hand, she came with him.

"Do you think he'll be there?" she murmured.

She meant Father Jeff. He could hear the edge of fear in her voice. Nick thought of the straight razor again, visualizing its impact on human organs. "If he's there, we'll meet him, and everything will be fine."

She didn't ask about her sister. Maybe it was too overwhelming to consider, or less of a concern because the girl wouldn't recognize her. Nick was confident that no one else would, either. They hadn't seen her since she was a child, twenty years ago. She was a full-grown woman now with lush curves and a mature face.

"You look nice," he said.

"In these clothes? Really?"

"Yes," he said, scanning her figure. She'd tucked the blouse into her skirt to disguise its voluminous shape. The outfit wasn't flattering, but it didn't matter what she was wearing. Avery Samuels, a.k.a. Ellen Dean, was a natural beauty. Her hair, which had dried in tousled waves, glinted in the moonlight.

"I feel naked without makeup."

"I feel naked without my gun."

She shuddered at this admission. They were alone on the path, so he wasn't worried about anyone overhearing their conversation, but maybe it was better to stay silent about certain things. He should work on being more a sensitive "husband." There was no need to remind her of the danger they were in. She knew he was unarmed, and she didn't trust him to protect her. He hoped he wouldn't have to kill anyone in front of her. If the mission went according to plan, she'd get out before hell broke loose.

"Sorry," he said gruffly. "I keep putting my foot in my mouth."

She seemed surprised by his apology. "Can we speak freely in the cabin?"

"Not yet. I'll inspect it tomorrow in the daylight."

The music recital took place inside the church, which was only a short walk from the cabins. It was a modest building that housed about a hundred parishioners. When Nick and Avery arrived, almost every pew was full. There were some furtive whispers and curious stares as they entered the space. Nick scanned the crowd for Jeff Silva, but didn't see him. There were a couple of open seats in the back row, so he guided Avery that direction. Before they reached it, a large man in overalls blocked the aisle.

"You must be the newcomers," he said, glancing back and forth between them. "I'm Brother Rupert."

Nick accepted Rupert's hearty handshake. "Nick Dean."

"Brother Nick," Rupert corrected. "And who's this pretty lady?"

"I'm Sister Ellen," Avery said with a smile. "Pleased to meet you."

"Likewise," he said, pumping her hand. He had a homely face, dotted with pockmarks. "Why'd you marry this ugly fella?"

Avery blinked in confusion. "Do you mean Nick?"

Brother Rupert laughed, slapping his knee. "I guess they can't all be as handsome as me."

A woman next to Rupert gave him a chiding look. She was a short, round woman with silver-threaded hair. "Are you scaring off the new members?"

Rupert kept chuckling at his own joke.

"Ignore him," the woman said. "I'm Sister Margot."

Avery said a polite hello. The older woman chatted about the recital and her granddaughter, who was one of the performers. Then a strange look came over her face, as if she'd realized something important.

"My goodness," she said, studying Avery intently.

Avery went still as a statue beside him. Nick grasped her elbow in warning. No matter what happened, they had to brazen it out. She couldn't run away at the first sign of trouble. He wouldn't let her.

"You're wearing one of my old blouses."

Her blouse. Nick released a slow breath of relief. False alarm. Sister Margot had recognized Avery's *blouse*.

"Sister Imogen gave it to me," Avery stammered.

"Did she? Well, that just won't do, will it? A lovely girl like you in old rags."

"I'm fine in this."

"Nonsense. I have some pretty outfits that belonged to my daughter, God rest her soul. She was about your size."

"Oh, I couldn't," Avery said.

"Of course you can," Margot replied. "I need to let go of those things, dearie. You can help me by putting them to good use."

There was no way to argue with that, so Avery didn't try.

"Which cabin are you in?"

"The last one," Nick said.

Sister Margot nodded with pleasure. "It's settled. Let's sit down."

Nick took the space next to Avery at the end of the pew. He could feel the tension in her body, still wound up tight. He threaded their hands together. Although she didn't seem comfortable with the contact, they had to do it. Every time they touched, it would get easier. The electric current of physical chemistry would start to feel normal, even humdrum.

Jonah Silva walked onto the stage and stood behind a podium. He waited for the crowd to quiet, his handsome face drawn into a jovial mask.

"Good evening, Haven."

"Good evening, Brother Jonah!" the entire flock replied. Avery jumped at the sound, though she must have expected it. Surely they'd done this twenty years ago. The same responses to the same statements.

"My father can't be here tonight. He sends his deepest regrets." The audience didn't seem surprised by this announcement. Jonah moved on quickly. "As you may have noticed, we have some special guests. I made the decision to invite two new members into our family. We'll celebrate their initiation tomorrow at holy service. For now, let's give them a warm welcome. Brother Nick and Sister Ellen, please stand."

When Nick rose to his feet, Avery stood with him. Her frozen smile matched the stilted clapping in the crowd. Nick scanned the members, noting the odd composition of family units. Groups of women, and scores of children, sat with single men.

Jonah gave the signal to quiet, so Nick and Avery took their seats again. Then Jonah introduced the music teacher, and the recital continued like any other. Children of various ages took the stage and began playing set pieces. They were quite good with their instruments. Without television or technology, mastery of this simple pastime flourished.

It was charming, despite the creepy undertones of bigamy and brainwashing. For the finale, a teenaged girl took the stage with her violin. She began a haunting solo that sent Nick back to Venezuela for the second time this evening. His mother had played the cello with passionate melancholy, every note bleeding from her fingertips.

He swallowed hard, blinking the tears from his eyes. The display of emotion bewildered and embarrassed him. He didn't cry in public. He didn't even cry in private. Something about this place, or the fraught situation, reminded him of his birth parents. They'd both been a pair of extremists in their own right. They'd died for their ideals—and he'd mourned them properly. He'd visited their graves, said goodbye and closed the door.

Avery's nudge reminded him to applaud. He'd been so wrapped up in his own thoughts that he hadn't noticed the performance was over. He covered for his inattention by standing and clapping. Margot and Rupert followed suit. Then the rest of the audience was on their feet, giving thunderous applause.

After the recital was over, families lingered to reunite with performers. Nick and Avery slipped away. He was eager to leave the close confines of the church. The events of the day had rattled him more than he'd realized; he was getting choked up over a kids' show. He didn't take Avery's hand on the lighted path. He felt too raw, his nerves on edge.

"Did you play an instrument?" she asked, tentative.

"No. You?"

"The harp."

He could imagine her strumming the harp in the church choir. If she hadn't escaped, this would have been her fate. Molded into a perfect angel, with pale, flowing hair. "My mother played the cello."

She studied his face with interest. He didn't know why he'd given that detail, unprompted. He tore his gaze away, clearing his throat. She tucked her arm in the crook of his elbow as they continued down the path.

Inside the cabin, there was no discussion of sleeping arrangements. No eye contact as he gathered a blanket and pillow from the bed. No words as he passed by her in the doorway. He was glad for the rug on the hardwood floor in the main room, which became his sleeping mat. He stretched out on his back. She turned off the lights. He could hear the mattress springs as she climbed into bed.

Then, no sound. No tossing and turning. Just stillness and tension.

Nick tucked his hands behind his head and stared into the oppressive dark. He was uncomfortable, but not for the reasons he'd expected. Instead of body aches or physical desires, he was plagued with feelings. Some were about Avery. Others were about himself, his disrupted childhood and issues unresolved. The closure he thought he'd attained seemed incomplete now. Moving on wasn't the same as mourning.

Music from the past and present echoed in his ears for many hours before he slept.

Chapter 11

Avery woke several times during the night, her heart racing.

She dreamed that they'd returned to the blessing pool for a second ceremony. She was wearing a white dress, with a crown of blossoms in her hair. When she waded into the dark water, her skirts turned red with blood. Gasping, she looked up at her companion, but it wasn't Nick who held her hand. It was Jonah.

She finally drifted off again in the wee hours of the morning. At dawn, she opened her eyes to a room filled with light. She was tired, but warm. Nick's wool blanket covered her from neck to toes. He must have gotten up already. A twinge of guilt struck her for enjoying the bed *and* the blanket. She squashed it, climbing out of bed. He'd brought her into this nightmare against her will. He wasn't concerned about her comfort and safety. Why should she be concerned about his?

The cabin was empty. As she tidied the bed, she heard Nick's voice outside, saying goodbye to someone. He came through the door a moment later with a loaded basket. "You're up," he said, eyes raking over her.

She touched her hair, which felt like a bird's nest. "How did you sleep?"

"Fine. You?"

"I got a few hours."

He extended the basket toward her. "Margot brought this stuff for you."

She accepted it from his outstretched arms and placed it on the bed. The basket held a treasure trove of items. A hairbrush, toiletries, two basic skirts, a shawl and five blouses of various colors. There was even a pair of soft leather shoes that appeared to be her size. She tried the shoes on first. They fit.

"There's a bell for breakfast," Nick said. He was watching from the doorway.

"Did it ring already?"

"No. I think it will ring soon. I can't tell what damned time it is."

She didn't remind him not to blaspheme. He must have searched the cabin thoroughly and deemed it safe. She gathered the toiletries she needed and visited the bathrooms. There were three young women inside, chatting excitedly. They went silent as soon as she entered.

"Good morning," Avery said.

"God's grace," they replied in unison, and hurried out.

Avery used the facilities before brushing her hair and teeth. There was a jar of mint powder toothpaste. She remembered it from her childhood. After she was finished, she returned to the cabin and handed the jar to Nick, along with a second toothbrush. He used it at the kitchen sink, unselfconscious. She wondered if he'd really been able to sleep last night. It was difficult to tell when he was lying. His face didn't reveal his thoughts or emotions often. He wasn't made of ice, however. Last night he'd been affected by the violin performance. Apparently it had reminded him of his mother. His eyes softened when he spoke of her. He'd lost his mother twenty-five years ago, but he still got sentimental about her.

She tried not to find that appealing, and failed.

He glanced over his shoulder at her before spitting in the sink. She realized she was staring at him while he performed an intimate, if ordinary, task. These moments were usually reserved for real married couples.

She grabbed the basket and retreated to the bedroom, her heart pounding. She told herself it was anxiety about the coming day. She shouldn't be feeling stirrings of sympathy for Nick, or stirrings of anything else. She had to focus on the task at hand. In a few minutes, they would join the others for breakfast, followed by holy service that would complete their initiation. There was a chance she would be recognized as a former daughter of The Haven. She might see Father Jeff. She might meet her sister.

Avery took a deep breath, overwhelmed. Then she selected the first blouse in the basket and put it on with shaking hands. The blouse was white with tiny blue flowers embroidered down the front. It fit comfortably loose, like a peasant blouse. Although the garment was modest, her neck and collarbone were exposed. She grabbed a gray knit shawl to wrap around her shoulders. Then she tied her hair back with a blue ribbon she'd found in the basket. Her hair was too short to braid, so the stubby ponytail would have to do. Trying to stay calm, she smoothed her skirt and returned to Nick. His gaze skimmed her outfit. He didn't say she looked nice again, but his eyes glinted with approval. She wondered if he was the kind of man who secretly preferred demure, docile women.

The next time I get on my knees, it will be for you.

Her cheeks flushed at the memory of his sexually charged comment. He wasn't the conservative, missionary-only type, judging by those words, and by their brief encounter on her couch. If his kisses were any indication, he enjoyed an enthusiastic partner.

The bell rang in the tower, bringing a fresh wave of panic. She went to the sink for a drink of water before they left. She didn't want to go, but she couldn't stay here, obsessing over what might happen next. It was better to keep moving forward, step by step.

They walked outside together. The sunlight felt too bright, the air too thin. There were other families heading toward the community's center. Avery pressed her palm to her stomach in an attempt to calm the butterflies.

"You've got this," he said, taking her hand.

She didn't believe him, but she nodded dutifully. "I've got this."

"You're doing great."

"I'm doing great."

"When in doubt, smile."

She smiled. It felt weird, like her mouth was warring with the rest of her face. He paused before they started down the path. They were alone at the edge of the commune. In the distance, two women in dresses walked behind a single man and five children of various heights. A girl chased after a little boy in a suit and bow tie. No one was paying attention to Nick or Avery—yet. They would be stared at in the breakfast hall.

"Watch what I do," he said. He took a meditative breath first. His expression went blank. Then he flashed a sincere-looking smile that began with his eyes. She realized that he'd used this technique to disarm her during their first meeting. His warm and charming manner was one of his many facades.

Setting that issue aside, she tried to mimic his actions in the same order. Deep breath, blank face, bright eyes, smile.

"You're a natural," he said, his gaze sharp.

There was no false positivity in his words, no pep talk. Just stated fact. He didn't seem surprised by her adeptness, either. The art of deception came easily to him. He assumed it would come easily to her, too. Maybe he knew it would, the way he seemed to know what she was thinking at any given moment. They shared similar trajectories in life. Childhood trauma, loss, being uprooted. Career ambitions. Relationship avoidance. She could identify the triggers. He could pull them.

He believed in her ability to do this job. His confidence boosted hers, and his unflappable attitude helped. She wanted to please him. He had an effective way of bending her to his will, but she wouldn't forget why she'd agreed to do this. She had her own agenda. At some point, it might diverge from his.

They continued down the path together. In full daylight, the place looked more quaint than sinister. Some of the cabins showed their age. Paint was peeling off the front of the old schoolhouse, which sat beside two new buildings. It was a clear, bright morning, without the misty overcast conditions that plagued Portland. She imagined the temperature would climb this afternoon. Right now, it was cool enough to make her shiver in the thin knit shawl.

Nick put his arm around her to chase away the chill. She leaned into him, the way a wife would, and sniffed his neck. She told herself it was for the role, but it wasn't. He smelled like soap and mint, mixed with earthy male. She'd read somewhere that scent was a major factor in physical attraction. If that was true, they were well matched, because she wanted to press her nose to his throat and inhale. Instead of breathing deep, she pulled away, frowning. She was a mature psychologist, not a giddy teenager. Her current fixation on Nick was a mental distraction. She couldn't process the fear and stress she was experiencing, so her mind had shifted to more pleasurable pursuits.

It was a defense mechanism. It was neuroscience.

"You don't have to sleep on the floor," she murmured.

He arched a brow. "No?"

"We can pull the mattress off the bed. I'll take the mattress. You take the bedsprings."

"I'm fine on the floor."

She opened her mouth to argue, then closed it. Haven wives didn't argue, and there was no reason to change their sleeping arrangements. She didn't know why she'd brought it up. She was in a strange headspace, torn between desire and dread.

They passed the church and entered the cafeteria together. There was a long line for breakfast. Members piled their plates high with pancakes, eggs and bacon. Children with sticky hands and faces ate happily at every table. It looked like any breakfast social, except for the old-fashioned clothing. And the polygamy.

Nick and Avery joined the others in line. After they got their plates, they found an open table and sat down. She didn't see Father Jeff or Brother Jonah in the crowd. She didn't see her stepfather, Gary, who would be in his seventies if he was still alive. Avery ate sparingly while Nick tackled his plate with methodical precision. She'd have to learn his trick for eating on a nervous stomach. Maybe he didn't get nervous. Similar trajectories or not, they hadn't developed similar personalities. She couldn't suppress her feelings.

When in doubt, smile.

She smiled.

He nodded his approval, taking a sip of coffee. "This is good."

"Farm to table," she murmured.

"No doubt."

She drank her orange juice, which tasted fresh-squeezed. They had fruit trees on the property, as well as several barnyards full of well-tended animals. These people treated their hogs better than their wives.

"I wonder if they buy flour or grow wheat. I can't imagine growing wheat here. It's so labor intensive, and the soil's rocky."

"Hmm."

"With the right crops, the meals will be even better."

Nick Dean proceeded to bore her with a litany of agriculture details. She was grateful to him for monopolizing the conversation. It kept the pressure off her and discouraged the strangers nearby from asking them questions. Before she knew it, she'd finished her eggs. He noted her empty plate with a wink. He was a sneaky operator.

After breakfast, they moved from the dining hall to the church. It was a full house. Nick and Avery took the same seats they'd inhabited the night before, next to Brother Rupert and Sister Margot.

"That blouse is lovely on you," Margot gushed to Avery. She cupped her hands together and placed them over her heart. "How old are you, dearie?"

"Thirty-one."

"My Beverly would have been thirty this year. She wore that blouse to her firstborn's blessing ceremony. Thank you for reminding me of her. I think she's looking down on us from heaven right now."

Avery was glad she'd practiced smiling with Nick. The expression felt more natural every time she tried it, and she'd experimented with several variations. The polite smile, the gentle smile, the pious smile.

Margot blinked tears from her eyes as Jonah took the stage. He began with a community prayer. They all bowed their heads as he read from his father's book, personalizing here and there with references to specific cult members. He spoke of their trials and triumphs with carefully chosen words. Avery didn't recall much about Father Jeff's sermons, but she knew they hadn't been temperate. Father Jeff had ginned up his followers with fire and brimstone, mixed with mystical ideas. Jonah had more substance, less flash.

The audience started fidgeting. Men shifted in their seats. Women scolded children in whispered hisses. A young mother with a crying baby exited through the back door. Several heads turned in interest.

Jonah didn't command the same respect or attention as Father Jeff. He wasn't crazy enough, or arrogant enough, to consider himself a messiah. He wrapped up his prayer and moved on to a hotter topic: Nick and Ellen Dean.

"If you joined us for the music recital, you already

know that I invited two new members into our flock. Brother Nick and Sister Ellen will complete the initiation during today's service. Please welcome them as warmly as you did last night."

The audience clapped politely while Nick rose to his feet, bringing Avery with him. They walked down the aisle like a newly married couple, hand in hand. Avery tried one of her smiles, but her face felt frozen. They were greeted on stage by Brother Sage and Sister Imogen, Jonah's creepy familiars. Nick and Avery stood next to Jonah, facing the crowd.

"Don't start without me," a man called out from the back of the church.

Avery's stomach dropped, because she knew that voice.

It was Father Jeff.

He was older than she remembered, but still tall and imposing. His white hair and beard flowed like an angel's wings. He wore a midnight-blue tunic and white trousers with his signature leather sandals. He strode down the aisle, arms open and raised in greeting, eyes bright with holy fervor. No less than three women and twelve children followed him. They took a pew in front that had apparently been reserved for Father Jeff's brood. Avery's sister wasn't one of the wives present. Where was she?

"Father," Jonah said stiffly. "How good of you to join us."

If Father Jeff was bothered by his son's cool greeting, he didn't show it. He climbed the steps to the stage and addressed his flock. "Family," he said in an adoring tone.

"Father," they shouted back in unison.

Yes, these were *his* followers. Not Jonah's.

"I apologize for missing the music recital," Father Jeff said. "I heard the performances were outstanding. Grace wasn't feeling well, so I stayed with her. She's been confined to bed rest until the baby comes."

Grace, Avery's mind whispered. Her sister's name was Grace.

"I will pray for her confinement to end," Jonah said.

Father Jeff squinted at this comment, which seemed to have a double meaning. Then he turned to her and Nick. He sized Nick up before moving on to Avery. Her breath caught in her throat as his gaze swept over her, lingering on her chest. She felt nauseated by his perusal, beyond nervous. It was almost like an out-of-body experience. She was staring down at herself, frozen in place.

"They are tainted," Father Jeff said.

"I've cleansed them," Jonah countered.

"We don't accept outsiders."

A hush fell over the crowd. Imogen stood like a deer in headlights. She seemed torn between her loyalty to Jonah and her natural inclination to agree with Father Jeff. She hadn't wanted the Deans to join the commune. It appeared that Jonah hadn't asked for his father's approval in this matter. The tension on stage was palpable.

"We've accepted outsiders before," Jonah said. "Our need is great, and they are worthy."

Father Jeff stroked his beard, considering. "How can you guarantee their worth?"

Jonah glanced at Avery, as if her worth was clear. Nick bristled beside her, affronted on her behalf. Or perhaps on his own. Nick Dean thought highly of his botany skills, and he was the true believer between them.

"New members can't be initiated without my blessing," Father Jeff said. "I will look into their souls and cleanse them by my own hand."

Jonah didn't object to this suggestion. His father held the power here, even if Jonah had usurped him momentarily. Nick straightened his shoulders beside her, ready to be judged. He was confident in Father Jeff's lack of psychic ability. Avery prayed the guru wouldn't notice any resemblance between her and Grace. Father Jeff stepped in front of Nick first. The two men were about the same height. Although Nick kept his eyes downcast in a deferential manner, Father Jeff wasn't satisfied.

"Kneel," he said.

Nick knelt without argument. She'd criticized him for kneeling earlier, but she'd done it only to goad him. There was no weakness in Nick Diaz, no fear whatsoever. He wanted to see Father Jeff nailed to the wall, at any cost. She was afraid of the actions Nick would take to accomplish that goal.

Brother Sage brought a bowl of holy water for the blessing. Father Jeff dipped his thumb into the water and swept it over Nick's forehead. He said a quick prayer before he shifted his attention to Avery. He didn't ask her to kneel before him, thank God. She stood very still as his thumb painted a wet mark between her brows. Then he grasped her chin with one hand and searched her face.

"You are one of us," he said. "Part of our family, as if born to us."

Avery's heart froze at this oddly accurate statement. Her eyes slid to Imogen, who might find the deeper meaning in those words. Father Jeff was a convincing performer. Avery felt like a rabbit caught in a trap, heart bursting with adrenaline. Was he making this up, or did he recognize her?

He moved his hand to her forehead, as if he could read her soul through his palm. "I see you barefoot in the woods. I see a newborn child."

Avery swallowed hard, blinking rapidly. She didn't know how to hide her fear, or how to suppress it, the way Nick did. Nick glanced up at her from his suppliant position. His hands were linked behind his back, his expression calm.

Father Jeff continued to surprise her. He grasped her shoulders and turned her toward the crowd. Embracing her from behind, he flattened her hands over her stomach. Her pulse raced and her skin crawled at his twisted exploration. She wanted to kick and scream and fight—for her sister, for her mother, for herself. Instead she stayed quiet, enduring his touch. The same way she'd endured it twenty years ago.

"No seed grows here," he declared. "You are barren."

Avery frowned at the strange diagnosis. She'd never tried to conceive a child, but she had no reason to believe she couldn't. It dawned on her that Father Jeff was inventing a medical problem to cure in front of his loyal followers.

The realization calmed her nerves. She'd watched him perform this routine before. He couldn't see into her past, and he couldn't predict her future. He was just putting on a show, like any two-bit faith healer.

"I see you with a babe," Father Jeff said. "You will be blessed in The Haven. Our land will be fertile and your belly will grow round with a child."

Nick, who was still on his knees at her feet, wrapped a hand around her ankle. She wasn't comforted by the gesture. Father Jeff continued to knead her stomach. She got the impression that he wanted to plant *his* seed there. She suppressed a shudder of disgust. Memories of him stroking her hair after her mother's death assailed her. This was his style of leadership. He preyed on the needy and vulnerable. But she wasn't a young, helpless girl anymore. She'd escaped him once before; she could escape him now.

She collapsed against him heavily, pretending to faint. Father Jeff wasn't ready for this maneuver. She slid from his grasp like a wet noodle. Nick caught her fall, as she'd hoped. He cradled her in his arms and pressed his lips to her hair. She was vaguely aware of Father Jeff taking a bow on stage. The audience roared with applause. They loved a good healing, or groping, or whatever had just transpired.

Avery clung to Nick, sobbing.

The rest of the initiation passed in a blur. Nick helped Avery to her feet. She wiped the tears from her cheeks. Father Jeff recited one of his mystical chants and spoke about the power of faith. Imogen looked disappointed by the proceedings.

So did Jonah, but for different reasons. He seemed irritated with his father for stealing his thunder. He closed his bible with a snap as soon as the ritual was over. Then he presented the new members to the crowd.

"It is done. Brother Nick and Sister Ellen are part of our family."

Father Jeff clapped Jonah on the back, a little too hard. He shook hands with Nick and Brother Sage. He ignored Imogen, who stood at Jonah's side like a proper little minion. When the audience filed out, Father Jeff returned to his wives and went with them. Jonah gestured for Nick and Avery to follow him into a small room tucked behind the stage. He sat down at a large wooden desk. Nick and Avery took seats across from him. Sister Imogen poked her head in to check on them.

"Do you need anything from me, Brother Jonah?"

"No," he said, waving her away.

"It was a great service."

"Thank you."

"I'll see you at lunch."

"God's grace."

"God's grace."

Jonah folded his hands on top of the desk, his expression grave. "You didn't tell me you couldn't have children."

Avery was still reeling from the ordeal on stage. She had no response for Jonah's accusation.

"We didn't know," Nick said.

"You said you wanted a baby, but hadn't been blessed yet."

"That's right."

"Have you tried to get pregnant?" Jonah asked Avery.

She moistened her lips, uncertain.

"You can tell him," Nick said.

Avery didn't know *what* to tell him. They hadn't decided on a specific script for every possibility. The best she could do was invent a plausible excuse and hope Jonah believed it. "We were going to let it happen naturally."

"And it didn't, after three years?"

"No."

"Weren't you concerned?"

"I was concerned about Nick," she said. "Managing his illness has been my top priority. I haven't thought of anything else."

"So you could be infertile," Jonah said.

"She's not infertile," Nick said. "Father Jeff just said she'd have a baby."

Jonah's mouth twisted with frustration. He couldn't

argue that his father was a charlatan whose word meant nothing. Nick grasped Avery's hand and kissed her knuckles. She smiled at him tearfully.

"I don't like being lied to," Jonah said.

Nick released her hand. "My wife doesn't lie."

"Consider my perspective," Jonah said to Nick. "I've invited two outsiders here for the first time in decades. I thought you were worthy of this honor, despite your illness. Her womb, and your ability to fill it, was a significant factor in your acceptance."

"Forgive me," Nick said, more contrite. "I downplayed the issue in the meeting yesterday, but Ellen is telling you the truth. We've been focused on my health instead of her desire for a child." He gave Avery an apologetic glance before returning his attention to Jonah. "The fault is all mine."

Jonah leaned back in his chair, dissatisfied.

"What can I do to prove my worth?"

"Get her with child as soon as possible. That will please my father."

"Will it please you?"

Jonah's gaze flitted between Nick and Avery. There was something melancholy about his expression, as if his pleasure couldn't be attained. "It will please me if you follow my orders without question."

Nick nodded his compliance. Avery stayed silent, her eyes downcast. They were supposed to be fruitful and multiply, not ask questions. Even so, Avery wondered about Jonah's unmarried status, and the tension between him and his father. Jonah was old enough to take a wife, but hadn't done so. He'd chosen Imogen to be part of his trusted inner circle. Avery had heard his critical tone when he'd spoken of Grace's confinement. Maybe Jonah disagreed with his father's treatment of women.

"Don't mention your brain disease to anyone else," Jonah said. "As of now, that matter is just between us."

"Of course," Nick said. "I feel better already."

"God's grace," Jonah said, dismissing them.

"God's grace," Nick and Avery parroted.

They walked out of the rectory and into the bright sunshine. It was warm enough that she didn't need her shawl, which she'd left behind. She hoped Sister Margot had retrieved it for her. As they headed down the path together, Avery noted the various groups of churchgoers chatting in the community's center. There was a garden on one side and a ballpark on the other. Boys were already playing a game, their Sunday sleeves rolled up to the elbows. Girls were picking wildflowers at the edge of the field.

Avery had gathered flowers here as a child while her mother socialized. They'd both worked in the garden every summer. She pulled her gaze away from the humble scene. Nick led her past the churchgoers and continued toward the cabin. He seemed to understand that she needed to retreat. She was drained from the morning's events, her head spinning with memories both dark and light.

They retreated to the cabin, which appeared even more cramped than before. She felt like a prisoner in a terrible sleepaway camp.

"Are you all right?" Nick asked.

"No."

"What can I do to help?"

Overwhelmed, she sank into a chair. He poured her a fresh cup of water and sat down across from her.

"It's okay to talk. I've checked every inch of this place."

She took a sip of water, saying nothing.

"I had to kneel again."

Her lips curved faintly. "I saw that."

"Did he touch you, before you ran away?"

Avery hesitated before answering. She wasn't eager to share the details of her past. She wouldn't feel safe here no matter how many times he checked the cabin for listening devices. "He didn't get the chance."

"What do you mean?"

"He stroked my hair the night my mother died, and promised to take care of me. He said he needed a new bride."

"Is that why you left?"

"It was a factor."

Nick stood, rubbing a hand over his jaw. He paced the room a few times, visibly agitated. "I don't think he recognized you. That's the good news."

"What's the bad news?"

"The bad news is he's not a fighter. He preys on defenseless girls, but he's nonconfrontational with men. He couldn't even look me in the eye. When the time comes, he'll surrender to law enforcement."

"Why is that bad news?"

"Because I'll have to take him alive."

Chapter 12

Nick prowled around the cabin while Avery retreated to the bedroom.

He hadn't slept much in the past forty-eight hours, but he was too wired to rest. Also, he wasn't eager to stretch out on the hardwood floor again. He still had a crick in his neck from last night. Massaging the ache, he thought about Jeff Silva. The unmitigated nerve of a man who would force a husband to kneel and watch while he felt up his wife.

Bastard.

Father Jeff's hands hadn't strayed too far beyond the bounds of propriety. He'd touched Avery's lower abdomen under the guise of healing her "affliction," so Nick couldn't protest, even though Father Jeff had stroked her stomach with the same relish he might have cupped her breasts. It was creepy, it was intrusive and it was blatant. Nick had wanted to break both of his mystical hands and smash his sandaled feet. Jonah Silva hadn't seemed comfortable with his father's actions, either. He'd stood by with an air of disapproval, which had reinforced Nick's first impression: Jonah was a possible ally. Not an innocent, but an ally. Jonah was complicit in his father's abuses.

Nick wished he hadn't told Avery that he would take Jeff Silva alive. He couldn't make any promises about the outcome of the investigation. He'd gone off the rails the moment he'd recruited Avery. He was no longer in communication with his department. For all he knew, the mission had been terminated.

Nick's SAC would probably wait for him to report back before deciding the next step. If Nick unearthed some actual evidence, his team would act on it. If he didn't... Nick was in serious trouble. He couldn't arrest Silva without support. He could only do recon and try to communicate his findings. There was a chance of Silva escaping prosecution, no matter what Nick discovered. Silva might take his own life, and encourage his followers to do the same. He might get off scot-free and continue terrorizing and impregnating young women, while also conspiring against the government.

Nick couldn't live with that kind of loose end. He wasn't above cutting it through illegal and immoral means. Exacting a personal revenge on Silva wouldn't bother Nick in the least. He'd welcome the opportunity. When he wasn't fantasizing about Avery, he was fantasizing about murder. Ms. Freud would have a field day with that, wouldn't she?

"Nick?" she called from the bedroom.

He walked to the doorway and looked in. She was lying on her side, staring at the blank wall. The bedroom had no windows. It was dark and confined, a closet with deep corners. "Yeah?"

She glanced over her shoulder at him. Her hair had come loose from the blue ribbon, creating a silky disarray. "Talk to me about your work."

He ventured farther into the room and stood with his back to the wall. There was an empty wooden chest at the foot of the bed that could double as a chair, but he didn't want to sit. He noted the irony of their positions. She was the shrink, reclining like a patient. She had an arm tucked behind her head. Softly supine, with feminine curves and a nipped-in waist. He tore his gaze away before his imagination wandered. "What do you want to know?"

"What happened to the other agent?"

"Ellen?"

"The man who was killed on the last assignment."

He studied his scuffed boots, unsure where to start. "His name was Chris."

"Chris," she said, as if committing it to memory. "How did he die?"

"He was shot twice. The first bullet went through his rib cage and grazed his lung. The second one was to the head. It wasn't survivable."

"Do you know who did it?"

"FBI arrested a guy named Beck. He's the leader of the White Army. Jeff Silva has been meeting him in private and helping him raise funds. Beck is a suspect in the bombing of a federal building in Sacramento. Two employees were injured. Chris went undercover to investigate the militia."

"Was Beck acting on Father Jeff's orders?"

"For the terror attack?"

"And the shooting."

"He didn't admit to the connection, but I'm sure of it. The members of the White Army are amateurs. They're your basic rowdy, disorganized bigots. Beck is a thug. He couldn't have identified our man on his own. The day after Chris was introduced to Silva, he was executed."

She lifted her head off her arm to examine his face. He kept his expression blank without really meaning to. The habit was so ingrained, he did it on instinct. He wasn't hiding his feelings so much as burying them.

"What did he mean to you?" she asked.

He glanced up at the ceiling, which was about as interesting as his boots. "I'd known him for more than ten years. We were friends."

"Work friends?"

"More than that. We hung out after work."

"How often?"

"Too often, in his wife's opinion."

"You said he cheated on her."

"Yes."

"Did you know he was cheating?"

"Yes," he admitted, after a pause.

"Did you disapprove?"

He massaged the nape of his neck, considering. "I told him he was going to get caught. That's as judgmental as I got."

"You didn't tell him to stop?"

"No. He wouldn't have listened."

"What about her?"

"His wife?"

She nodded. "What's she like?"

He grappled for an apt descriptor. "She's…nice."

"Nice-looking, or nice personality?"

"Both."

Avery propped her head on her hand, elbow bent. "Did you tell her he was cheating?"

"Hell no."

"Why not?"

"He was my best friend, and it was none of my business."

"Would you have lied, if she'd asked you about it?"

He didn't answer.

"*Did* she ask you about it?"

Nick pushed away from the wall and started pacing the room. She was pretty good at ferreting out emotions from the dry well of his soul. He could lie to her, or refuse to speak on this subject. He could shut down and blank his face. The problem was, he needed her on his team. Giving her the cold shoulder wouldn't help them work together. She'd already been subjected to the degrading whims of Jonah and Jeff Silva. She'd played her role well. If psychoanalyzing him reduced her stress level, so be it. He could open up.

"She didn't ask me about it until after they separated," Nick said. "She'd already caught him sneaking around, and he'd admitted to an affair. She called me from a bar one night, crying. I offered to give her a ride home."

"Did she accept?"

"Yes."

"What did you tell her?"

"Very little. I don't think she wanted the details."

"What did she want?"

"Comfort," he said. "Revenge."

Avery rose to a sitting position. "Did she get it?"

He rubbed a hand over his mouth, shrugging.

"You slept with your best friend's wife?"

"They were separated."

She gaped at him, incredulous.

"It wasn't my finest moment," he allowed.

"Why did you do it?"

He tried to articulate his reasons. "She was upset with me because I'd covered for him. She was hurting. I knew that she'd gone to that bar to find someone to make her feel good. Better me than a stranger."

"You considered this an act of kindness?"

"I didn't say that."

"Was it just once?"

"It was just one night."

She studied him for a moment. "Did she tell him?"

He braced an arm against the doorframe. "I don't know. They weren't on speaking terms, and he never mentioned it."

She rose from the bed. "Have you considered that she did it to punish him? Not to assuage her hurt, but to hurt *him*?"

"Yes," he ground out.

"Do you feel guilty?"

"Of course I feel guilty. I went back and forth about telling him myself. I made excuses to avoid him. I didn't want to lose him as a friend or jeopardize our professional relationship. Then he picked up the undercover assignment and that was it. I never saw him alive again."

"You blame yourself," she said, studying him.

He didn't want to admit she was right. He felt responsible for Chris's death. Maybe Chris had taken on a dangerous assignment because his marriage was ending and his best friend had betrayed him.

"Have you spoken to her?"

"Only at the funeral."

"And?"

"And what?"

"He's out of the picture now."

Nick scowled at her wording. "I don't want to date her."

"What's wrong with her?"

"Nothing."

"Was the sex disappointing?"

"No. It was good."

"But not good enough to repeat."

"It was a mistake," he said, his voice clipped. "We both knew that. I wouldn't ask her out because she's the widow of a fellow agent. The guys in the department would never let me live it down, and Chris's death would hang over us like a goddamned shroud. Plus, I haven't even looked at another woman since…"

She moistened her lips. "Since what?"

"Since I met you," he said, holding her gaze. "I haven't looked at another woman since I met you."

Color rose to her cheeks at his admission. She crossed her arms over her chest, which had the spectacular effect of plumping her breasts against the neckline of her blouse. The modest undergarment acted like an old-fashioned corset.

He couldn't prevent his eyes from dipping. The best he could do was raise them again, because her face was even more arresting than her figure. He watched with bated breath, waiting for any hint of encouragement.

She wanted him to talk about his feelings, but he'd much rather express himself physically. He wanted to take her to bed. Sexual release was a guaranteed stress reliever. He'd make sure to give her pleasure, kneeling and worshipping in his preferred style. Plus, he'd be following Jonah's orders.

The last thought had a chilling effect. Nick couldn't take the risk of unprotected sex, and that was the only kind they could have here. These backwater zealots didn't believe in birth control. His chances of scoring a condom were nil. He imagined asking Jonah for one, along with his watch and a straight razor.

Ha.

She arched a brow. "This is funny to you?"

"No," he said, erasing his smile. "It just feels good to confess my sins. Like a weight's been lifted off my shoulders."

She didn't appear to believe him, which was perceptive of her. He was giving her a line. Stepping forward, she poked a finger at his shirtfront. "Do you want to know what I think? I think you do this to avoid feelings."

"Do what?"

"Turn on the charm. Make it physical."

"I'm not 'making it physical' on my own," he said, capturing her hand against his chest. His heart pounded under her fingertips. He knew the attraction between them wasn't one-sided. He'd encountered the evidence firsthand in her apartment. She'd kissed him with enough heat to incinerate them both.

"When a woman asks you for emotions, you give her sex."

He couldn't evaluate the plausibility of this theory; he was too fixated on her mouth. The words *sex* and *ask* sent blood rushing to his groin. He rubbed his thumb over the pulse point in her slender wrist. "I'll give you whatever you need."

Her pulse leaped at his touch, but he didn't have to count the beats to gauge her responsiveness. It was clear from her flushed skin, her dilated pupils and parted lips. Her chest rose and fell with rapid breaths.

When he slid his free arm around her waist, pulling her close enough to align their lower bodies, she didn't resist. Quite the opposite; she lifted her lips to his. He made an animal sound and crushed his mouth over hers. He was already aroused, his senses clouded by lust. He kissed her with a hunger that bordered on desperation.

There was no charm or finesse in it. He wasn't kissing her to avoid his feelings, or to regain control of the situation. He was kissing her because he had to kiss her, emotional consequences be damned.

She didn't seem too concerned about his motivations, or bothered by his inelegance. She pressed her breasts to his chest and tangled her tongue with his eagerly.

Santa Maria.

His erection went stiff as a board between them. When she moaned into his mouth, grinding her softness along his length, he lost the ability to think. He filled his palms with her supple backside and lifted her against him.

Instinct had him heading toward the bed, where he fell on top of her. The curves of her body felt like heaven underneath him. He thrust into the cradle of her hips, groaning. It was crude and clumsy and hot as hell. She purred her approval, so he kept doing it, plundering her mouth with his tongue at the same time. The firm mattress made a perfect surface for rough-and-tumble sex. He gathered a handful of her skirt and pushed it up, fumbling for bare skin.

A knock at the door caused her to freeze underneath him.

He broke the kiss, panting. His erection throbbed with frustration, rock-hard.

"Sister Ellen?"

It was Margot.

"Just a minute," Avery said, her voice strained.

Nick couldn't roll over on the narrow bed. With a groan, he lifted his weight from her and stood. The buttons of his homespun pants strained to contain his arousal. He was almost embarrassed by the exaggerated tent. When she caught sight of him and bit her lower lip, brow furrowed with want, he had to turn away. He was so close, a hot look could set him off. The bedsprings squeaked as she scrambled to her feet.

He stayed in the bedroom, trying to will away his raging hard-on, while she had a short conversation with Margot. To his relief, the woman didn't ask to come in. By the time Avery thanked her for stopping by and shut the door, Nick had his body under control. He went to the sink to fill a mug with cold water. He drank several gulps before hazarding a glance at Avery. She held another basket in her arms.

"Do you think she heard us?" Avery asked.

He shrugged. It was the least of his troubles.

Avery set the basket on the table. "We can't get carried away again."

"I know."

"You do?"

He nodded. "I shouldn't have started anything. I apologize."

She crossed her arms over her chest. "You apologize?"

"Would you rather I didn't?"

Her eyes narrowed at his surly tone. He knew what they'd both prefer: a steamy resolution in the bedroom. She seemed offended by his agreement that they should not, in fact, do that. She rifled through the items in the basket, her brow furrowed.

He could have mentioned condoms, but he was reluctant to use that excuse. They could get each other off without using protection. If she was up for that, he didn't want to know—because he wouldn't be able to resist. His control was hanging by a thread, and he needed to keep his distance for professional reasons. He'd crossed the line by making her his partner. His recruitment tactics had been highly questionable. He hadn't been straight with her, and the information he'd fabricated might come back to haunt him. He couldn't afford to complicate the situation with sex.

There were emotional repercussions he didn't want to deal with, as well. Avery Samuels was relationship material. They'd had an instant and undeniable connection. He'd told her more about his past than he'd told any of his previous girlfriends. He'd confessed his deepest secrets to her with an air of nonchalance, but he didn't feel like a weight had been lifted from his shoulders. He felt like he was standing at the edge of a precipice, about to fall off.

Avery gasped as she discovered an item in the basket. She lifted a tiny garment between her thumbs and forefingers. It was an infant onesie.

Nick, who'd just taken another sip of water, coughed it out in a spray of disbelief. Avery doubled over with laughter at his reaction. Nick laughed with her, wiping his face.

"Jesus," he said. "They could at least wait for us to finish doing it."

She wiped tears from her eyes. It was encouraging to see her cry with laughter, rather than sadness. He was glad she could find some humor in their situation. If they couldn't engage in one stress reliever, they'd take another.

"You have to remember not to use the lord's name in vain," she said.

He made a sign of the cross. "I'll do ten Hail Marys."

She smiled at his religious reference. "You were raised Catholic?"

"Yes."

Instead of using this opportunity to grill him about his tragic past, or psychoanalyze him, she let the subject drop. "Margot invited me to her garden club."

"When is it?"

"This afternoon."

He wanted to examine the land that was available for growing crops. He couldn't plant his seed in Mrs. Dean, as ordered, so he might as well do his other job properly. "I need to take a tour of the fields."

"I'll go with you."

"You don't have to."

"I know."

He didn't argue, because her input would be helpful, and staying together was wise. Someone else might drop in for a visit while he was gone. Someone like Father Jeff, or Brother Jonah. Nick didn't trust either of them with Avery.

He waited as she changed her soft leather shoes for the heavier boots and retied her hair with the blue ribbon. She looked stronger than she had after the service. She'd been pale and distant, even numb. Now the color had returned to her cheeks and there was sparkle in her eyes. The retreat to the cabin had done her good. Maybe their make-out session had revved her up a little, too. It had certainly gotten his blood pumping. He'd pay the price tonight, when he couldn't sleep for wanting her.

As they strolled down the main path, they ran into Rupert. He winked at Avery and said hello to Nick. "Where are you two off to?"

"I wanted to check out the summer crops," Nick said. "See what's growing."

"Have you seen the garden?"

"Yes."

"That's it."

"You're kidding."

"I wish I was."

"You don't have anything planted in the fields?"

"It's been a tough year for farming," Rupert explained. "First Brother Michael passed, God rest his soul. Then we lost his apprentice to holy service. In the spring, Father Jeff decided we needed more guards because of the reckoning. There wasn't anyone left to tend the fields." Rupert patted Nick on the shoulder. "You've got your work cut out, Brother."

"What's the reckoning?" Nick asked.

"It's the destruction of the outside world. Father Jeff has visions about it. Evil forces are gaining ground all around us, which I'm sure you know. We're safe here, but we have to protect ourselves."

Nick didn't mention the obvious, that stable food resources and self-sufficiency were better safety measures than armed guards. "And holy service?"

"That's a rite of passage. Every young man in The Haven journeys beyond our borders to perform a spiritual task. Some stray off the holy path when they cross into the secular plane and don't come back."

Avery appeared surprised by the description of this practice, as if she hadn't heard of it before. Maybe holy service was a new strategy for culling the flock of strong male competitors. Nick grasped Avery's hand. She changed her expression to a sunny smile.

Rupert looked back and forth between them. If he suspected they were anything other than devout worshippers of Father Jeff, his face didn't show it. "I know who can give you a tour of the fields," he said, waving at someone nearby. "Brother Jonah asked me to fetch him for that very purpose, in fact."

"Who's that?"

"Brother Jeremiah."

Chapter 13

Avery feared Father Jeff more than any other Haven member—with one exception.

Jeremiah Silva had been her worst tormentor as a child. His careless cruelty and hair-trigger temper had plagued her throughout grade school. Over time, however, the specter of Jeremiah had faded. She supposed that getting her braids yanked and her shins kicked by a prepubescent boy paled in comparison with losing her mother. Suffering his abuse wasn't as disturbing as almost becoming a teen bride, or surviving for months in the woods alone. But her nightmares of the storm cellar continued to haunt her.

Some horrors stayed fresh.

She'd been so anxious about facing Father Jeff and Brother Jonah that she'd almost forgotten about Jeremiah. She hadn't seen him at the music recital, or this morning's breakfast. One glance at him revealed a formidable opponent who might have eclipsed his father as the scariest person in the cult. No longer a boy, he still radiated belligerence. He'd grown tall and heavy-limbed, with long hair and an unkempt beard reminiscent of Father Jeff, circa 1980. He didn't have the photogenic good looks of the young guru, whose handsome face had helped give rise to his cult stardom. Jeremiah's nose was too large and his eyes were too close together. He was probably considered attractive despite these flaws, and because of his social status. He looked strong enough to hold his own in any fight he picked.

As he approached the trio, Jeremiah turned his head and spat in the dirt. Avery's smile slipped, and no amount of reassurance from Nick could bring it back. She held on to his hand like a lifeline. Luckily, Jeremiah didn't focus on her. He gave Nick a close study, scanning his physique as if to make sure the new guy wasn't bigger than him.

"Brother Rupert," Jeremiah said in greeting.

"Have you met the new members of our flock?"

"No."

Rupert made the introductions. Jeremiah wore an impatient, put-upon expression. Nick wasn't bigger than Jeremiah, but he was big enough to pose a serious threat. Jeremiah appeared to dislike him on sight, and Avery by association. His gaze skipped over her without lingering. She gathered that she was unworthy of his attention.

Avery wasn't offended by his disinterest; she was relieved. He clearly didn't recognize her, and the less he cared about her, the better. When they were kids, she'd gone out of her way to avoid his notice. She would use the same strategy now, and stay quiet. Jeremiah had none of the polish or civility of his brother. He lacked the natural charisma of his father. The gift he'd been given was brute strength. She wondered if he wielded it at the urging of Father Jeff, or followed his own whims.

"Brother Jeremiah oversees the guards and manual laborers," Rupert said.

Avery's stomach sank at the implication. Jeremiah was Nick's boss. She hoped they wouldn't butt heads.

"Nick's going to be our lead farmer."

Jeremiah arched a brow. "Is that right?"

"Brother Jonah wanted you to give him a tour."

"He said that?"

"He did."

"Great," Jeremiah said, unenthused. "I'm heading back to the ranch after lunch, so we'll have to do it tomorrow."

"How about now?" Nick said.

"No time like the present," Rupert agreed.

Jeremiah shrugged and spat in the dirt again.

"I can't wait to see the fields," Nick said in an earnest voice, as if he hadn't noticed Jeremiah's reluctance. He smiled at Rupert and squeezed Avery's hand. "Working on a small farm is a dream come true for me."

Jeremiah grunted a response.

"I'd come with, but I've got a sow in labor," Rupert said. "I was just looking for Dr. Winslow."

"He's over there," Jeremiah said, gesturing toward the shade. His tone sounded wistful, as if he'd rather be resting under the oak branches with the elders, or retreating to the luxury of his father's estate.

"Thanks," Rupert said. "God's grace."

Jeremiah had a golf cart nearby. It stood out like a sore thumb in the pioneer-style village. Things had changed since Avery had lived here twenty years ago. She'd heard of the reckoning; Father Jeff had been talking about that forever. Holy service was unfamiliar to her. In her day, truculent boys had been whipped into shape, literally. Solar power was new, and there were other upgrades. Jeff Silva's compound. The church had been renovated. For the most part, life in the commune remained unchanged.

Jeremiah lumbered toward the golf cart and got behind the wheel. Nick took the passenger space. Avery climbed into the back seat, which faced the opposite direction. The vehicle lurched forward before she'd gotten settled. She gripped the side of the cart to keep from toppling out.

· "Hang on," Jeremiah said, smirking at her near fall.

As they zoomed through the community's center, she noted its distinctive features. The brick schoolhouse sat in the same corner, across from the church. There were various outbuildings for storage and workshops. The men of The Haven made their own tools and furniture. Women made soap, candles, clothes, bread and cheese. They had a blacksmith, a builder and a veterinarian. Jeremiah gave a terse account of these accomplishments, with minimal details.

"Is there a doctor?" Nick asked.

"Dr. Winslow."

"Isn't he the vet?"

"He's both," Jeremiah said. "We're faith healers."

Avery waited for Nick to ask why animals couldn't be healed by faith. When he didn't, she applauded his restraint. Nick Dean knew when to shut up and smile. He wasn't curious or argumentative, like the hardnosed Nick Diaz. They zipped past the barn and grazing fields. Jeremiah informed them that Rupert was in charge of livestock, somewhat begrudgingly. Beyond the grazing fields was the cemetery. There were grave markers in neat rows to commemorate the dearly beloved. Her mother's grave would be there. Avery sat up straighter, her heart racing. Jeremiah drove by too fast for her to read any of the headstones. She vowed to return at her first opportunity.

The Marble Mountains loomed in the background, protecting The Haven's east side. At the base of this craggy range was a stretch of rolling hills. This land had always been used for crops. Even to Avery's untrained eye, it was in a sad state of disrepair.

Jeremiah pulled to a stop beside an equipment shed. Nick hopped out and strode across a weed-strewn field. The foxtails were waist high in some places. Avery stood at a distance, her arms crossed over her chest. Jeremiah stayed in the golf cart. He wasn't interested in making conversation, so she didn't try. Her thoughts wandered to the explosive encounter with Nick. She touched her lips, imagining his taste on them.

I'll give you whatever you want.

He had a way with words. His voice had dragged over her like a rough caress, stirring her overwrought senses. The sexy comments he made struck her as both impulsive and defensive. Impulsive, because he wanted her, even though he knew he shouldn't. Defensive, because he wasn't comfortable with his emotions. He'd rather take her to bed than answer personal questions.

She wondered why he'd agreed to no further contact. He'd been polite so far, giving her the space she'd asked for. He hadn't grabbed her and kissed her against her will. If anything, she'd invited him to touch her—and she'd encouraged him to keep touching her. His fierce response had thrilled her beyond belief. When he'd slid his hand up her skirt, she'd shuddered with excitement.

His arousal had been unmistakable. They'd been *this close* to consummating their fake marriage.

After the interruption by Margot, Avery had come to her senses. He'd accepted her rejection without argument. She hadn't expected him to be so casual about it. He hadn't even seemed disappointed. He'd apologized for crossing the line.

Ugh.

She watched Nick wade through the overgrown field. Dandelions clung to his trousers, their puffs floating in the stirred-up air. She had to admit that the setting complimented him. The homespun shirt clung to his broad shoulders and well-muscled arms. She dragged her gaze away and found Jeremiah glaring at Nick's back. His eyes were narrowed, his lips curled around a straw of hay.

Something about Nick bothered Jeremiah. Avery didn't think it was his athletic build. Maybe it was his eagerness to clear the field. Maybe the presence of an outsider grated on Jeremiah's nerves for other reasons.

She glanced across the dirt road, where an apple orchard grew wild. The trees were mature and appeared healthy enough to bear fruit come fall. Avery remembered apple season vividly. Every member of The Haven pitched in at harvest time, when the air was cool and crisp. She'd helped her mother jar the fruit and make apple butter. They'd had apple pie every October on her birthday, with homemade ice cream straight from the churner. She pressed a palm to her stomach, nostalgic.

Nick inspected the fields and the contents of the shed before returning to Jeremiah. "Can you tell me what crops grew here?"

"Corn, wheat, hay," Jeremiah said. "Sometimes other stuff."

"Like what?"

"Potatoes and squash. There's seed in the storage house."

"What are the livestock eating?"

Jeremiah squinted at him in annoyance. "You'll have to ask Rupert."

"Does he have goats?"

"Yeah."

"I need them out here as soon as possible. How many workers can I get?"

"We're short on labor," Jeremiah said. "Brother Sage has a crew working with him on a drainage system. We had heavy rains last year. Almost every home has weather damage, too. Those repairs can't wait."

"Neither can this."

Jeremiah chewed his straw, unmoved.

"You can't spare anyone? Teenaged boys? Girls?"

"Girls?"

"Sure," Nick said. "I'll take all the help I can get."

Jeremiah chuckled at the thought of girls doing manual labor.

"I can ask the garden club," Avery offered.

"Great idea," Nick said, brightening. "If I can get a herd of goats and a dozen helpers, we can clear an entire field this afternoon."

The lunch bell sounded, a faint clang in the distance. Jeremiah gestured for them to get back in the cart. Avery hurried to comply, afraid he'd take off without her. Nick didn't press him about the labor situation. For a man in charge of overseeing workers, Jeremiah seemed disinterested in actual work. He wasn't as surly on the way back to the center, however. He made small talk, his body language more relaxed. Perhaps he'd dismissed Nick as a threat. Anyone who would clear fields with females was beneath Jeremiah's contempt.

Lunch was a simple meal of ham and cheese sandwiches. There was a bushel of peaches at the end of the chow line. Avery grabbed one, turning it over in her hand. She didn't remember a peach tree. Instead of dining with them, Jeremiah disappeared in the crowd.

"Good riddance," Nick muttered as they sat down.

Avery bit into the peach, which was fresh picked and warm from the sun. Nick watched her devour it with interest. He polished off his sandwich and half of hers before trying a peach. She flushed as he bit into the ripe skin. There was something sexy about it, as if he was thinking about feasting on her. She squashed that notion by recalling what he'd said about Father Jeff earlier. Nick didn't want to arrest him. He wanted to *kill* him. He hadn't said those exact words, but she'd understood him well enough. He'd listened to her spare account of the guru's past actions without expression. He hadn't raised his voice or shaken his fists. No veins had bulged out of his neck. Even so, she got the impression that he had strong feelings on the matter, and was more than willing to do violence in her honor.

The conversation had given her a dark sense of foreboding. She needed his protection, not vigilante justice. She hoped he didn't get the chance to square up with Father Jeff. Or with Brother Jeremiah, for that matter. Nick Dean might be a genial guy, borderline spineless, but Nick Diaz was dangerous—and he wasn't as emotionally removed as he pretended to be. There were hidden depths in him.

"June is late to start planting," he said. "It limits my choices. I need short-term crops that will seed in hot weather."

"You need workers, too."

"Yes. It's not a one-man job."

They split up after lunch. Avery walked to the garden while Nick went in search of Rupert's goats. A group of women in wide-brimmed hats had gathered by the fence. Sister Margot was among them.

"Sister Ellen," she exclaimed. "How wonderful of you to join us."

Avery accepted a warm hug from Margot, who introduced her to the other women before taking her aside.

"I'm so sorry about this morning," Margot said. "I interrupted you."

Avery felt heat climb into her cheeks. "Not at all," she lied.

"I didn't hear the bedsprings squeaking until after I knocked. You two must have been eager to start making that baby Father Jeff blessed you with."

"Um."

"It's nothing to be ashamed of, dearie. What a gift from above, to have a lusty husband so well favored in face and form. Your children will be beautiful."

"Thank you," she said.

Margot leaned in to whisper. "Be careful of the young women. They might cause mischief out of jealousy."

"I need to ask a favor," Avery said, changing the subject.

"Anything."

She explained Nick's predicament regarding the summer crops. Margot listened with a sympathetic ear.

"Say no more," Margot said, beaming. "My Rupert's been up in arms about feed for his livestock, not to mention the rest of us humans. You two are a godsend. I'm so thankful we have a real farmer again, and one who's such a go-getter."

Avery donned a matching smile. Yes, it was wonderful to have a lusty, well-formed go-getter for a pretend husband. If she could continue to play her role, resist Nick's rugged sex appeal and keep him from murdering Father Jeff, everything would be great!

Within twenty minutes of their talk, Margot had rallied the troops. Every member of the garden club, plus several husbands and quite a few children, marched toward the fields with tools in hand. They looked like a prairie mob, complete with pitchforks. Rupert couldn't be there because of the pregnant sow, but he'd sent two strapping helpers and four hungry goats. Brother Sage came with a pretty young woman.

The girls of The Haven were thrilled to be included in a coed activity. They raked and weeded alongside the boys. Everyone was sweaty-faced but happy. Avery used a shovel to dig up thistle roots, panting from exertion. The older women of the garden club tired first. They left in a pack, only to return with canteens full of fresh water. Avery drank with gratitude, parched beyond belief. Margot gave Avery her wide-brimmed hat before retreating to the shade. Avery donned it and kept digging. She wanted to ask Margot about the teenaged girl with Sage, whose hairstyle indicated she was married. The young woman giggled more than she worked, which caused Sage to glower at her. Avery had questions about Imogen, also. She wondered how Jonah's secretary had remained unmarried. Jonah's bachelor status was another mystery, but men were allowed their freedom.

Jeremiah didn't make an appearance, which wasn't a surprise or a disappointment. He probably wouldn't have approved of women clearing fields with men. In the commune, labor was highly stratified. Gardening was women's work; farming wasn't. Women didn't do men's chores, and men didn't do women's. The girls looked amazed, as if they'd been granted the keys to a secret kingdom. Their delight wore off a little as the afternoon wore on. It was hot, dirty, backbreaking work.

Nick hauled away wheelbarrows heaped with weeds, over and over again. When he wasn't doing that, he was swinging a pickax with impressive force. His shirt clung damply to the muscles of his chest.

Avery heeded Margot's warning about other women. Their eyes had been alighting on him all afternoon. She couldn't blame them for looking. He was a fine specimen of masculinity, lean and sinewy. He'd taken charge of this project with the ease of a natural leader. He also had an earthy, elemental vibe that suited the communal setting. It was almost as if he'd been born here instead of her.

They called it a day when the dinner bell clanged around sunset. They'd cleared a field and a half, which was remarkable progress. Nick asked everyone to gather around and thanked them profusely.

"Who can come back tomorrow?" he asked.

Two teenaged boys raised their hands. A younger boy and his three sisters followed suit.

Nick smiled with relief. "You're all hired. We'll meet here after breakfast."

They walked down the dirt road together, exhaustion dogging every step. As he took her hand, she felt the broken blisters on his palm.

"You're hurt," she murmured.

"It's nothing."

She made a mental note to bandage the wounds after

dinner. If she could stay awake long enough to eat. She hadn't slept more than two hours the night before. The stress of the assignment was catching up with her. It appeared to be catching up with Nick, as well. He had dark circles under his eyes.

They washed up before entering the dining hall. The meal was a hearty chicken and vegetable stew with oatmeal cookies for dessert. Avery had no trouble finishing her meal. Nick went back for seconds. They skipped the coffee and conversation afterward.

"I need to shower," Nick said on the way back to the cabin. "I smell like a goat."

"I can't tell," she said, glancing at him. "Maybe I smell worse."

He shook his head, as if this wasn't possible. Then he studied her disheveled appearance. Her hair was mussed, her skirts were dusty and her blouse was wrinkled. She touched her neck, which felt gritty and sunburned.

"You smell like wildflowers," he said gruffly.

She laughed, though he sounded serious. Either way, she was glad for the soap and supplies Sister Margot had brought to their cabin. Nick found a change of clothes in the second basket. There were towels and toiletries in the first. They both headed to the showers with arms full. Avery didn't mind the lukewarm water or the rustic stall. She shampooed her hair and washed her weary body, rinsing away the grueling day.

When she returned to the cabin, Nick's boots were on the front step. He was inside, already stretched out on the floor. The woven rug made a barrier between him and the hardwood, but it couldn't be comfortable. He'd taken the sheet off the bed, leaving her the wool blanket. She didn't detect the scent of goats or wildflowers in the close confines. There was only him. Warm male skin and a hint of homemade soap.

Desire stabbed through her, triggered by nothing more than this faint aroma. She couldn't see his features in the dark, but she didn't need to. His face was imprinted in her mind, along with his touch, his taste, his hard-muscled body.

She retreated to the bedroom before she did something stupid like invite him to join her. She hung the towel over the bedpost and climbed in. The squeaky springs reminded her of Margot's embarrassing comments, and of the delicious weight of him on top of her. She burrowed into the pillows, biting her lower lip.

As much as she tried to dispel the arousing images and memories, they were stuck. An erotic movie featuring the two of them played in her mind on an endless loop, and she couldn't stop watching. Her nipples pebbled with arousal and an ache pulsed between her legs. She heard him shift positions in the dark. She imagined he was plagued with the same malady, his body throbbing for release. It took every ounce of willpower she possessed to stay quiet instead of offering him succor.

The agony was short-lived. Within a few minutes, fatigue swept over her and brought sweet oblivion.

Chapter 14

Nick slept like the dead, literally.

The floor beneath him felt about as cozy as a pine box. The walls seemed to close in on him from all sides, creating a sense of pressing doom. He dreamed of being laid to rest in a green pasture. It was an unsettling scene that shifted into something even darker. Instead of a Haven-style funeral pyre, he was placed in a mass grave with a pile of decomposing bodies. He rolled over in horror, only to find the mutilated faces of his parents.

He woke with a gasp, one hand over his heart. It was bouncing around in his chest like a pinball.

Jesus.

After a drink of water and a quick visit to the men's room, he settled down again. Exhaustion took him swiftly back to sleep. His dreams returned, more pleasant this time. He was having a picnic with Avery on a misty hillside. She wore a white dress with buttons down the front, half-undone. He climbed on top of her, feasting on her mouth. Her breasts spilled out of the bodice. He tried to fill his hands with her, but his range of movement was restricted. His elbows bumped into wood. At first he thought it was the picnic basket. Then he lifted his head and saw a gravestone with her name on it. She wasn't lying on a blanket, underneath him. She was resting in a coffin, eyes closed.

The second nightmare was disturbing enough to wake him, but it wasn't as gory or graphic as the first. It was more gothic fantasy than horror. Avery was beautiful, even in death. Her breasts were pink-tipped and lush.

And he was predictably aroused.

Smothering a groan, he stared at the crosscut beams in the ceiling. It must have been close to dawn, because muted light filtered in from the single window. Despite the bad dreams and general discomfort, he'd slept at least eight hours. He'd drifted off in the same condition he'd awoken, with an erection as stiff as the hardwood floor. He could hear her soft, steady breathing in the next room. He imagined her sleep-warm body, her unbound breasts. His erection throbbed and his jaw clenched.

He could get up and take a cold shower, or he could stay put and furtively seek his own release. Neither option appealed to him. He didn't want to get off with the mental picture of her half-naked corpse still lingering in his psyche. It was sick to be aroused at all. Wryly, he wondered how Ms. Freud would psychoanalyze *this*.

"No," she murmured, bedsprings squeaking. "Don't leave me here."

He sat up and listened. It sounded as if she was having a nightmare of her own.

"Don't lock me in," she cried.

Nick lumbered to his feet, wincing at the various aches and pains that had nothing to do with his groin. He entered the bedroom, where she was thrashing wildly. He grasped both wrists and pinned them to the mattress, afraid she'd strike him.

"Avery," he said in a quiet voice. "Wake up."

"No!"

"You're having a bad dream."

Her eyes sprang open and she stopped struggling. She stared at him, her chest heaving. The old-fashioned undergarment she was wearing had tiny buttons down the front. They were partially undone, revealing the inner curves of her breasts.

Nick wasn't picky about breasts. He'd never handled a pair he didn't like. To him, they all looked and felt pretty nice. He didn't care about size or symmetry. Avery just happened to be blessed with the most perfectly shaped breasts he'd ever seen. They strained against the home-spun bodice, large enough to fill his hands.

"Let go," she said, breathless.

It took him a few seconds to drag his gaze to her face and process those words. He released her wrists, chagrined. She pulled the blanket over her chest. "I'm sorry," he said. "You were crying out in your sleep."

"What did I say?"

"'Don't lock me in here.'"

She flinched in recognition, but didn't explain. She was as reluctant to share childhood experiences as he was. He let it go, because he needed space as much as she did. He rose from the bed, aware that he was in his underwear. The form-fitting long johns didn't hide his physical reaction to her. His arousal was half-mast, but still noticeable. He left the room, feeling like a damned pervert.

He donned the same pants he'd worn yesterday, along with a fresh shirt and socks. Then he shoved his feet into boots and visited the men's room. He passed by her on his way back. Inside the cabin, he filled the washtub with an inch of water and tossed his dirty things into it. He gave them a scrub against the washboard with bar soap. When she returned to find him doing laundry, she blinked in surprise.

"Do you want me to wash something for you?" he asked.

"It's considered women's work."

He shrugged and got back to it. She didn't bring him her blouse or underwear, which was just as well. The water was already dingy. He wrung out the fabric as best he could and looked for a place to hang it. She took the wet garments from him and went outside to a clothesline he hadn't noticed before. He watched from the window as she performed the task for him. Maybe it was okay for him to do women's work as long as no one saw.

He filled two mugs with fresh water and sat down, wishing it was coffee.

Spiked coffee.

She joined him a moment later.

"Thanks," he said, gesturing to the clothesline.

"I forgot to bandage your hands last night."

He turned his palms over to study the broken blisters. The right was worse than the left. "They'll callus faster without bandages."

"What about gloves?"

"Jeremiah probably can't spare any."

She smiled at his joke and tore a muslin cloth into strips. He let her wrap his right hand. Then he closed his fist, testing the utility of the bandage. He had to admit it felt better with the protective layer.

"How are you holding up?" she asked.

"I'm sore."

"What hurts?"

"My entire body."

"You don't have to work so hard."

He didn't necessarily disagree. Working hard was just what he did. It was who he was. "I'll be all right."

"They like you."

"Who?"

"These people."

"Not all of them," he said, thinking about the holy trinity. Jeremiah, Jonah and Jeff Silva. They weren't impressed with him.

"You'll have to watch out for Jeremiah."

"I don't like the way he treated you."

"The way he treated *me*?"

Nick cited the golf cart incident. Jeremiah had taken off before she was even seated, and he'd seemed amused by her near fall.

"You were his main target," she said. "He was glaring daggers at your back."

"What's his problem?"

"I don't know. He's a jerk, and you're a threat."

"A physical threat?"

"Not only that," she said, tapping the table. "Sister Margot warned me about young women causing mischief, because you're so lusty and handsome."

"She said I was lusty?"

Avery nodded, her cheeks pink.

He supposed he was guilty as charged. He certainly had been since he'd met Avery, and Sister Margot had almost interrupted them in flagrante delicto. "Do you think I should let girls work in the fields?"

Her face softened. "Yes. It's a breath of fresh air for them."

He considered his options, which were limited. Nick Dean wasn't a throwback sexist. He hadn't been drawn to the cult because of its track record with women. He was here to till the earth and faith-heal. He needed workers too much to turn the girls away. If Jeremiah had a problem with it, he could bring some men to take their place. Nick doubted any of the girls would flirt with him, regardless. This was an extremely restrictive environment, and he was twice their age.

They sat in silence for a few minutes. He tried to focus on a game plan. He needed to get his watch back or find another way to communicate with his team. He wanted to check out Silva's compound, but it appeared heavily guarded. At this point, playing his role and gaining the trust of the cult members was paramount. The hard work had a dual purpose. It could act as a sleep aid and anesthetic, dulling his desire for Avery.

When the breakfast bell rang, they left the cabin. He expected a hearty meal and wasn't disappointed. These fanatics loved bacon. They did seem to like Nick Dean, and they'd embraced Ellen just as warmly. The dining hall was noisy and comfortable. He took a seat at an empty table, across from Avery. Nick noted some familiar faces, including Brother Sage. He was with the same young woman he'd brought to the fields. It dawned on Nick that the pretty, dark-haired girl was his wife, not his daughter.

"How did my goats do?" Rupert asked as he passed by.

"Great," Nick said. "Thanks for sending them."

"My pleasure."

"I was going to ask you about silage for livestock. It's too late to start wheat or corn. What do you think about oat hay?"

"I'll take whatever I can get, Brother."

Rupert promised to send Brent, one of his farm-hands, before he moved on. Nick turned his attention back to his breakfast plate. His eyes met Avery's as he swallowed a bite of eggs. She looked away, but not before he read the censure in her gaze. She thought he was fitting in too well, even enjoying himself. And, to be fair, he was. He hadn't forgotten the trauma she'd endured here. He would never forget Chris, who'd died at the behest of Jeff Silva. Nick understood that this assignment was stressful and scary for Avery. He'd coerced her into becoming his partner.

Although his recruiting tactics were questionable, he didn't regret bringing her in. She was a perfect wife, sexy and angelic looking. She had a natural instinct for this kind of work. Her social skills and emotional insights were impeccable. Her company was a factor in his enjoyment. He liked being with her. He liked what they were doing. This was the most important assignment of his career, and he thrived on it. He was aroused by danger. He also couldn't wait to make Silva pay for his sins—in blood. If Nick had to take him alive, he would, but he'd beat the fear of God back into him first.

After breakfast, Avery accompanied him to the storage building where seed was kept. He loaded several bags into a wheelbarrow before they walked to the fields. Jeremiah's golf cart would have come in handy. Nick could put the man to use, as well. He wondered what, exactly, Jeremiah supervised. He never seemed to be around.

"I want to visit the cemetery," Avery said as they passed it.

Nick stopped in the middle of the dirt road, the sweat chilling on his body. Images from his nightmares floated in his mind. "That's not a good idea."

"Why not?"

"You know why not."

"I just want to look."

"You'll get emotional."

She proved his point by crossing her arms over her chest and blinking tears from her eyes. She couldn't be seen weeping over her mother's grave, but that wasn't the only reason he opposed the idea. There might be a second grave nearby, revealing a truth he had compelling reasons to hide.

"You got your closure," she said. "Can't I get mine?"

He kept his expression blank as he massaged the nape of his neck. Throwing his past in his face was an effective strategy. When he'd opened up to her about his parents, he hadn't imagined she would use the information against him. Maybe he was being too soft with her, sharing too much of himself. He heard the electric whine of the golf cart approaching and made his decision.

"You'll do what I say, and that's final."

Her eyes darkened with hurt. The order came out harsher than he'd intended, but had the desired effect of shutting her up before the golf cart reached them. Nick didn't want to get caught in the middle of this particular argument.

The driver of the golf cart wasn't Jeremiah. It was Jonah, with Brent in the passenger seat. The teenaged farmhand was a welcome sight, as he was six feet tall and worked tirelessly. When Jonah pulled to a stop, Brent hopped out. They exchanged greetings.

"Can I take that for you, Brother Nick?"

"Sure," Nick said, stepping away from the wheelbarrow. "Thanks."

"See you over there."

Jonah rested his forearm on the steering wheel, splitting a glance between Nick and Avery. He seemed pleased to have interrupted a tense moment. "I heard you've done wonders with the fields."

"I had a lot of help," Nick said. "Are you joining us today?"

Jonah laughed, shaking his head. He didn't do farm-work. "I actually came for Ellen. I hope you don't mind sharing her."

Nick kept his smile in place. "Not at all."

"You'll report to the health office every morning," Jonah said to Avery, who nodded her compliance. He gestured to the cemetery behind them. "Did you have a question about our dearly departed?"

She looked over her shoulder at the headstone-speckled hillside. The epitaphs couldn't be read from this distance. Jonah must have assumed they'd stopped here for a reason. "I wanted to visit the graves," she said. "The grounds are lovely."

"I told her we didn't have time," Nick said.

"What a shame," Jonah said. "I'd be happy to take her in your place."

Nick suspected that Jonah was deliberately trying to provoke him with suggestive word choices. The younger man's smirk invited Nick to call him on it. Instead of rising to the bait, Nick deferred to Avery.

"That's a kind offer," she said, "but not necessary."

"Are you sure?" Jonah asked.

"I'll come with Nick another day."

"As you wish."

Nick couldn't decide which brother he disliked more, Jonah or Jeremiah. As Avery moved toward the pas-senger side of the golf cart, Nick surprised her with a goodbye kiss. He wasn't sure why he did it. Maybe he felt guilty about scolding her, and grateful she'd refused Jonah. Maybe he just wanted to show Jonah whom she belonged to. She made a soft squeak as their lips met.

He kept it chaste, releasing her after a brief peck. He doubted she appreciated his send-off, but at least she didn't slap his face. She climbed into the passenger seat, her eyes flashing and her cheeks flushed.

Jonah wasn't smirking as he turned the golf cart around and drove back toward the community center.

Nick continued to the fields, his mood tempered. He hoped Avery would be busy with nursing duties in the health office, not hanging out with Jonah all day. Nick didn't trust the young prophet with his wife. He also worried about Avery's stress level. This was a harrowing experience for her. She was having nightmares about her childhood trauma. If something went wrong when they were apart, he couldn't protect her.

The work in the fields kept his mind occupied for the next few hours. Four girls and three boys reported for duty. He sent everyone except Brent to the second field to continue clearing. Nick and Brent stayed in the first field to start tilling. There were two vintage tillers. It required considerable effort to move the heavy blades across the earth. By midday, his hands ached and his back muscles quivered from exertion. He finished the last row, soaked in sweat. Brent was in the same condition, but appeared energized rather than wiped out. Nick felt every one of his thirty-eight years and then some. They retreated to the shade of a nearby oak tree.

"You want to keep going?" Brent asked.

"I don't think I can," Nick said.

Brent grinned with relief. "Thank heaven. I was worried you were going to work me to death."

"Maybe after lunch."

"You're a beast, man. My arms feel like rubber."

After a short rest, they started the process for planting seeds. It was painstaking work, but not difficult. Nick showed Brent how far apart to place the seeds, and how deep in the earth. Then he went to check on the rest of his crew. He needed a few extra hands to haul water, and he probably shouldn't leave them unsupervised for too long. He was pleased with their progress on the second field. The girls were working as hard as the boys, if not harder. They would have the field cleared this afternoon.

Nick was examining the outside edge of the farmland, where the undergrowth had become unmanageable, when the lunch bell clanged. He waved to dismiss everyone, but his attention got snagged on something beyond the fence. It looked like a tarpaulin. As he got closer, he identified what appeared to be a camouflaged net stretched across an area the size of a basketball court. He couldn't make out the shapes underneath it, but his special-agent senses went into overdrive. The military-style camouflage, and whatever it was covering, hadn't shown up in the drone photos. What was under there? An arsenal? A bomb shelter? Enough explosives to blow up a federal building?

Nick's heart pounded with excitement. Purely by accident, he'd stumbled across a secret hideaway. It could hold the evidence he needed to nail Father Jeff. It could be the reason Jeremiah didn't want him clearing these fields.

Nick studied the fence line with a sharpened gaze. He spotted a tall oak tree with branches that extended over the top of the razor wire. Although the climb would be challenging, it was doable. He glanced around the deserted fields, considering. He was alone right now. He could climb the tree, hop over the fence and investigate.

There were a few problems with taking that sort of risk. The first was Avery. She'd worry if he failed to show up for lunch. He was already on thin ice with her, and others would notice his absence. He also couldn't afford to get caught in the wrong place. The fence marked the commune's outside border. Guards patrolled the area so regularly that they'd worn a footpath around the perimeter.

The real clincher was the tree itself. The sturdy branches that reached across the fence were inaccessible from the opposite side. He could drop down from that height, but he wouldn't be able to jump back up. He'd be stranded.

Vowing to return later with a length of rope, he walked the opposite direction. He rubbed the empty spot on his wrist, wishing like hell for his watch. He estimated he was about five minutes behind the others. As he passed the equipment shed, he decided to pick up his canteen, which needed to be refilled. He heard a strange noise inside, sort of rhythmic thumping. Experience had him guessing at the origin of the sound before he wrenched open the door. Sure enough, there was a boy with his pants down, on top of a girl with her skirt up. They both froze at the intrusion.

Nick clapped a hand over his eyes. Two days in this puritanical place hadn't turned him into a prude, but he did *not* want to see teenagers doing it. Letting out a stream of curse words, he stumbled backward.

The pair emerged from the shed in less than a minute, red-faced. The boy was Brent, proving he still had energy to burn. The girl wasn't on his crew, thank God. Nick couldn't be blamed for failing to protect the virtue of one of his female workers. With her head bowed and her eyes downcast, he struggled to place her. She looked about Brent's age, which was eighteen. Her hairstyle revealed she was married.

Recognition dawned.

She was Brother Sage's wife.

Chapter 15

Avery folded her hands in her lap as they headed back to the communal center.

Jonah was a careful driver, unlike his brother. She could feel his eyes on her flushed face, gauging her reaction to Nick's kiss. Although it was normal for a husband to kiss his wife goodbye, the contact hadn't felt practiced or commonplace. She was worried that Jonah would pick up on the sexual tension between them. Married couples weren't supposed to have that kind of tension. Nick and Ellen had been ordered to make a baby. They should be in a state of relaxed, postcoital bliss.

Jonah pulled to a stop behind the church, next to the door to his rectory. "Is everything okay with Brother Nick?"

"Of course," she said.

"It looked like you were arguing."

She bowed her head, as if in shame. In reality, it

was anger. She couldn't believe Nick had ordered her to obey him, and then kissed her two minutes later. He was lucky she hadn't bit him and drawn blood.

"Do you think he's working too hard?"

"It's not my place to criticize," she demurred.

"A husband should please his wife."

Avery didn't know what to say, so she stayed quiet. Jonah was difficult to read, like a master chess player. She couldn't guess his next move. Did he want her to agree with him, or demonstrate loyalty to Nick?

"Our ways must seem strange to you," Jonah said.

"I'm settling in," she said. "Everyone has been so welcoming."

He arched a brow. "Even Sister Imogen?"

Her lips parted with surprise.

Jonah chuckled at her reaction. "She can be a little uptight."

Avery got the impression that he was trying to disarm her with his casual tone and conspiratorial attitude. It was working. His eyes glinted with sincerity. His clean-cut good looks gave him a boyish appeal. He wore black slacks and a white cotton shirt with the cuffs rolled up to his elbows. She wouldn't forget that he'd made her strip and walk naked through the woods, but she could have a civil conversation with him. He wasn't needlessly cruel, like Jeremiah. Jonah was deliberate in every action.

"Don't be afraid to come to me if you have any problems," Jonah said. "Giving spiritual guidance is my favorite part of the job. My door is always open, and that goes for my home as well as my office." He pointed to the house where Father Jeff used to live. "Drop by anytime. Day or night."

"I appreciate that."

"The health center is right here. We're neighbors."

She glanced at the building he indicated. The front door was about ten steps from the church rectory where he wrote sermons and guided wayward spirits.

"I'll give you a tour."

She rose from the passenger seat, swallowing her unease. She wasn't eager to be alone in an enclosed space with him. Handsome or not, he was still creepy, and his twenty-four-hour availability struck her as overkill. She doubted he invited every member of his flock to call on him in the middle of the night. He had an ulterior motive for taking her under his wing. Maybe he wanted to antagonize Nick. The two men had acted like adversaries earlier. Maybe Jonah found her attractive and considered her a ripe candidate for an affair. Even in this staunchly religious sect, people committed sins of the flesh. Powerful men of all walks of life couldn't seem to resist. There was also the possibility that Jonah imagined himself as her next husband—after Nick died of his "illness."

Disquieted by the thought, she stalled him before he reached the door to the health center. "There is something you could do for me."

He puffed out his chest. "Name it."

"I can't see properly without my glasses. I'm afraid it will interfere with my nursing duties."

"No problem," he said. "Your glasses are in my office. I'll get them for you."

"Do you have Nick's watch?"

He hesitated. "A watch isn't a medical necessity."

"It is for him," she said. "He loses track of time and forgets things because of his condition. He can recall a wealth of scientific information about plants and growing seasons, but he struggles with daily routines. The watch helps him immensely."

Jonah's brow furrowed with disapproval. He wasn't as enthusiastic about bending the rules for Mr. Dean.

She touched his arm, which felt strong despite his slender build. "Please. I'll be so grateful."

Her breathy request did the trick. He was a clever strategist and a dedicated preacher, but he was also a man. A lonely man, if her feminine instincts were correct. A man who hadn't yet chosen a wife, perhaps because a teenaged bride didn't appeal to him. "Come with me," he said, changing directions.

They entered through the back door of the church and continued to his rectory. Both were unlocked; there was no crime here. She filed that information away as Jonah rounded his desk. The top drawer held her prescription lenses, wrapped in soft cloth. He rummaged through another drawer for the watch, which appeared to have been tossed inside without care. He gave the watch a cursory inspection. It was a dated analog timepiece, harmless looking and clunky. She wondered if it truly held any sentimental value for Nick.

"These items aren't to be flaunted," Jonah said. "You will wear the glasses only when you need them to care for a patient. Brother Nick can keep the watch in his pocket. Is that understood?"

"Of course," she gushed. "Thank you so much."

"You're welcome," he said, studying her. He seemed to be contemplating a recoupment for his generosity. She stuck the treasures in the pocket of her voluminous skirt and left his office before he could make a suggestion. They returned to their original destination, the health center. Now there was a woman standing outside the building. She wore a buttoned-up gray dress with a spotless blue apron. Her hair was pulled back into a severe bun. She looked like an older version of Imogen. With a start, Avery realized she was Imogen's mother.

Imogen's mother...and Gary's first wife. Avery's mother had been Gary's second wife. Avery had lived in this woman's household in the years before she'd escaped.

"Sister Katharine," Jonah said. "How lovely to see you."

They exchanged greetings, and Jonah introduced Avery as Katharine's new assistant. Katharine studied her without comment. There was no flicker of recognition in her eyes. She didn't remember Avery as the skinny girl who'd babysat her children.

Avery breathed a sigh of relief. She'd dodged another bullet. Every time she met someone from her past, she tensed in anticipation of discovery. The possibility hung over her like a dark cloud. Her anxiety doubled when Nick wasn't around to monopolize the attention. She wondered if her luck would run out eventually. It could happen any moment. Someone could look twice at her this afternoon, or tomorrow morning. A single whisper of her former name could jeopardize the mission.

Instead of giving the tour he'd promised, Jonah made an excuse to leave. He wasn't as interested in spending time with Avery when there was a chaperone around. Katharine led Avery through the medical center, which had first aid supplies, an exam table and some basic equipment. There were herbs growing on the windowsill. Jars of ingredients for homeopathic remedies lined a shelf. They appeared neatly labeled, but Avery couldn't read them without her glasses. While Avery had nothing against alternative medicine, she had misgivings about Katharine. She remembered her as a stern woman, even cold. Avery wondered if she'd been selected for the job, or if she'd volunteered.

"Have you been trained as a midwife?" Katharine asked.

"I'm afraid not," Avery replied. "I was a pediatric nurse."

"So you've handled newborns."

She nodded, though she didn't have much experience with infants. She'd held both of Chuck's sons when they were only a few weeks old. They'd been so wrinkled and helpless, like little hairless possums. She remembered smiling as Tyson clutched her thumb in his tiny hand. She might have an aversion to all things maternal, due to her mother's untimely death, but she could hold a baby without having a panic attack.

"I have to make a house call," Katharine said. "You can come with me."

"Where are we going?"

"To Father Jeff's. Grace is in her final month."

Avery's stress level skyrocketed. She couldn't think of a reason to decline, so she didn't. Staying behind might mean spending the morning in Jonah's company. As much as she'd like to avoid Father Jeff, she was curious about her sister. The prospect of seeing Grace filled her with equal parts anxiety, dread and hope.

Sister Katharine collected a leather satchel from the health office before they set out. They walked along the same path Avery and Nick had taken to enter the commune. She wondered if Katharine had any real medical supplies, or just backwoods remedies. Imogen had confirmed what Avery already knew from experience: the members of this community didn't believe in modern medicine. Modern golf carts, however, were acceptable.

"Can I carry your bag?" she offered.

"It's not heavy," Katharine replied.

"What's in it?"

"Bandages, antiseptic, ointment. The usual assortment."

Avery didn't remark on the content. It was better than toadstools and milkweed. "Are you related to Imogen?"

"She's my daughter," Katharine said.

"You look alike."

Katharine touched her face, as if she'd forgotten the resemblance. Avery regretted broaching the subject, because it might invite Katharine to make a similar comparison. The woman had known her mother.

"Is Imogen married?" Avery asked, hoping to distract her.

It worked. Katharine's eyes narrowed with pique. "No, she's not."

"Does she wish to stay independent?"

"She's very dedicated to her secretary position."

"Hmm."

"My younger daughter, Isobel, is married," Katharine said. "She's expecting, too. We'll check in on her during the home visit."

Avery vaguely remembered Isobel, who'd been a toddler twenty years ago. "Is she married to Father Jeff?"

"Brother Jeremiah," Katharine corrected proudly.

It was clear that Katharine approved of her younger daughter's life choices. Isobel had married the son of the prophet. She lived on the elite compound with a husband who wasn't an old man. Jeremiah's awful personality didn't seem to bother Katharine as much as Imogen's single status.

"I supposed you're used to secular ways," Katharine said. "Women having careers instead of families."

"Some have both," Avery replied.

"It's poison."

"What do you mean?"

"Those kinds of ideas infect a woman's body and keep her from increasing. You're lucky Father Jeff cleansed you."

Avery withheld comment. It wouldn't do any good to assert that her beliefs had no scientific basis. Access to birth control was the key to fewer pregnancies. She wondered if any natural contraceptives grew in the woods around here. These poor women needed all the help with family planning they could get.

"Do you have a husband?" Avery asked.

"He passed," Katharine said. "Five years now."

"My condolences," Avery said.

She felt no sadness over the death of her stepfather, who had slapped her the last time she'd spoken to him. Katharine didn't appear broken up about it, either. She didn't miss a step as she strode forward.

They approached the gate where a teenaged boy was standing guard. He opened it with a mumbled greeting. As they walked through it, a wave of memories washed over her. Twenty years ago, there had been no armed guards to stop her, and no razor wire. She'd climbed the fence easily. As soon as she was on the other side, she'd run like the wind. The desire to do the same thing now was difficult to resist.

You'll do what I say, and that's final.

Nick's highhanded command didn't keep her grounded. If anything, it encouraged her to flee, because screw him and his stupid orders. She wasn't his employee. She wasn't his *wife*. She didn't care about his investigation. She wanted to see her sister.

It was a short walk to the Silva compound. A second guard let them inside a wrought iron gate. He looked as bored and callow as the previous one. She hoped these boys had been given training on weapons safety, because the automatic rifles they carried were no joke. Beyond the gate, there was a mini-commune of sorts. A ranch-style home loomed large in the distance. Several smaller buildings in the foreground resembled guesthouses, or servants' quarters. The estate itself was neither grand nor well cared for. The grass needed cutting. There was a playground with children's toys strewn about.

"We'll visit Grace first," Katharine said. "She lives in the garden house."

The garden house was more of a groundskeeper's shack. The no-frills structure was nestled amid an overgrown bramble of rosebushes at the end of a cobblestone path. As the front of the building came into view, Avery spotted a young woman with a rounded belly sitting in a lounge chair. She jumped up with impressive alacrity and tossed something into a murky-looking miniature pond. Then she rushed into the cottage and slammed the door.

The pungent odor of marijuana hit Avery's nostrils as they ventured forward. It was as much of a shock as the disorganized grounds. She glanced at Katharine, who said nothing. The midwife either didn't notice the scent or couldn't identify it. Had she never encountered the drug in her sheltered existence?

Katharine rapped her knuckles on the door. "Grace?"

"Go away."

"You're supposed to be confined to bed rest."

"I'm resting."

"You're up and about."

"I feel fine. Leave me alone."

Short of busting down the door, there wasn't much

Katharine could do. She wore a sour expression as they retreated.

"She's a difficult patient," Katharine said. "Always has been."

"Why is that?"

"She doesn't think I'm qualified to be a midwife, for one. I took over for her mother, who passed away last year."

Avery had wondered who raised Grace. The most logical choice was Katharine, because Grace had been born in her household. Imogen, Isobel and Grace were half sisters. They all shared the same father. Katharine could have kept the child. Instead, it seemed she'd gotten rid of the evidence of her husband's second union.

"Grace wanted the job," Katharine continued. "Father Jeff forbid it. Her place is here, serving him."

"Why is she confined?"

"It's just a precaution," Katharine said. "She fell off a bike last week. She shouldn't have been riding, of course. But as you can see, she's headstrong. That's why she lives by herself. She hasn't learned how to get along with the other wives."

Avery remembered how difficult this situation had been for her mother. Sarah had never been accepted by Katharine. The two wives had occupied different areas of the same house. Avery and her mother had been treated like intruders instead of family members. They'd known they weren't welcome.

"Does Grace get along with Isobel?" Avery asked.

"Not as well as she used to," Katharine admitted. "They were like sisters as children."

They were *literally* half sisters.

As they ventured farther into Father Jeff's lair, Avery studied their surroundings. Between the gate and the main house there was a structure that appeared to be a guard tower. It sat on a raised platform, high enough to overlook the rest of the compound, as well as the neighboring commune. There were a couple of cabins at the base of the tower. Dirt bike trails zigzagged in every direction, with various ramps and jumps. A trio of teenaged boys stood around a ping-pong table, arguing in boisterous volume.

"The guards live here?" Avery asked.

"Most of them do. They need to be available around the clock. Keeping us safe is an important job."

Avery assumed the guards were also making sure no one escaped. They looked bored with their duties, but security detail was easier than farmwork. There were perks in the form of recreation activities, and private cabins with no parental guidance.

"This is Isobel and Jeremiah's house," Katharine said.

Avery turned her attention to a basic modular home opposite the guard cabins. The front door was open. Katharine announced their visit and let herself in. The space was as tidy as a pin, with homespun decor. Yellow curtains fluttered in the kitchen window. A vase filled with wildflowers adorned the dining table.

"Isobel?" Katharine called.

There was no response.

Frowning, Katharine continued out the back door. Avery followed, curious. A trim young woman with a wicker basket was standing with her back to them, hanging freshly washed clothing on a line to dry.

Isobel didn't turn at the sound of Katharine's voice. She didn't turn when Katharine touched her shoulder, either. The young woman sank to her knees in the grass and covered her face. Avery rushed to join them, concerned about her medical condition. Isobel's gently rounded stomach indicated she was in her second trimester. Katharine knelt beside Isobel and moved her hands away from her face. She had a split lip and a swollen eye.

Jeremiah.

"What happened?" Katharine asked.

Isobel embraced her mother, weeping.

"Did you anger him?"

"I didn't mean to. I just asked him why he was going over there, and he—"

Katharine cradled her daughter's head to her chest and smoothed her hair. "You mustn't question him, darling."

Avery was disturbed by Katharine's advice, but not surprised. Women held no power in their community. They simply had to endure whatever abuse they were dealt. Isobel couldn't argue with Jeremiah. If she reported his behavior to someone who might care, like Jonah, she risked incurring more of Jeremiah's wrath.

They went inside the house, where Katharine performed a basic exam in the living room. Isobel rested on a sofa with a cool washcloth on her forehead. She resembled Imogen so much the two could be twins. Both were pretty, petite and dark-haired. Katharine placed a cold compress on Isobel's left eye. Katharine might not be the kindest soul, but she appeared to love Isobel. Avery felt a pang of sympathy for both of them. No mother wanted to see her child in physical or emotional pain.

"Did you take her breakfast?" Katharine asked.

"How could I?" Isobel wailed. "This is all her fault."

Katharine made a sound that was part soothing, part shushing. "She's supposed to be confined, sweeting."

"She doesn't need any help. I'm the one who's hurt."

Avery realized this conflict was about Grace. Jeremiah and Grace? Avery couldn't sort through all the different levels of dysfunction and twisted connections around here. Katharine spent the next few minutes fussing over her daughter. Before they left, Katharine packed a breakfast in a wicker basket. She left it on Grace's doorstep.

"Tomorrow, you're getting an exam," Katharine said through the door. "Father Jeff's orders."

Grace's response was unintelligible. Avery desperately wanted to barge in and see her sister face-to-face. She wanted to ask her a thousand questions. Most of all, she wanted to rescue her from this nightmare. Grace was confined in the garden house like a prisoner in a penitentiary for wayward wives.

Katharine didn't speak as they walked back to the commune, which gave Avery time to consider her options. Maybe she could return to the compound with Katharine tomorrow and get a chance to meet Grace.

Or maybe she could return *without* Katharine, and find a way to help Grace escape.

Chapter 16

Nick had no idea what to do with the disheveled pair.

They'd complicated his lunch break by deciding to have a tryst in the equipment shed, of all places. Brent stood silent, his hair sweaty and his neck flushed. He couldn't defend his behavior, so he didn't try. The young lady he'd been caught with threw herself at Nick's feet in the most dramatic fashion possible.

"Please," she sobbed. "Don't tell anyone. He'll be exiled."

Nick figured she should be worried about herself more than Brent. Adulterous women were probably stoned in the town square, or hung from the church rafters in this hellhole. She continued to beg and plead, looking up at him with teary eyes. It was incredibly uncomfortable. "Get up," he said.

She stood, but didn't let go of him. "Please, Brother Nick. Promise you won't tell."

Nick wasn't sure how to extricate himself from her. He raised his hands at his sides instead of pushing her away. Brent slid his arm around her waist and hauled her back a few steps. She clasped her palms together, still weeping.

"Don't come back here," Nick said.

"I won't."

"Go on, then. Before I change my mind."

When Brent released her, she hurried up the hillside and took off toward the commune. She ran like the devil was on her heels.

Nick turned to Brent. "Brother Sage's wife?"

"Her name is Nadine."

"You two have done this before?"

Brent didn't answer. So that meant yes.

Nick raked a hand through his hair, unsure where to begin. He gestured to the shed. "That can't happen again."

"It won't."

Nick didn't believe him. He also didn't blame him, or Nadine. She was married to a man in his forties. Teenagers had no sexual outlet in an oppressive religious community like this. They couldn't date or experiment. What were they supposed to do? "If you keep messing around with her, you're going to get caught. By someone who won't stay quiet."

Brent nodded, his jaw clenched.

"Are you taking precautions?"

"Precautions?"

"Against pregnancy."

Brent gave him a curious look. "What kind of precautions?"

"Forget it," Nick said, dropping the subject. It wasn't his place to school this kid on the withdrawal method—

which wasn't reliable anyway—or lecture him about poor judgment. Brent was a good farmworker. As long as he stopped using the shed as his hookup shack, Nick didn't care what he did. He collected his canteen before starting off down the road. Brent walked with him, his demeanor subdued.

"Do you know anyone who's been exiled?" Nick asked.

"Brother Caleb," Brent replied.

"What happened to him?"

"They say he got the devil in him and attacked one of the guards. But I don't believe it."

"Why not?"

"He was in love with Grace."

Nick snapped his head around. "Father Jeff's wife?"

"That's the one."

"How long ago was he exiled?"

"Nine months," Brent said.

The significance of this time frame wasn't lost on Nick. Grace was almost ready to deliver. Holy hell. Had they ousted a teenaged boy for having a sexual affair with the leader's wife? And had he really been allowed to walk away after committing such an egregious sin?

"I wouldn't mind being exiled, if Nadine could come with me," Brent said.

"Do females get exiled?"

"No."

"Then put that idea out of your mind."

"She was my girl before she was his wife," Brent said.

Nick didn't respond to this statement, which was rife with despair and longing.

"He doesn't even like her. He hardly touches her."

"Even more reason for you to stay away."

"Why is that?"

"If she gets pregnant, he'll know it's not his."

Brent went quiet again. Nick hoped he was thinking about the consequences of his actions, which should scare the bejesus out of him. But Nick also knew how the teenage mind and body worked. All of those fears and anxieties faded in moments of extreme excitement, leaving only one thought—to have her.

Nick had a grown man's experience and control, and he was still struggling to keep his hands off Avery.

They washed up and parted ways before entering the dining hall. Nick grabbed a plate and joined Avery. Lunch was soup and a grilled cheese sandwich, with a ripe peach for dessert. He was too hungry to make conversation. Avery had finished her meal before he'd arrived, so she watched him eat. She wore a standoffish expression, which didn't surprise him. He'd bossed her around and kissed her in front of Jonah. He supposed he should apologize, but he didn't regret the kiss. That moment had been the highlight of his day.

She slid an object across the table, hidden under her hand. "Put this in your pocket."

His watch! Hot damn. He could have kissed her again. "How'd you get it?" he asked, tucking the item away.

"I asked Jonah for it."

"Did you get your glasses, too?"

"Yes."

He picked up the peach, impressed. "Nicely done."

"You have to keep it out of sight."

"No problem."

Getting his watch back lifted his mood considerably. So did her presence. He enjoyed being with her, even when she was mad at him. She made him feel less jaded about humanity. He'd been wallowing in darkness too long, fantasizing about revenge.

Now he was fantasizing about her.

When they were alone in the cabin, he'd fill her in on what he'd learned today. For now, he just sat back and admired her. He liked the contrast between her sooty eyebrows and golden hair. He liked her wary blue eyes and the freckles across her nose. He liked her skin, when she was flushed and when she wasn't. He liked the color and shape of her lips.

While he studied her, she studied the crowd around them.

"How's your day been?" he asked.

"I'll tell you later," she said in a low voice. She tilted her head to the right. "Why is that girl staring at you?"

Nick glanced in the direction she indicated, where Nadine was dining with Brother Sage. She averted her gaze quickly, her cheeks red. Nick imagined she was afraid he would tell someone about her indiscretion. It might get discovered, regardless. In a community this small, her trip to the fields wouldn't have gone unnoticed. Instead of acknowledging her, Nick scanned the other tables and polished off his peach. "I'll tell you later."

Avery frowned at this answer. She rose with her tray and left him sitting there. He took care of his own tray and followed her outside. He sensed that she was upset about something beyond his domineering behavior earlier. He hoped she hadn't been harassed by Jonah, or any other creepy bastard. This place was crawling with them.

"I'm sorry about this morning," he said.

"Are you?"

"I didn't want to get caught arguing."

"You didn't want me to visit the graveyard. Why?"

"I told you why," he said, holding her gaze. Damn her psychologist's insights. He hadn't been completely honest with her, and when she found out the truth, there would be hell to pay. Nick's only option right now was brazening it out.

She didn't continue her interrogation because there were other people milling around. Before she left, she returned this morning's favor by leaning close to him and lifting her mouth to his. Any onlooker might have described the kiss as soft and loving. It wasn't. She caught his lower lip between her teeth and bit him. Not hard enough to draw blood, but hard enough to get his attention.

"God's grace," she said sweetly, and walked away.

Nick watched her until she disappeared around the corner. A feeling he couldn't name welled up inside him. This woman affected him like no other woman had. She was keeping him on his toes. She was driving him crazy. And, if he wasn't careful, she was going to be the death of him. He touched the watch in his pocket, his heart pounding with unease. Then he headed back to the fields, ready to work until he dropped.

Brent jogged into step beside him. Nick wasn't in the mood for company. He wanted to tell the kid to get lost, but he restrained himself. He could endure the earnest teenager's presence, as long as he didn't picture him with his pants down.

"How old is your wife?" Brent asked.

"Thirty-one."

Brent seemed surprised. He probably didn't believe hot women could be over thirty. "How old are you?"

"Thirty-eight."

"Is that normal for outsiders? To marry someone close in age?"

"Not everyone does, but most do."

Brent glanced around to make sure they weren't being listened to. "Have you, um, used precautions?"

Now Nick understood why he'd started this conversation. Brent wanted to learn how to continue his dalliance with Nadine, sans consequences. Nick was annoyed by his ignorance, and he blamed Brent for rousing Avery's suspicions. "What I do with my wife is none of your business, Brent."

"Oh," Brent said. His mouth went slack. "I'm sorry."

"You should be."

That shut him up. They continued to the fields, where Nick rewarded Brent with an afternoon of tilling. As he supervised the planting and watering, his eyes strayed to the tree near the fence line. He'd found rope in the shed, but he couldn't hop over the fence and peek under the camouflage in broad daylight. He'd have to come back tonight.

The plan of attack helped him focus. He was getting too distracted by his feelings for Avery, too wound up with physical desire. He vowed to concentrate on the investigation and stop worrying about the peripheral details.

People. Relationships. Unnecessary complications. Who needed them?

Nick buried himself in manual labor for the rest of the afternoon. Brent tilled the earth as if his salvation depended on it. Neither of them found peace, as far as Nick could tell. Backbreaking work was a poor substitute for sexual release.

When the dinner bell rang, they returned to the commune to wash up. Avery was late for dinner. She arrived

ten minutes after Nick. He devoured everything on his
plate and finished the leftovers on hers.

"Where were you?" he asked.

"With a patient."

"Which one?"

"Brother Joseph. He has a broken ankle."

He wiped his mouth with a napkin. "Do they faith-
heal broken bones here?"

She smiled faintly. "Dr. Winslow set it."

They headed to the cabin, which seemed smaller and
more confined than ever. The tension of the day boiled
inside him, needing release. He pulled his shirt over
his head, tossed it in the sink and started scrubbing. He
didn't expect her to do "women's work" for him,
and she didn't offer. When he glanced over his shoulder, she was watching him.

"Well?" she prompted.

He went back to scrubbing. "Well, what?"

"Why was Sage's wife staring at you?"

Nick explained what he'd interrupted earlier.

"You promised not to tell on them?"

He shrugged, rinsing the soap from the fabric. "I
didn't want to get involved."

"That's very permissive of you."

"No, it's not," he said. "I told her not to come back,
and I told him to stop messing around with her."

"You think he'll listen?"

"As long as they don't use my toolshed as their love
shack, I don't care." He wrung the moisture from his
shirt with more force than necessary. He felt her eyes on
him, spanning his shoulders and biceps. He wondered
if he looked as good to her as she did to him. His muscles were sore from the hard work, but still primed for
action. The veins in his forearms stood out in harsh re-

lief. He was sweaty and dirty, but the discomfort didn't bother him. *She* bothered him. This conversation bothered him. His guilty conscience bothered him.

Nick tossed the shirt aside and gripped the edge of the sink, his head low. "There's something else."

"What?"

He recited the information he'd heard about Caleb and Grace.

Avery's cheeks went pale at the implication. "This boy was exiled after getting caught with Grace?"

"That's what Brent suggested."

"What do you think happened to him?"

Nick didn't say that he suspected "exile" was a euphemism for "execution." He wondered if there was an unmarked grave in the nearby woods. He made a mental note to search the immediate area during his recon mission tonight.

Instead of disclosing those plans to her, he picked up his wet shirt and twisted the fabric to wring the excess moisture from it. Her gaze slid down his torso like melted ice. He guessed she liked what she saw, because she kept looking. He turned his back on her, jaw clenched.

Avery had accused him of using sex to avoid his feelings. He wished he could do that now, because he ached to touch her.

Unfortunately, there was an insurmountable obstacle between them. The deceptive tactics he'd used to gain her as a partner meant he'd never have her as his woman. In her apartment, he'd convinced himself that the sacrifice would be worth it. He'd been wrong.

"You're angry," she said in a soft voice.

"Yes."

"Why?"

Because he wanted her, and he couldn't have her. He wanted her on the kitchen counter with her blouse open and her skirt hiked up. He wanted to be inside her.

Her fingertips skimmed his naked back, and he hissed with pleasure. Arousal throbbed in his veins and his groin flooded with heat. Her breaths quickened, fanning his skin. She slid her slender arms around his waist and touched her lips to his shoulder.

His entire body responded to the contact. This cabin wasn't big enough for the both of them, plus his erection.

Instead of turning around and lifting her against the sink, he removed her hands from his clenched abs. He imagined those smooth hands lower, exploring his swollen length. He imagined her fingers stroking him. With a tortured groan, he twisted away and thrust his shirt at her. "Hang this up for me, will you?"

Her mouth dropped open. Twin flags of color stained her cheeks. She accepted the shirt, eyes flashing, and stormed outside.

If Nick knew anything about women, it was that they didn't take rejection lightly. They were used to being chased, not doing the chasing. Any sexual offer they made was expected to be snapped up with eager appreciation. A woman like Avery didn't have to beg a man to take her to bed. If she issued an invitation, and he passed… It was over.

It was over.

In the meantime, he would die from this hard-on. RIP, Nick Diaz.

He watched from the window as she hung up his damp shirt and snatched the dry one off the line. She returned from the task in less than a minute. His arousal hadn't abated. He couldn't hide it, so he didn't bother trying. She surveyed his bare chest and distended fly. Then she threw the dry shirt at him. The lightweight fabric didn't have enough heft to reach him. It sailed to the floor, short of her target.

Making a sound of frustration, she retreated to the bedroom. If there had been a door, she'd have slammed it in his face.

He picked up his shirt, smiling a little. The situation wasn't particularly funny. It was painful, and awkward, and emotionally wrought. It was passionate. It was everything he'd never wanted, and everything he hadn't known he was missing.

He was probably in love with her. That was why he felt like his guts had been yanked from his abdominal cavity and his dick had turned to stone. Draping the shirt over a chair, he settled down on his mat on the floor. Although it was barely twilight, he needed to get some rest if he was going out later.

He closed his eyes, but didn't sleep.

Chapter 17

She had the nightmare again.

She was trapped inside the storm cellar. It was pitch-black and felt like a tomb. She searched blindly for a way to escape. Her shaking hands encountered nothing but dirt floor and splintered wood. She sank to a sitting position in the oppressive dark. Sensing a presence, she turned around and reached out. Her fingertips touched something wet and sticky. Blood, she realized with a start.

Nick's blood.

She woke with a scream on her lips, sitting up in bed. She didn't know if she'd cried out in her dream or in real life. Her heart was hammering in her chest, her breaths ragged pants. She kicked away the blanket and rose to her feet.

It wasn't pitch-black inside the cabin, but she couldn't see clearly. She was aware of the same aloneness she'd felt in the storm cellar. The same…wrongness. She walked to the open doorway and stood barefoot on the threshold, listening. She couldn't hear any sound above her own pulse pounding in her ears. While she waited, shapes materialized in the gloom. The sleeping pallet appeared empty.

"Nick?"

No answer.

She tiptoed forward and knelt down to touch the flat space. He wasn't there. He wasn't inside the cabin at all. Moving quickly, she returned to the bedroom and got dressed in the dark. Slipping on shoes, she went outside. There were no lights on in either of the communal restrooms. She walked over there anyway, glancing in every direction. She didn't see or hear a soul. It was completely quiet. After using the facilities, she returned to the cabin. Her eyes weren't playing tricks on her. This wasn't a dream.

He was gone.

Bastard!

She kicked at his sleeping pallet in frustration. He hadn't told her he was leaving. He'd gone to bed early. She'd assumed he was tired, or just avoiding her company. Avoiding the temptation she presented. By initiating contact with him, she'd broken the ground rules they'd established. They'd agreed on separate sleeping arrangements from the start. She'd insisted on it. After their last encounter, they'd both agreed that they shouldn't be intimate. His desire for her was unmistakable, but that didn't matter. His words were clearly stated, and his body language—other than the obvious arousal—communicated reluctance.

She'd puzzled over his restraint. They didn't have any condoms, so that was a major obstacle. He was a commitment-phobe. She was wary of relationships. They were colleagues, bound by professional ethics. They lived in different states.

She acknowledged that these were all excellent reasons for him to keep his distance. They were excellent reasons for her to do the same. And yet, when she'd seen his bare chest, she'd snapped. She'd watched his muscles flex and ripple as he'd scrubbed his shirt. Maybe the tension of the assignment was getting to her, because she'd just reacted. She couldn't resist touching him, pressing her lips to his skin.

What was a girl to do? The man radiated sex appeal. His biceps were a thing of beauty and his erection could drive nails.

He was also a sneaky son of a bitch, evidenced by his current disappearance. He was probably spying on someone or communicating with his team somehow. She didn't need to shadow him everywhere he went, but she'd like to know if he was leaving. He'd waited until she fell asleep to circumvent that conversation.

Ugh.

She crossed her arms over her chest, pacing the room. She hadn't been completely honest with him, either. After his withdrawal, they hadn't talked about her day. She hadn't wanted to tell him about her visit to the compound. If Nick found out she had access to Father Jeff's estate, he would make demands of her. He would ask for information about the layout and the inhabitants. Larger demands might follow.

You'll do what I say, and that's final.

Yeah, no. She wasn't signing up for more sleuthing responsibilities, or whatever else Nick might have in mind. Grace was her first priority. Her only priority, maybe. She needed to consider her options, and sort out her feelings. At some point, she had to make a decision: help Nick investigate, or help her sister escape.

Grace was almost full-term. She wasn't taking care of herself. Genetically she had a higher risk of a difficult birth. Their mother had died bringing her into the world. Avery had to tell her sister about the danger as soon as possible. Her life could hang in the balance. What if she died, or lost the baby? Avery would be devastated. She'd feel responsible. The problem was, Avery had no idea how to warn Grace without breaking her cover. She also had no idea how to escape this guarded fortress.

She'd tossed and turned half the night, searching for answers. In the meantime, Nick was out searching for clues. She wondered if they'd both come up empty. She resented him for adding to her stress, after refusing to relieve it.

She went back to bed and punched her pillow. She stayed awake for what seemed like hours. She hoped he was okay, because as soon as he got back, she was going to kill him. When the front door opened, she surged upright.

"Nick?"

"Go back to sleep."

"Where were you?"

"Out."

She scrambled from the bed, incensed by his curt response. "I was worried about you, you insufferable oaf!"

He choked out at laugh at the insult.

"It's not funny."

"Sorry," he said, getting a cup of water. He drank in thirsty gulps, and his breathing indicated an elevated heart rate.

"Have you been doing this every night?"

"It's better if you don't know."

"Better for who?"

"Both of us. I can't have you following me or giving away my location. It's too dangerous."

She narrowed her eyes. "So you're just going to keep me in the dark?"

Instead of answering her, he opened a cabinet near the sink and reached inside. When he struck a match, she saw that he held a stubby candle in his other hand. He lit the wick and placed the candle on the center of the table. They both sat down on opposite sides.

"You want to talk," he said. "Let's talk."

"Okay."

He folded his hands in front of him. "Why don't you tell me about your day?"

Although his tone and body language seemed innocuous, his suggestion sent a chill down her spine. Was he aware of her visit to the compound? She wondered why he hadn't asked her about this earlier. A phrase she'd learned in Latin came to mind. *Cui bono?* Who benefits? Every choice Nick made benefited him. Maybe he'd waited to question her for this very purpose—to direct the subject away from his own shady acts. She'd caught him sneaking around, but she was the one sitting in the hot seat. Not fair.

"I went to the compound this morning," she admitted.

His brows shot up. Either he hadn't heard, or he was good at faking surprise. "You went to the compound?"

"Yes."

"Father Jeff's compound?"

"What other compound is there?"

"Who did you go with?"

"Sister Katharine. The midwife."

"You two have a history."

"That's right."

"Did she recognize you?"

"Not that I could tell."

Avery outlined her day with Katharine, omitting her brief glimpse of Grace. She didn't feel obligated to disclose every detail. She focused on the visit with Isobel and the abuse Jeremiah had inflicted on his pregnant wife. The description of her injuries captured Nick's full attention. Avery got the impression that he'd added Jeremiah to the list of people he'd like to kill. Then he interrogated her about the compound, as expected. He wanted to know who lived where. She told him about the guard quarters, the ranch and the guesthouse. She even told him about the garden house. She drew a layout on the surface of the table with her fingertip for him. He appeared to commit the invisible lines to memory.

"I need more information about Jeremiah," Nick said. "Who he talks to. Where he goes during the day. He's supposed to oversee the guards and laborers, but he's never around. I think he's up to something."

"Like what?"

"I don't know," he said.

She drummed her fingertips on the table, annoyed with his vagueness. "This partnership doesn't feel very equal, Nick."

"I never said it would be. I said I would protect you with my life, and I will."

"How can you protect me if you get caught out there?"

He pulled the watch from his pocket and turned the face like a combination lock. When it opened, he showed her three tiny buttons inside. "This is how I communicate with my team. Green means I'm okay. Yellow is a call to stand by, because I might need assistance soon. Red is a request for emergency pullout. It will bring immediate support by air."

An unsettling thought occurred to her. "Is it recording us?"

He pocketed the watch, avoiding her gaze.

Oh God. *It was.*

She stood on shaky legs. The device had recorded their heated exchange after dinner. Had she issued a verbal invitation? She couldn't remember, but now she understood why he hadn't accepted her offer. "What if you don't communicate? You haven't been able to."

He rose with her. "We're being monitored by the same technology we used to collect intel. Drones at night. Aerial photography from a distance. I use signals. One fist raised is all good. Two waving arms is a distress call."

She dragged a hand through her sleep-tangled hair. She was glad he could ask for emergency assistance in multiple ways. She wondered if he would actually do it, however. Calling for air support would end the mission. The risks he was willing to take for this investigation seemed infinite. He wouldn't leave without a fight.

He came up behind her and clasped her upper arms. "I'm sorry," he said again.

She understood what he meant. He wasn't sorry for worrying her, or for deceiving her. He was sorry he hadn't taken her to bed. His regret was genuine, and palpable, but misplaced. She broke from his hold. "I had a nightmare."

"About what?"

"The storm cellar. It's where they sent children for punishment."

"Jesus," he muttered, shaking his head.

"They left me in there all night once. Jeremiah pulled my hair, and I retaliated by stomping his foot."

"Who put you in there?"

"Sister Joyce. A teacher. She's dead now."

"Good," he said.

Avery had hated Sister Joyce for a long time. After spending the day with Katharine, Avery's perspective had changed. All of the women here were victims. It didn't excuse the mistreatment or abuse, but they weren't the main offenders. Evil trickled down from the top. Father Jeff and his ilk were to blame.

"In my dream, I reached out in the dark and felt blood. Your blood."

A muscle in his jaw flexed. He didn't dismiss her nightmare as meaningless. He also didn't promise to be careful. He wanted this mission to end in bloodshed, with the bodies of his enemies in his wake.

"Do you want out?" he asked finally.

"Do I have a choice?"

"Of course you have a choice. You're not my prisoner."

"How would I get past the guards?"

"I found a way. You'd have to go at night, and walk several miles in the dark. Then a member of my team would meet you."

"What would you tell the others?"

"I'd think of something."

She supposed he could claim she ran away, or that he didn't know where she went. The idea struck her as dangerous, not to mention detrimental to his investigation. Maybe he was making the offer to mollify her, with no intention of following through. Either way, she didn't want to leave him. Or her sister.

"You don't have to decide now," he said.

"Are you asking me to go, so that you can—"

"No," he interrupted fiercely. "I'm not."

The words she hadn't spoken were "start your revenge spree." She had no proof that he intended to kill anyone. He had no weapons, other than garden tools. Tensions were running high enough between them without her making wild accusations. They were both tortured by the same desire. He tried to be cold and removed, but she could see the storm of emotions on his face. Passion had brought him here. Passion was driving him now.

"I'll stay," she said.

He exhaled a ragged breath and retreated a step. She assumed he was relieved by her agreement to remain. His gaze swept over her in a slow drag. She was wearing the clothes she'd put on in the dark, which consisted of yesterday's skirt and the gray shawl. She hadn't bothered with a blouse. Her old-fashioned undergarment covered almost as much as a tank top. She clutched the shawl over her breasts, self-conscious.

"If you change your mind, let me know."

"I will."

He turned his back on her. "Get some rest. It's late."

She went to the bedroom without another word. She finally drifted off after lying awake for hours. The clanging breakfast bell roused her from a deep slumber. She'd overslept. Jumping out of bed, she saw that Nick had done the same.

He groaned from his pallet on the floor. "I'm too old for this."

She dressed quickly and found her shoes in the doorway. "Too old to work in the fields, sleep on the floor or stay up half the night?"

He rose and stretched. "All three."

From her perspective, he looked extremely fit. He'd slept in his clothes, so he only had to put on his boots to get ready. His ruggedness appealed to her. The grooves and lines on his face only made him more attractive. So did the shadow of beard stubble along his jaw. He was the type of man Laura would have pointed out at the Tulip Festival. Avery could picture her sister-in-law elbowing her as he passed by. He'd be the kind of hot dad whom women of all ages smiled at. When he put a child on his shoulders, female hearts would melt.

Avery, who'd been in the middle of tying her shoes, straightened so quickly she almost fell over.

What. The. Hell?

She'd lost her mind. Sometime between trying to throw herself at him last night, and waking up alone in the dark, she'd completely lost it. The stress of the assignment, plus a virile man in close proximity, had short-circuited her brain. There was no other explanation for her happy-family fantasy.

"What's wrong?" he asked.

"Nothing."

She erased those images from her psyche before they could settle in. Then she grabbed her bag of toiletries and ran to the bathroom. By the time she returned, she'd convinced herself that the brain glitch was an anomaly. She hadn't meant to daydream about Nick Diaz and a baby. It wouldn't happen again.

Instead of eating breakfast with him in the dining hall, she asked for a meal to go. He gave her an odd look.

"I'm taking this to a patient," she said. "I'll see you at lunch."

He didn't object to her leaving him. He also didn't

lean in for a kiss goodbye, maybe because he was holding a breakfast tray. The cook handed Avery a wrapped cloth with several blueberry muffins inside. Nick continued through the line without her.

Avery hurried to meet Katharine at the health office. Katharine grabbed her medical bag, seeming impatient to get started. She walked toward the front gate with a stalwart expression and a clipped gait. They were allowed to exit the commune and enter the compound. Avery wondered if she could come and go without Katharine as escort. They approached the garden house just as they had the day before. Avery didn't detect the scent of marijuana in the air this time. Grace opened the door on the first knock.

"God's grace," Katharine said in greeting.

Avery repeated the phrase.

Grace crossed her arms over her chest. "Whatever. Who's this?"

Avery was flummoxed by the sight of her heavily pregnant sister. Grace looked no older than the students at the high school where Avery worked. At nineteen, she was still a teenager and it showed. Her face had the luminosity of youth. Her pale hair was caught up in a messy bun atop her head. She wore denim overalls on top of her undergarments, sans blouse. Both the hairstyle and the clothes were a rebellion against the commune's strict codes. Up close, the resemblance to their mother wasn't as pronounced. She was beautiful in a sullen way. Her eyes were an ordinary brown.

Avery realized the girl was waiting for an introduction. "I'm Ave—Ellen."

"Avellen?"

"Ellen," Avery said quickly. She stuck out her hand. "Pleased to meet you."

Grace ignored the gesture. "What's she doing here?"

"You're not in bed," Katharine said.

"Give me a break," Grace said. "I had to answer the door, didn't I?"

"You could leave it unlocked."

Grace snorted and went inside. Avery followed Katharine into Grace's living quarters. The one-room cottage was dark and sparsely furnished. There was an unmade bed in the corner of the room. Grace flopped on her back on the mattress in a dramatic fashion, awaiting her exam. While Katharine took a seat at the foot of the bed and snapped open her medical bag, Avery watched Grace hide a paperback book under her pillow. Judging by the cover, it was a romance novel. Another contraband item, like the marijuana she'd been smoking yesterday. That sort of reading might even be considered more dangerous than drugs in this stifling, male-dominated environment.

Grace's petulant expression dared Avery to mention it. Avery just stared at her, memorizing the contours of her pretty face.

"Sister Ellen is a new member," Katharine said. "She's my apprentice."

Grace's mouth dropped open. "Your apprentice?"

"Yes."

She squinted at Avery in disbelief. "You *can't* be serious."

"How have you been feeling?"

"Ugh," she said, punching the mattress. "I hate my life."

"Any pain?"

"Just the usual. In my lower back."

"Contractions?"

"No."

Katharine donned a stethoscope and placed the drum over Grace's stomach. While she listened for the baby's heartbeat, Grace glared at Avery with contempt. Tears flooded Avery's eyes, unbidden. It wasn't because the girl seemed to loathe her. It was because—she had a sister! Avery had a sister, right here in front of her.

"What's your problem?" Grace asked.

Katharine removed the earpieces. "Hmm?"

"What's her problem?" Grace repeated, gesturing at Avery.

"I'm sorry," Avery said. She wiped the tears from her cheeks. "I just love babies. You're so blessed."

Grace made a skeptical sound. Katharine replaced the earpieces and moved the drum of the stethoscope around on Grace's distended belly.

"What did you say your name was?" Grace asked Avery.

"Ellen."

"You look familiar."

It was ironic that the one person who'd never seen Avery before recognized her. Avery didn't know how to respond to Grace's astute observation, so she remained silent. She hoped Katharine hadn't overheard the exchange.

Katharine put her stethoscope away. "How's your morning sickness?"

"Gone," Grace said. "I'm starving."

"I brought muffins," Avery said. She held up the bundle.

No one acknowledged her.

"The baby's heartbeat is slightly elevated," Katharine said. "You need to stay in bed. If you can't follow my instructions, I'll recommend moving you to the big house, where your activity can be monitored."

"You wouldn't dare," Grace snarled.

"Try me," Katharine replied.

They stared each other down for a moment, dragon lady versus rebel youth. Then Katharine picked up her medical bag and gestured for Avery to precede her. Avery cast a glance over her shoulder as they left. Grace looked ready to hop up and dance around the room the minute they were gone. Avery wanted to ask Katharine if she ever did pelvic exams. Monitoring cervical dilation at this late stage in the pregnancy seemed like a no-brainer. Katharine probably had no medical training, however. She didn't know the basics.

"I can come back later to check up on her," Avery offered.

"I don't think that's necessary," Katharine said.

Avery stayed quiet, because she intended to do it anyway. Seeing Grace in person had brought the urgency level up to ten. Her sister wasn't taking care of herself. She might be devastated by Caleb's exile, or traumatized in other ways. Katharine wasn't qualified to assist in a difficult birth or read any warning signs.

Avery had to help her sister escape as soon as possible.

Chapter 18

At Isobel's house, Katharine's bedside manner was much warmer.

Avery stood by as Katharine listened to the fetal heartbeat and palpated Isobel's baby bump gently. The swelling around Isobel's eye was down, replaced by a spectacular bruise. Avery's heart went out to her.

"You'll have to wait until it fades," Katharine said, touching Isobel's face.

Makeup would help disguise the injury, but that was another contraband item around here. It was ironic that men were free to abuse their wives, but wives weren't allowed to hide the evidence.

"I know a home remedy for bruises," Avery said. "It reduces pain and swelling and helps cover the mark."

Isobel perked up. "Really?"

Avery named a few everyday pantry items that would create a makeup substitute. While Isobel gathered the ingredients, Katharine turned to Avery.

"I have to visit the main house. They're very private, so I'll go alone."

Avery tried to look disappointed. In actuality, she was happy to avoid Father Jeff's lair, and splitting up suited her other objective perfectly. She agreed to meet Katharine back at the health office and said goodbye.

Isobel set the necessary items on the kitchen table, along with a porcelain bowl and a fine paintbrush, at Avery's request.

"Do you have any berries?" Avery asked.

"I have boysenberries."

"That will do."

She brought them to the table. Avery whipped up a pale beige paste with baking soda, tea and calamine. She painted the tincture on the affected area around Isobel's eye. Then she rinsed the brush and made a second mix with tea and crushed berries. She applied it to Isobel's lips to disguise the injury. When she was finished, Avery studied her work, pleased with the results. Isobel was pretty to begin with, which helped. The simple remedy made her black eye and split lip almost indiscernible.

Isobel went to the bathroom to look in the mirror. "It's like magic," she exclaimed.

Avery, who was standing in the doorway, smiled at her response. "Do you think Jeremiah will mind?"

"He's not here, so it doesn't matter," Isobel said.

"Oh?"

"He's due back tonight, but he'll be busy with Father Jeff. They meet for hours every time he takes a trip."

"Where does he go?"

"I don't know. He goes somewhere to talk to the outside militia about the reckoning."

"He talks to outsiders?"

"They aren't really outsiders," Isobel said. "They're members who work on the outside. Some of them grew up here."

Avery wanted to collect more information about the militia, its members and Jeremiah's clandestine activities, but she was afraid to rouse Isobel's suspicions. "Does Imogen know?" she asked gently.

"Does she know what?"

"That Jeremiah…has a temper."

Isobel tore her gaze from the mirror, her face pale. "You must have misunderstood. I had an accident. I was clumsy."

"I'm sorry," Avery said. "I didn't meant to pry."

"You should go now."

Avery nodded, swallowing hard. She saw herself out. Although she felt sorry for Isobel, she couldn't save every woman here. She had to prioritize her efforts. She didn't see Katharine outside, so she returned to the garden house. Her pulse pounded with trepidation as she knocked on the door.

"Grace?"

"What do you want?"

"It's, um, Ellen. Can I come in?"

Grace let her in. She seemed curious about Ellen's reappearance. "First it was Avellen. Now it's Umellen."

Avery didn't know if she'd get another opportunity to speak privately with Grace, so she decided to go for broke. "My name's not Ellen," she said in a low, steady voice. "It's Avery. When I lived here, it was Hannah."

Grace tilted her head to one side, puzzled. "Hannah?"

"I'm your sister."

"I don't have a sister."

Avery led the girl by the arm toward the bed and

urged her to sit down. "I escaped the day you were born. Our mother died in childbirth. I ran away and lived as an outsider for almost twenty years."

"My mother died last year."

"That wasn't your mother. Our mother's name was Sarah. She was cowives with Katharine."

"No," Grace said. Her eyes filled with tears. "You're lying. My mother's name was Louise. My father was Henry. He died before I was born."

"Your father was Gary."

Grace stood, wiping the tears from her cheeks. "You're lying. You know how I know? Because no one in their right mind would come back here."

Avery rose with her. "I came back for you. I'm going to get you out."

"How?"

"I don't know yet."

Grace let out a shrill laugh. "You're crazy, Umellen. Hannah-Anne. Whoever you are."

"I can help you escape."

Shaking her head, Grace opened a drawer by the bed. Inside was a joint and lighter. She sparked it up, defiant. "This is what helps me escape," she said, inhaling deep. "I don't need you."

Avery wanted to take the joint away from her and smash it, but she restrained herself. "Marijuana is bad for you and the baby."

Grace took another drag. "That's why I like it."

"Who gives it to you? The guards?" An idea occurred to her. "Jeremiah?"

The young woman avoided her gaze, exhaling smoke in a ragged breath. Her eyes watered again.

"Are you having an affair with him?"

"Ugh," Grace said. "I'm so fat right now. I'd rather die."

"But you accept drugs from him. In exchange for what?"

She shrugged, evasive.

"Did he kill Caleb?" Avery asked.

This question appeared to strike a nerve. Grace set the joint aside. "Where did you hear that?"

"If you know something about his disappearance, I can help you talk to the authorities. We'll go together. If there's evidence of a serious crime, they'll come to shut this place down. Everyone will be free."

Grace picked up the joint again, shaking her head in disbelief. "Are you a cop?"

"No."

"Maybe I'll tell Jeremiah about this conversation."

The air rushed from Avery's lungs. She'd miscalculated. She'd assumed that Grace's rebellious attitude meant she'd be open to leaving the commune. But there was no foundation of trust between them. Of course the girl didn't believe Avery could help her. The level of indoctrination in the cult, as well as the fear of reprisal, kept its members obedient. Grace had chosen Jeremiah over Avery for a reason. He was the devil she knew.

"When are you due?" Avery asked.

"Any day now."

"Okay. I'll try to get proof of my identity." Surely there were birth records, school photographs or some evidence of Hannah's existence. "If you go into labor, send for me. I have more medical training than Katharine."

"A monkey has more medical training than Katharine."

"Remember that our mother died in childbirth. Factor in the marijuana, and you're at very high risk for complications."

Grace didn't appear swayed by this argument. In fact, she continued smoking with relish. Avery realized that there was another kind of escape the young woman might be considering. Death was the ultimate respite from pain and loss.

Tears flooded Avery's eyes as she watched Grace get high. It was ironic that Ellen's fake backstory featured a sister on drugs. Avery left the cottage before she could do any more damage. She'd already broken her cover and risked the entire assignment. If Grace followed through on her threat to tell Jeremiah, the consequences would be dire.

Avery had to get proof—before Jeremiah returned from his trip.

When she reentered the commune, she went straight to the health office to search for records. There were two important-looking leather-bound journals on the shelf next to the homeopathic remedies. One had Births embossed on the cover in gold. The other said Deaths. Avery donned her glasses to flip through them.

She located her birth year and date near the middle of the book. Someone had written "Hannah, daughter to Gary and Sarah," in neat script. Avery flipped forward thirteen years, scanning for Grace's name. There was an entry under the correct year, but wrong month: "Grace, daughter to Louise and Henry (deceased)."

Four months earlier, in the middle of June, there was another entry: "Baby girl (deceased), daughter to Gary and Sarah (deceased)." Avery assumed that Louise, the previous midwife, had kept these records. Avery only vaguely remembered her. It was obvious that Louise hadn't wanted Grace to know about her real mother. She must have falsified this information.

The steps she'd taken to cover up the truth frustrated Avery. She'd hoped to find evidence, not obfuscations.

Frowning, she moved on to Deaths. Baby Girl and Sarah made an appearance here, on the same day as the birth. There was a short description of the reason for death in a slanted scrawl. Someone else wrote the death records. Dr. Winslow, perhaps. He might be the coroner, as well as the doctor and the vet. Three days after Baby Girl and Sarah, Hannah's name appeared. The reason for death? Broken neck.

Broken neck?

She hadn't realized she'd spoken the words out loud until Katharine entered the office with Imogen at her side. Imogen looked like a tidy storm cloud in her charcoal-gray dress. Avery wanted to close the book and put it back on the shelf, but Imogen swooped in to peer over Avery's shoulder.

"What are you reading?" Imogen asked.

"Death records."

Katharine glanced at the page Avery had landed on. "Tragic story. That poor girl ran into the woods after her mother died. They found her at the bottom of a ravine. She must have fallen in the dark."

Avery wondered if there was a headstone in the cemetery with Hannah's name on it, and an empty grave underneath.

"Do you remember Hannah?" Katharine asked Imogen. "She used to babysit you."

A crease formed between Imogen's brows. She stared at Avery for a long moment. Avery didn't avert her gaze, even though she felt like her hair was on fire, and her former name was stamped on her forehead. She closed the book with silent dread. Her heart pounded like a drum inside her chest.

Imogen turned to her mother and said, "No. I don't remember her."

"Don't worry," Katharine said to Avery. "We don't have accidents like that often."

"You got your glasses back," Imogen said.

Avery took off the glasses and hid them in her pocket. She realized that they indicated a favor from Jonah. Imogen was fixated on this, not Avery's resemblance to a girl named Hannah. Avery drew in a breath of relief. "I only need them for reading."

"How's Isobel?" Imogen asked, changing the subject.

"Busy," Katharine replied shortly. "As am I."

If Imogen felt slighted by the brush-off, she didn't show it. These were the starchiest women Avery had ever met. Avery supposed it was a survival mechanism, a sort of armor against the harsh conditions in the commune.

After Imogen left, Katharine and Avery continued to make house calls. There were four other pregnant women to visit, and a number of babies who needed checkups. Summer was the season of teeth cleaning, as well. Katharine encouraged all of the mothers to make an appointment.

Avery was about to take lunch when a young woman rushed into the health office carrying a screaming toddler. She thought the boy had been bitten by a snake, maybe a rattler. Avery examined the affected area.

"It's a beesting," she said, smiling.

By the time the boy and his mother calmed down, the lunch hour was almost over. Avery saw Nick only in passing. After a quick bite, she went back to work. Katharine kept her busy for the rest of the afternoon. When the dinner bell clanged, Avery rushed to meet Nick. He greeted her with a kiss on the cheek.

"I need to shower first," he said. "I'm filthy."

She walked to the cabins with him. She didn't know what to say about her exchange with Grace, so she said nothing. Maybe he was too tired to notice her silence—or he was thinking about his own secrets. He grabbed a bar of soap and a fresh set of clothes before heading to the showers. She decided to do the same. When she emerged from the bathroom with damp hair and clean clothes, he was waiting for her.

"How was your day?" he asked as they walked to dinner.

"Eventful," she admitted. "Yours?"

"Exhausting."

She reached for his hand and held it. His palm felt rough and warm. The blisters had already turned into calluses. He used his other hand to massage his neck. She remembered how his muscles had flexed the night before, when he'd washed his shirt in the sink. He was working hard and it showed.

"Sore?" she asked.

"Yeah."

"I'll give you a back rub."

His gaze glinted with sexual interest, even though he'd spurned her less than twenty-four hours ago. She looked away, flushing. She hadn't meant to tease him. Or herself, for that matter. Offering to touch him was a *bad idea*.

She didn't speak at all during dinner. He made conversation of the farming type that required no response from her. Anyone listening in would assume that Nick Dean had a one-track mind. Avery marveled at his ability to do this in a way that appeared sincere and effortless. It was almost as if he'd memorized a very dull script. He was probably some kind of genius. And she was, without a doubt, in love with him.

She'd always thought the moment she knew she loved someone would be joyous, like the elation of standing at the top of a mountain after a long hike. Instead, she felt a mixture of anxiety and dread. Because she had to tell him what she'd said to Grace earlier. He would be horrified. This case was everything to him. She wished she'd come up with some evidence that she was Hannah, or that she and Grace were sisters. Short of convincing Grace to escape the commune and become a star witness, Avery didn't know how to fix her blunder.

Being in love sucked.

She managed to eat most of her meal, so maybe she'd become numb to stress. It was Wednesday night, and there was church service after dinner. She sat next to Nick and held his hand as Jonah regaled the audience with moral stories. She hadn't slept well the night before, because of Nick's escapades. She could hardly keep her eyes open now.

At the end of the service, Imogen trotted up to them. "Brother Jonah needs to see you in the rectory."

Avery's heart sank at her smug announcement. Had Grace reported her?

"Of course," he said easily. "You look pretty tonight, Sister Imogen."

Imogen thanked him for the compliment, which sounded sincere. Nick Dean wasn't always boring. He could turn on the charm when it suited him. Imogen escorted them to Brother Jonah's office, where she was summarily dismissed. Nick smiled at her on the way out. She bumped into the doorframe.

Avery focused on Jonah. His expression was serious, his hair slicked back. Nick congratulated him on a rousing service. Jonah wasn't as starved for flattery as Imogen. His smile didn't reach his cool green eyes.

"How are the two of you adjusting?" he asked.

Nick launched into his farming soliloquy, which Jonah cut off.

"The last time we sat down together, we discussed Sister Ellen's fertility issues. Can you give me an update on your progress?"

Nick cocked his head to the side. "It's only been three days."

"And?"

Avery squirmed in her seat. This wasn't the interrogation she'd expected, but it was an uncomfortable one nonetheless.

"I think it's too soon to tell," Nick said.

"I'm asking if you've made an effort."

"Of course we have."

Jonah turned to Avery. "Is your husband pleasing you every night?"

Nick held up a hand in objection. "Brother Jonah, can we continue this conversation in private? These are personal matters—"

"She's got a right to know what you've been doing."

"What I've been doing?"

"Brother Sage reported an incident to me this afternoon. He caught his wife, Nadine, sneaking in after a rendezvous last night. When he went out in search of her companion, he spotted you returning to your cabin."

Avery's palms turned sweaty and her pulse raced.

"I can explain," Nick said.

"Please do."

"I couldn't remember if I turned off the water pump yesterday. I woke up in a panic, so I went out there to check. It was a false alarm."

"You never saw Nadine?"

"No."

"There's a problem with your story, Brother Nick."

"What's that?"

Jonah leaned forward. "Nadine admitted to her transgression with you."

Nick appeared stunned by this turn of events. He'd done Nadine and Brent a kindness by not reporting them, and this was the thanks he got. If he told the truth now, Jonah probably wouldn't believe him.

"She's lying," Avery said, with conviction. "Nick couldn't have done it."

"How do you know?"

"He's impotent," she said.

Nick turned toward Avery, his jaw slack. Instead of issuing a denial, he covered his eyes with one hand in shame.

"He couldn't cheat if he wanted to."

Jonah studied Nick intently. "Is that true, Brother Nick?"

Nick actually shuddered, as if suffering from acute embarrassment. Then he lifted his hand from his face and focused on Jonah. "It's a temporary side effect of my illness. I just need more time to build faith and heal my body."

Jonah tapped his fingertips on the surface on the desk. "This should have been brought to my attention earlier, Brother Nick. Instead of humbling yourself before God, you hid your affliction and pointed the finger at your lovely wife."

"Have mercy on him," Avery pleaded, her voice breaking. "He already feels like less than a man."

Nick made a wounded sound and rose from the chair. "It's a *temporary* affliction. Should I have announced it on the pulpit, next to Father Jeff? Maybe he could have focused his healing powers on my manhood instead of Ellen's womb."

Jonah narrowed his eyes. "You question my father's methods?"

Nick didn't answer. "I'll recover soon enough, and I'll do my husbandly duties. In the meantime, I'd rather cut off my own hand than betray my wife." He gestured toward Avery. "Look at her. Why would I go elsewhere? I would die to touch her again. No other woman compares."

Avery was moved to tears by his passionate entreaty. She wished with all of her heart that he meant some of those words, but she knew it was just a performance. She was torn between loving him for being so damned good at his job, and hating him for the same reason. His deceptions were so convincing, she never knew when he was lying.

"God's grace," Nick snarled, and left the room.

"Well," Jonah said, after a pause. "That struck a nerve."

Avery came to her feet, still weeping. Jonah stood to console her. He wrapped his arm around her shoulders and offered her a monogrammed handkerchief. She remembered when Nick had done the same. She dabbed her eyes with the fabric, which smelled faintly of antiseptic. She preferred Nick in every way, but especially by scent. No other man compared.

She pressed her face to Jonah's shirt. "Why aren't you married?" she murmured.

"I haven't been blessed yet."

"Who does the blessings?"

"My father."

"You've never asked him to select a wife for you?"

"I asked him once."

"What did he do?"

Jonah stroked her hair with a careful hand. "That's a story for another day."

"All I ever wanted was a baby," she whispered.

"Let me know what I can do to help."

She could guess what he *wanted* to do. She gazed up at him. "If Nick doesn't recover…"

"I'll be here."

With a grateful nod, she fled.

Chapter 19

Nick had borrowed a straight razor from Brent.

As soon as he entered the cabin, he removed his shirt and soaped his jaw. The routine of shaving, plus the challenge of an unfamiliar tool, calmed his nerves. He wicked the blade over the sharp contours of his face, his mind blank. The task required a steady hand and total concentration.

When he was finished, he wiped away the excess soap and studied himself. Ricardo Diaz's eyes stared back at him, alight with idealism. The resemblance hadn't bothered Nick in Vegas, when he'd been brimming with triumph. Now it did.

He gripped the edges of the sink, his head low. Nick's father had been a political zealot, full of reckless fervor, willing to die for a cause. He'd died fighting—and he'd taken Nick's mother with him. It was an unforgiveable offense, but Nick hadn't assigned any blame when he'd learned of the tragedy. He'd mourned his parents in a detached, dutiful way. Then he'd shut the door on his heart.

He refused to follow in his father's footsteps. It was one of the reasons he'd stayed single. If he never fell in love and had a family, he couldn't repeat the same mistakes. He wouldn't endanger or abandon anyone.

Nick strove to be calm and calculated, not driven by emotion. He'd failed at this spectacularly. His need for revenge had brought him here. He'd dragged Avery along with him, heedless of the consequences. He was hot-blooded and obsessive, just like his father.

He wanted to smash the mirror in denial, but the truth stared him in the face. He was no better than Ricardo Diaz. His father had been a jealous man, prone to bouts of machismo. Nick couldn't deny that the trait had been passed down to him. He'd practically been spoon-fed it from birth. It still lived inside him, straining like a beast on a chain.

Avery entered the cabin, and the beast quickened.

She studied him with nervous eyes. "You shaved."

He nodded curtly. "How did it go with Jonah?"

"Fine."

"Did you have to get on your knees?"

She flinched at the low blow. "What's your problem, Nick? Are you mad that I said you were impotent?"

He choked out a laugh. They both knew it wasn't true, and he didn't give a damn what Jonah thought of him. The impotency excuse had been a stroke of genius, one that played perfectly with Jonah. She had him wrapped around her finger. "My problem isn't what you said. It's what he did after I left."

"He didn't do anything."

"He didn't comfort you? Tell you he could be my stand-in dick?"

She crossed her arms over her chest, flushing. "You wanted him to want me, remember? You counted on it. You paraded me around naked in front of him."

"I didn't parade you around," he said, teeth clenched. "I tried to shield you."

"You didn't try very hard."

"That's not true."

She made a skeptical noise. "The bottom line is that Jonah is doing exactly what you expected him to do. You orchestrated this. Why are you balking?"

"I'm not balking," he said, nonsensically. He closed the distance between them, until his body was inches from hers. "I just can't stand the thought of him touching you. I can't stand the thought of anyone else touching you."

Her gaze darkened with sensual interest. She lifted her hand to his face, exploring the newly smooth angles. He tensed at the contact, his jaw clenched with longing. Her fingertips left a sizzling path on his skin. Every nerve ending stood at full attention, vibrating for more. Heat pooled to his groin.

She stood on tiptoe, her lips brushing his ear. "Why don't you touch me, then?"

The beast broke free, roaring.

He clutched a handful of her hair and tilted her head back. She didn't blink or pull away. He studied her for a taut moment, mapping the places he wanted to kiss. Her mouth, her neck, her chin. The tender spot beneath her left ear. The pulse point in her throat.

He imagined pinning her arms above her head and kissing her from wrists to elbows. Then from elbows to mouth, and mouth to breasts. Breasts to belly, and beyond. The fantasy was so powerful he doubted reality could match it, but he dipped his head nonetheless. The first kiss made him groan. Her mouth was hot, wet, receptive. She tasted like the peach tea they'd served before Jonah's sermon.

God.

Nick followed his fantasy without conscious thought. After plundering her mouth with his tongue and backing her up against the wall, he kissed all the places he'd imagined. Her silky throat, the tender undersides of her arms. She didn't object to him holding her wrists high above her head. She moaned and begged for more.

He gave it to her. He tugged her blouse over her head and unfastened her skirt. Standing in her underwear, she unbuttoned his shirt and pushed it off his shoulders. He lifted her onto the counter by the sink. Then they were kissing again, his hands roaming her curves. Her bodice fell away, exposing her breasts. For a few seconds, he just looked at her, his heart pounding like a jackhammer inside his chest. She was beautifully shaped, with creamy skin and taut nipples. He cupped her breasts reverently, rolling the tips between his fingers. Her head fell back and she clutched his hair, moaning. He wanted to spend days with his mouth on her nipples. He laved them with unselfconscious enjoyment, excited by her eager response.

"Please," she said, panting. "More."

Jesus. She sounded ready to come.

He yanked off her bloomers, or whatever they were, and shoved his hand between her parted thighs. She was deliciously wet. He plunged two fingers into her slick heat. She sobbed in ecstasy, her breasts heaving.

Nick was a big believer in foreplay. He cared about being a good lover with any woman, but he *loved* Avery.

He'd planned on taking his time with her. He'd fantasized about falling to his knees and feasting on her right here at the kitchen sink. His mouth watered and his erection throbbed at the thought.

He didn't quite get there, because her hand found him first. She released the buttons on his fly and reached into his long johns. He released a hiss of breath as her fingers wrapped around him. He watched her face as she stroked him. She bit her lower lip, eyes half-lidded. Her breasts jiggled from the motion.

His knees almost buckled. "Stop," he rasped. "I'm going to—"

She did stop, but only to place the tip of him against the center of her. She guided him toward heaven, and that was all she wrote. His hips thrust forward on instinct, until he was fully seated inside her.

Damn. Damn.

He managed to stay still, giving her a few seconds to adjust, and him a moment to think. "I'm not wearing a condom," he ground out.

"It's the wrong time of month."

Famous last words, but he wasn't arguing. He was almost weeping with joy at the bare-skin contact. She wrapped her legs around him, driving him deeper. He couldn't hold back a strangled groan, because she surrounded him with sultry perfection. He withdrew and plunged in again, and again, and again.

It wasn't his best performance. It was a fast-and-furious coupling at the kitchen sink, with his pants around his ankles.

He knew he wouldn't last. Her hot body undid him. Her nipples were damp from his mouth, brushing his chest with every thrust. Her lips parted, making breathy little sounds. It was all he could do to remember to get her off first. He slipped his hand between them and stimulated her with as much finesse as he could muster.

It was just enough, apparently. She bit down on his arm to muffle her cry as she shuddered with a climax that felt earth-shattering, at least to him. He withdrew seconds before he spent against her stomach. Then his knees did buckle, and he slumped against her so hard the back of her head bumped into the cabinets.

When he'd recovered enough to speak, he choked out an apology.

She laughed softly. "I'm fine."

They were already at the sink, so he washed his seed from her belly with cool water. After fastening his pants, he carried her to the bedroom. Once there, he made up for the frantic first round with a second, more leisurely session. He spent the time between her legs he'd dreamed of, and she wasn't shy about expressing her enjoyment. She also wasn't shy about returning the favor. She sucked and stroked him with the same fervor he'd shown her. Even after two orgasms, they were both insatiable. The third round was a blur of erotic positions and Spanish gutter talk that drove her crazy. He didn't come again, but she did. Then she curled up beside him, damp with perspiration, and fell asleep.

It was the best night of his life. The best sex of his life, by far, but that was only half of the equation. The other half was emotion. This wasn't a fling, or a fluke, or a side effect of playing a married couple on a dangerous assignment.

He was in love with her. Which made it that much more difficult to take the next step.

He had to leave her. He couldn't stay here in bed with her, no matter how tempting. The beast inside him was quiet now, drowsy and satiated, but he could not rest.

There was work to be done. He hoped he'd worn her out thoroughly, because he wanted to slip away without waking her. It was imperative that she not follow him.

He needed to communicate with his team as soon as possible. The modified watch wasn't good enough. It wasn't recording audio, despite what he'd let Avery believe. The drone was his backup system. He'd used it to signal for a drop, and there was no margin for error. The drone would deliver a package to the far field at midnight. Nick had to pick up the package, evaluate the contents and come back.

Easy.

Except that he'd been spotted by Brother Sage last night, in addition to getting caught by Avery, and that damned Nadine had lied about Nick being her lover. Nick didn't know if Jonah believed the impotence bit, or the story about him checking the water pump. He assumed the guards would be on high alert, regardless. He would proceed with caution.

He rose from the bed in silence, his muscles aching from overuse. He was tired, and her naked form beckoned. He stood and stared at her for a long moment. He memorized every line and curve. She reminded him of a blush rose, pale and petal-soft. Maybe being in love was turning him into a poet. Another trait passed down from his father.

It probably wasn't fair to blame his father for his mother's death, but Nick couldn't change how he felt. He believed a man should protect his wife at any cost. He should never knowingly put her in danger. His father had failed on both counts.

So had Nick.

The comparison to Nick's current situation made his gut clench. Smothering a curse, he covered Avery with a sheet and got dressed in the dark. He'd left his boots outside the door, because they smelled like goat dung, and it made for a quieter getaway.

There was no one outside. No guards milling about. No Brother Sage, searching for the man who'd cuckolded him. Nick was angry with Brent and Nadine for putting him in a bad spot, but he was angrier with himself for getting seen, and for not seeing this twist coming. The young lovers were stupidly indiscreet. Brent had disregarded Nick's advice, like any horny teenager. It was only natural for Nadine to lie about his identity. She was protecting Brent from exile. Why not point the finger at the new guy?

Using considerably more stealth than the night before, Nick skulked toward the fields. Whenever he heard a noise, he dropped to his belly like a lizard, listening and waiting. It took him thirty minutes to traverse a half mile. It took another thirty to find the package among the tangled weeds at the edge of the fields. He tore it open. There was a cell phone inside. He probably couldn't use it to make a call, due to the remote location. There were three text messages available to view.

The first was from McDonald:

You've got a lot of explaining to do, Diaz.

The second, longer message indicated that several grave sites had been found in the area via a drone with LIDAR technology, which was some kind of laser scanner that identified objects underground. Nick didn't know how that worked, but he could read a map with X marks. There was a printed copy inside the package. A third message ordered him to delete after reading.

He followed that instruction and contemplated his

next move. He could hide the phone and return to Avery. Or he could grab a shovel and do some in-depth investigating.

An unmarked grave was a strong indicator of foul play under normal circumstances. Unfortunately, these circumstances weren't normal. The members of The Haven didn't follow interment codes or file death reports. A few strange burials, in a commune full of unconventional beliefs, might not be enough to justify a search warrant. And if there was no evidence of trauma or unlawful death in those graves? They'd be back at square one.

Nick had to make sure.

He went to the equipment shed for a shovel. While he was there, he grabbed a pruning hook he'd had his eye on. He'd considered carrying the straight razor, but it was a poor weapon for self-defense. The pruning hook could gouge and puncture. It was small, sharp and curved like a scythe. He tucked it into his boot and headed out.

Chapter 20

Avery didn't have any nightmares after falling asleep in Nick's arms.

Something else jolted her awake. It wasn't a sound, or a movement. It was a feeling of foreboding, of words unspoken. She hadn't told Nick about her meeting with Grace—who had threatened to rat her out to Jeremiah as soon as he returned from his trip.

Intuition told her that Grace was bluffing, but Avery still had to warn Nick. Because intuition also told her that their covers were crumbling. Jonah's suspicions were aroused, and he was an intelligent adversary. He'd accused them both of lying on separate occasions. If he caught Nick sneaking around tonight, he wouldn't believe another excuse.

She sat up in bed, aware that he was no longer next to her. She didn't have to reach out to make sure. The space wasn't big enough for him to be there without touching her. She didn't have to say his name to know he wasn't in the cabin, either. She felt his absence as acutely as she'd felt him inside her.

Throwing off the blankets, she scrambled to her feet. Moonlight coming through the window in the main room illuminated her discarded clothes. She dressed quickly, her heart racing, and emerged from the cabin. The moon was high in the sky, bright and bisected with billowy clouds. She covered her head and shoulders with the gray shawl. As she hurried down the path, she realized that she didn't know where to look for him.

The fields seemed like a good place to start. He'd told her that he'd found a way out, and he'd been spending most of his time there. Also, he'd told Jonah that he'd gone to check the water pump last night. He'd probably engineered the lie to match the route he'd taken.

She headed that direction, her steps swift but silent. Her drowsiness wore off and anger set in. They were supposed to be *partners*. Instead of communicating his plans with her, he'd left her in the dark again—after screwing her senseless.

She smothered a gasp as a terrible thought occurred to her. He was a man who used sex to avoid feelings. To circumvent difficult conversations. To escape.

He'd done that with her. He'd done that *to* her.

He hadn't wanted her to accompany him or ask him any pointed questions about his nefarious activities, so he'd taken her to bed. The fact that she'd invited him to touch her didn't matter as much as his motivations for doing so. He'd spurned her advances the night before, and nothing had changed between them. Nothing except the fact that she'd caught him sneaking out, and could expect him to make another attempt.

"That bastard," she whispered.

She was in love with him, and he'd slept with her to get away.

Pushing that thought from her mind, she continued toward the fields with urgency. She was going to slap his face off when she found him. As she neared the cemetery, she heard the sound of voices carrying on the wind. She looked over her shoulder and her stomach dropped. There was a trio of figures carrying torches, like an old-fashioned witch hunt.

She was the witch. Or Nick was the monster. Either way, they were closing in. She picked up her skirts and ran into cemetery. It was a poor choice of hiding place, because there weren't many trees, and most of the grave markers were modestly sized.

She ducked behind the largest headstone she could find. Pressing her back to the granite, she tucked her knees to her chest and prayed. Please don't let them find her. Please don't let them find Nick.

As she cowered there, shivering with fear, she became aware of the grave markers directly in front of her. Even without her glasses, but she could read the epitaphs at this distance. Three names were carved into three simple headstones in a neat row, sized from largest to smallest:

Sarah.

Hannah.

Baby Girl.

Avery clapped a hand over her mouth to stifle her scream. She was staring at her own grave! It sat between her mother's, and her sister's. Tears filled her eyes, but she was too scared and confused to process her sadness. Instead, she considered the implications of what she was seeing. She'd already assumed that they'd buried an empty coffin in her place. She could infer that they'd done the same thing for "Baby Girl."

Something felt wrong with that theory, however. The headstone for Hannah made sense, because she'd run away. Father Jeff and the elders couldn't allow word to spread about a girl who'd made a successful escape. Why would anyone go to the trouble to carve a headstone for a baby who had lived? If the midwife had raised Grace as her own child, there was no need for fudging records or faking grave sites. The members of The Haven remembered Sarah and her pregnancy. They wouldn't be fooled.

You'll do what I say, and that's final.

Nick's command had bothered her then, and it haunted her now. Yes, he could be arrogant and implacable, but the domineering words had still seemed out of character. He *really* hadn't wanted her to visit the graveyard. He'd known these grave markers were here, and he'd been afraid she would see them.

Because it wasn't an elaborate cover-up.

It was the truth, staring her in the face.

Grace wasn't her sister. Avery's baby sister had died with their mother. And Nick, damn his beautiful eyes, had lied.

The pain of this betrayal cut so deep, she felt like she'd been sucker punched. She curled up on her side and clutched her stomach. He'd brought her a photo of Grace, and claimed it had been genetically matched to her. What a fool she'd been to fall for that. The technology probably didn't even exist. She couldn't believe the lengths he'd gone to—and the levels he'd stooped to—in pursuit of vengeance. She supposed she should have guessed, but the magnitude of his deception rocked her to the core.

Maybe everything he'd said was a lie. Every word he'd spoken in bed, every tender caress. Every story he'd told about his childhood. She was so wrapped up in her own misery that she almost didn't care that her pursuers were closing in. There was nowhere else to hide, regardless. They must have spotted her running through the graveyard. Now they were searching the area methodically, torches blazing.

When they reached her, she rose to her feet.

It was Jonah, Brother Sage and Imogen.

"I told you," Imogen said, triumphant. "She's at her own grave."

Jonah glanced from the headstone to Avery's face. "Who are you?"

"I'm Ellen," she said. "Ellen Dean."

Jonah lifted his torch higher. "Where's Brother Nick?"

"I don't know."

"Did you come out here looking for him?"

"Yes."

"Why did you hide?" Imogen asked.

Avery didn't answer. She couldn't think of a reasonable excuse, and what did it matter? Imogen had put two and two together. It was over. She'd been recognized.

"Let's go," Jonah said, grasping her arm.

Avery went without a struggle, her mind numb. She wondered what they'd do with her. Maybe Jonah would take her to the rectory and interrogate her until she broke. They walked back to the road in silence.

"We should keep looking for him," Sage said, his eyes narrow.

Jonah shook his head. "Jeremiah will find him."

"I want to find him now. The fields are close."

"Wounded pride makes you reckless," Jonah replied. "It's a job better suited to my brother's strengths."

Avery realized that Sage still thought Nick had corrupted his sweet Nadine. She could also guess why Jonah didn't want to go after Nick. It was Jonah's mess, because he'd invited the Deans to the commune, but he'd let Jeremiah do the dirty work.

"We're unarmed," Jonah said.

"So is he."

"You don't know that."

"You're afraid of him," Avery said to Jonah.

Jonah's response was swift and cruel. He released Avery's arm and backhanded her across the face. The impact knocked her off balance. She fell to her knees, holding her cheek. Blood trickled from her lips.

Imogen appeared stunned by his actions. She stared at Avery with wide eyes.

"If I did that to Nadine, you'd punish me," Brother Sage said to Jonah.

"Nadine isn't an outsider spy!"

Imogen helped Avery to her feet again. This basic kindness seemed to enrage Jonah. He regained his hold on Avery's arm and started dragging her toward the commune. Imogen fell in line with Jonah, but Sage didn't. He must have stayed behind to look for Nick, disobeying Jonah's orders.

Avery's brain was rattled from the blow. The inside of her cheek felt swollen and raw. She wiped the blood from her mouth with a trembling hand. Jonah yanked her arm, causing her to stumble. Any misconceptions she'd had about him being a decent person were gone. He was no better than his father. No better than his brother. Just another power-hungry leader with a violent temper and a God complex.

He didn't haul her into the church rectory, or the health office. He headed past the schoolyard, to the setting of her worst nightmare.

The storm cellar.

"Open it," he said to Imogen.

She flipped the hasp and wrenched the heavy door aside. Jonah pushed Avery down the steps, into the dark abyss. When Imogen tried to follow them, he shook his head, denying her access to the interrogation.

"Leave us."

Imogen's face crumpled with emotion. Despite Jonah's flaws, she was devoted to him. The sight of him doing violence to another woman didn't sit well with her. Avery imagined he planned to do more as soon as they were alone. Imogen must have suspected the same thing, but she didn't voice an objection. She closed the door quietly.

Nick was immersed in digging when he heard an ominous sound.

Golf cart.

He glanced up from the grave, where he stood knee-deep. He'd chosen this site because it looked the most recent, with loose-packed dirt. He'd just unearthed the heel of a boot, which indicated the body was facedown. That was consistent with foul play, not a proper burial. The overwhelming stench of decomposing flesh emanated from the dark soil. He'd bet his badge that this man was Brother Caleb. If the poor bastard had his hands tied behind his back, execution-style, or a visible gunshot wound, Nick could call in his team.

First he had to survive the night, however. The grave wasn't deep enough to hide in, so he tossed the shovel and dived behind the nearest tree. The golf cart didn't zip past and keep going. It stopped in the middle of the road, idling nearby.

That was unlucky.

Even unluckier, someone in the cart had a flashlight.

Its beam penetrated the forest and zeroed in on the grave site. The business end of the shovel glinted in the dark.

Damn.

Nick realized they knew he was here. They were looking for him. He considered running, but he figured the motion would be noticed, his steps heard. It would be a footrace. Could he outrun the driver, who knew this terrain and probably had a shotgun?

Nick didn't run.

He climbed.

The tree he'd ducked behind had a sturdy trunk, but it wasn't easy to climb. He grasped the nearest branch and hauled himself up anyway, adrenaline giving him a much-needed boost of energy. He went hand over hand, limb over limb, until he was high enough to hide among the thicker branches. Then he stayed very still, because two men had entered the space below him. He glanced down, his pulse pounding.

Jeremiah was there with one of the guards. They searched the immediate area for a few minutes and returned to the grave.

"He was here," the guard said. "We just missed him."

"Doesn't matter. He won't get far."

"What if he went back?"

"Why would he do that?"

"For his wife."

"It's not his wife, stupid."

The next exchange was intelligible. Then Jeremiah said, "Stay here and keep digging. We've got to move the body now."

Nick waited for Jeremiah to walk away. Then he opened the face of his watch and pressed the emergency button. It was over. His cover was broken, and Avery was in danger. He shouldn't have left her alone.

He thought she'd be safer in the cabin. She would have been, if he'd been there with her. He'd been so intent on collecting evidence that he'd disregarded the risks. He'd wanted to get the photos and get out, with Avery. He'd imagined them leaving the commune together before dawn. He'd meant to stay one step ahead of these bastards. Somehow he'd fallen behind, and he'd completely failed to protect her.

Nick watched from above as the guard started digging. He figured he had only a few minutes before a second man showed up to help. Moving a body was hard work. Nick had to sneak away now. He'd like to tackle the guard, beat him unconscious and finish documenting the evidence. A week ago, he might have made that choice. His quest for justice had outweighed everything else, including professional ethics.

Over the past few days, his priorities had changed. Now all that mattered to him was saving Avery.

He descended the tree with quiet stealth and crept away from the grave site. If the guard had spotted him, Nick would have attacked. He still had the pruning hook tucked in his boot. Lucky for the guard, he didn't look up from his task. Nick continued walking until he was at a safe distance. He checked the cell phone, which had no service. He tried to send a text and failed. Instead of chucking it into the woods in frustration, he put it in his pocket.

His best option was to head to the main road and wait for backup. He could search for a better reception area and try the phone again. His team was already mobilizing. They might not bring in air support in the middle of the night, but they'd get here as soon as possible. By daybreak, at the latest.

He checked his watch. It was 2:00 a.m.

He couldn't wait four hours to rescue Avery. There were a lot of unspeakable things that could happen to her in that time frame. The odds were stacked against him, however. He had to face a militia of armed guards. He didn't have the element of surprise. He had a garden tool, an unusable phone, his fists and his wits.

Nick considered the most likely scenario, that he'd get captured immediately and tortured alongside her. It didn't dissuade him. If he died trying to save her, so be it. At least he could keep his promise to protect her with his life.

Decision made, he headed toward the commune. He managed to avoid the guards, who were out in greater numbers, combing the woods. They were untrained boys, for the most part, unfamiliar with their weapons and ill-prepared for combat. Nick didn't want to hurt them. He still wanted to hurt Father Jeff and Jeremiah, and he wouldn't mind taking a crack at Jonah while he was at it. The rest were innocent bystanders.

He reached the area with the camouflage netting that he'd discovered yesterday. It seemed like a week had passed since then. Underneath the camouflage was a crop of maturing marijuana plants. The pot was an interesting discovery, but not the smoking gun he'd hoped for. Nick figured the plants were Jeremiah's, which explained his touchy attitude about Nick poking around the fields. The crop might be a side hustle he didn't want Father Jeff or Jonah in on. Maybe Jeremiah exchanged drugs for guns. Either way, the number of plants exceeded the legal limit and could be added to his list of crimes.

Nick was more interested in murders than marijuana, naturally. A few dead bodies were enough to bring the law down on this ungodly place.

He used the rope to climb the overhanging branch

by the fence line. He'd tied several knots in it to use as handholds. His muscles ached from working, digging and that final round in bed with Avery. He'd overdone it, but no regrets.

He'd meant what he'd said in Jonah's office. He'd die to touch her again, and no other woman compared to her.

He brought the rope with him with the intention of stashing it in the equipment shed like he'd done the previous night. As he approached the shed, the hairs at the nape of his neck pricked with awareness. It was too quiet, too deserted. They were supposed to be looking for him. Even if they assumed he'd went for the road, instead of returning to the commune, Nick had expected more vigilance.

He decided to leave the coil of rope by the side of the road. He knelt to hide his cell phone in a notch of a fence-post before continuing down the path. He gave the shed a wide berth, all of his senses on high alert. No one jumped out to ambush him. The scent of burning wood carried on the wind, along with the acrid odor of male sweat.

A stranger's sweat.

The crunch of gravel indicated a presence at Nick's back. Someone had been lurking behind the shed, not hiding inside it. The man had moved around the perimeter to escape detection as Nick passed by.

Nick couldn't believe it. He'd let an amateur sneak up on him.

He whirled around to see a dark figure wielding a wooden club. It was Brother Sage, and he swung his weapon with the fury of a man scorned. The club connected with Nick's temple. Nick staggered to the ground, his head exploding. He watched the stars bleed across the sky. Then utter darkness.

Chapter 21

Jonah shoved her to the dirt floor as soon as they'd reached the last step.

Avery crawled to a dark corner and stayed there, hugging her knees to her chest. Jonah lit a kerosene lamp to illuminate the space. The torch he'd discarded lay flickering between them. She thought about going for it, and trying to defend herself against further harm, but she was afraid to anger him. Her face still stung from the blow he'd dealt her. Challenging him didn't seem wise. He was bigger and stronger than her, so she couldn't overpower him. Trying to outsmart him was the better option.

She would let him calm down. Reason with him.

He kicked the torch aside, out of her reach. "I remember you," he said. "I remember Hannah."

She stayed quiet, her heart pounding. She wondered how he knew. Had Grace told Jeremiah about her visit, or had Imogen recognized her?

His gaze wandered down her body. "You've changed."

"I'm not Hannah."

"I had a crush on you, even then. I saw how my father looked at you." He stepped closer. "It's ironic, isn't it? If you hadn't left The Haven, he would have taken you as a bride. He would have ruined you long before I got the chance."

Panic gripped her. She stared at him in silence.

"You escaped that fate, but you won't escape this one."

She started scooting backward, against a row of dusty shelves. "Don't do this."

Jonah followed her. He crouched down and touched her hair, rubbing the strands between his fingers. "You're a little old for his taste, but you fit his type. Natural blonde. Pretty blue eyes. He was practically salivating over you on the pulpit."

She cringed, turning her head to one side.

He swept his fingertips over her bruised cheek. "Tell me, was he aroused during the faith healing session?" When she didn't answer, he grabbed a handful of her hair again. "Speaking of arousal, I never believed your ridiculous lies about Nick. I went to your cabin tonight, after Imogen came to me with her suspicions. I smelled the sheets." He leaned closer, inhaling deep. "You still reek of him."

"What suspicions?" Avery asked.

"Hmm?"

"What were Imogen's suspicions?"

"She brought me an old photo of Hannah. I admit, I didn't see the resemblance at first. You look very different now. I wasn't convinced it was you until we found you in the cemetery, weeping at your mother's grave."

Avery's mind raced at this news. Jonah knew who she

was, but he didn't know why she was here. She could use that to her advantage. She could use psychology to her advantage, too. Jonah wasn't making sexual threats out of the blue. All behaviors had a reason. Avery remembered what he'd said earlier about asking his father to bless him with a bride. It must have been a fairly recent request, because Jonah hadn't been eligible for marriage for that long. There were only a few young, unwed women available.

He would have had to pick from Nadine, Isobel, Imogen or… Grace.

"It was Grace," she murmured, in a flash of insight. "You asked for Grace, and Father Jeff denied you."

Jonah's gaze sharpened. "Very astute."

Avery studied him quietly. Grace would have been eighteen when Jonah turned twenty-eight. Her pale blonde beauty made her the best prize of the bunch. She looked angelic, and that was enough. Jonah wouldn't have been deterred by her headstrong attitude. He controlled his world and everyone in it. The challenge of molding her into a proper bride had probably appealed to him. Of course, Grace would have also caught the attention of Father Jeff, who favored innocent blondes. Instead of waiting for Grace to mature and giving her to Jonah, Father Jeff had taken her as his own bride.

"I'm sorry he did that to you," Avery said. "He's a cruel man."

"Spare me your false empathy."

"You should be the leader here. The only leader." She placed a hand on his shoulder. "We can help each other."

He smiled at the offer. "Can we?"

"You can have it all, Jonah. The commune, the compound, Grace. Your father is a sinner, and he's slipping. He doesn't care about The Haven anymore. When he goes down, everything will be yours for the taking."

"What about you?"

"What about me?"

"Will you be mine for the taking?"

Avery moistened her lips. She wanted to stroke his ego, but she could go only so far. Surely he didn't believe she would stay here with him.

"Maybe I'd rather have you than Grace," he mused. "In retrospect, she was a bad match. Immature. Unimaginative. You're much more intriguing. Plus, I've seen you naked. I have to agree with Nick. No other woman compares."

She flushed at the compliment. He was toying with her.

"Who is he to you? I know he's not your husband. He looks at you with too much desire. A hired investigator, perhaps?"

"Go to hell."

"You were always clever," Jonah said. "But not clever enough, apparently. I can't imagine why you would come back here. You have no family in the current membership. It doesn't make sense."

"Your father is going to be arrested for his crimes," she said.

"What crimes?"

"Caleb's murder. I'm sure he ordered it."

Jonah frowned. "Caleb's not dead. He's in the outside militia."

"Who told you that?"

"Jeremiah."

"You think they let Caleb live, after he fathered Grace's baby?"

Jonah shoved her down on the ground and crushed his palm over her mouth. "You're a liar and a whore. I don't care what happened to Caleb. He got the punishment he deserved, and so will you."

Avery tried to scream, but she couldn't draw breath. She tasted blood from the inside of her cheek again. He was pressing his fingers into the bruise. She groped the dirt floor for a blunt object to strike him with and came up empty. She was about to use her fists to pummel his back when a knock sounded at the door above them.

"What?" Jonah asked.

"They found Brother Nick by the cemetery." It was Imogen. "Jeremiah wants you there."

Avery struggled against Jonah's hold. He released her and rolled away, breathing heavily. She didn't know what kind of assault he'd intended. She was glad for Imogen's interruption, and terrified for Nick. Tears flooded her eyes.

"Don't hurt him. Please."

Jonah laughed at the pathetic request. "What should I do, slap him on the wrist?"

"He's not a private investigator, Jonah. He's FBI. His team is coming as we speak."

"How does he communicate with this team? He has no means—" Jonah broke off as he realized his mistake. "The watch."

She stayed quiet, afraid to confirm his guess.

"You bitch," he said, his jaw slack with disbelief. He wasn't used to being outmaneuvered.

Above them, Imogen knocked again. "Jonah?"

"I'm coming," he shouted, rising to his feet. He kicked dirt at the torch to extinguish it. Then he pointed at Avery. "If he's not dead yet, I'm going to kill him. Then I'll come back and deal with you."

He took the lamp with him and climbed the steps. Casting her into darkness.

* * *

Nick came back to life, little by little.

He was no longer on the dirt road by the shed. He was still on his back, staring up at the stars, but the ground beneath him felt like grass. His hair and face were dusty. His head throbbed from the knockout blow. He touched the goose egg at his temple. Blood had dried in gritty streaks along his jaw.

When he tried to sit up, nausea gripped him. Bile came rushing up his throat. He rolled onto his side and retched in the grass. Thankfully, he didn't have much in his stomach. He wiped his mouth and glanced around, trying to take stock of his situation.

It was bad. He wasn't restrained, probably because he'd been unconscious, but there was no hope for escape. He was surrounded by armed guards. Brother Sage stood at a distance, holding his caveman club. Nick realized it was an extinguished torch. Either way, it packed a wallop.

Nick reached into his pocket for his watch. Gone.

Although his vision was fuzzy, he could make out rectangular shapes nearby. They were placed in neat rows, evenly spaced. There was something familiar about this place. Had he seen it in the aerial photos?

Nick's stomach lurched again as the shapes came into focus. They were headstones. He was in the graveyard.

And he was a dead man.

He closed his eyes, wincing. He felt like a corpse, stiff-limbed and numb, but he wasn't actually dead. Dead men didn't vomit. He couldn't move, and it was hard to think. He tried to remember what had happened.

Brother Sage had clocked him. He knew that much. Nick didn't know why he'd done it. The minutes before the incident were blank. There had been stars in the sky.

He'd been near the shed for some reason. He strained for more details, his brain pulsing like a sore thumb.

Avery. He'd been with Avery.

He grasped that memory and held on tight. He'd been in bed with Avery. Was that a dream, or a fantasy? It seemed too good to be true. Images and sensations drifted across his fractured psyche. Her naked body, like rose petals. Cool water from the sink. Her mouth moving up and down on him.

Yes. That was real.

He couldn't puzzle out the sequence of events after leaving her bed, so he didn't try. He replayed the good parts of the evening, half-conscious. There were a lot of good parts. He sank into them.

A slap of cold water brought him back to his senses. He sat upright, gasping for air. Someone had doused him with a bucket. Nick wiped his face with the edge of his shirt. He felt more alert now, but his thoughts were still muddled.

Jeremiah stood over him with a 9mm handgun. "Rise and shine, Princess."

Nick recognized the gun as the same model that had been used in Chris's murder. A ballistics test could prove the match with 100 percent certainty, but Nick didn't need it. He'd never believed the man who'd confessed to the crime had done it. Jeremiah had killed Chris. He'd probably killed Caleb, too. And now he would kill Nick.

"Nice Ruger," Nick said, lumbering to his feet. As he stood, the pruning hook he'd tucked into his boot pressed against his ankle. Whoever had searched him for weapons hadn't done a thorough job. "Is that an SR-9?"

"The last guy who looked at my gun didn't live to tell about it. Was he a friend of yours?"

"You mean Brother Caleb?"

Jeremiah's gaze narrowed. "You know who I mean. He begged for his life. Offered me all kinds of favors. Cried like a girl, too."

At one time, an insult to Chris's memory would have sent Nick into a blind rage. Now it had no impact whatsoever. Nick didn't believe Jeremiah, and he didn't care. This mission had never really been about Chris. It had been about Nick's guilt. Avenging Chris would never absolve Nick of his sins.

Jonah arrived on the scene. Not close enough to get hurt, but close enough to listen. The rest of the men, including Sage, had left the area. That was a mistake. By eliminating the witnesses, they'd given Nick better odds. Now it was two against one. If Nick could get the blade out of his boot, he might have a chance.

Jeremiah switched tactics. "I like your woman, Brother Nick. I'm going to visit her as soon as I'm done with you."

This threat was more effective than his previous taunts. "Where is she?"

Jeremiah laughed, enjoying himself. "She's waiting for us. We're going to take turns, right, Jonah?"

"Quit toying with him," Jonah said. "We still have to get rid of his body."

"You can bury me with Caleb," Nick suggested. "The grave's already open."

Jeremiah raised his gun. "Shut up."

"I've been wondering about something," Nick said, splitting a glance between them. "I know you'll kill for Father Jeff, but are you expected to share your wives with him, too? Is that what passes for quality family time around here?"

Jeremiah hit him across the face with the butt of his gun. Which hurt like hell, and made his vision blur again. Nick staggered to his knees, gasping in pain. "I'm going to have a shiner like Isobel."

"I told you to shut up," Jeremiah said.

"Finish him," Jonah said.

Jeremiah was a belligerent moron who didn't like being told what to do. "Why don't you finish him, brother? This is your mess, not mine. You invited him here. You're the one who wants him dead."

"Father wants him dead."

"Yeah? He didn't give me the order."

"What difference does it make? He's a cop."

While they argued, Jeremiah lost focus. He let the gun drop a few inches. Just enough to give Nick an opening to attack. Nick couldn't afford to waste his chance by fumbling in his boot, so he used his body as a weapon instead. Nick drove his shoulder into Jeremiah's midsection and took him to the ground. The gun fired, but the bullet went wide, ricocheting off a nearby headstone. Nick had the better leverage, and he took advantage of it. He grasped Jeremiah's wrist and slammed his gun hand against the hard ground in three rapid successions. When this didn't work, Nick head-butted him.

Desperate times called for desperate measures.

Jeremiah's weapon hand finally loosened. The gun slid from his fingers, out of reach. Nick's brain was rattled, the wound at his temple bleeding into his eyes, but he still had the will to fight. He drew back his right arm and punched Jeremiah in the jaw. Jeremiah returned the favor with a brutal cross. Nick's mouth filled with blood.

They rolled across the grass, locked in battle. Nick could feel himself weakening. Jeremiah was the stronger opponent, and he wasn't suffering from a head wound.

Nick had to go for the kill, or he would lose.

The next time Jeremiah landed a blow, Nick went limp. He let Jeremiah pummel his midsection and bruise his ribs. Nick absorbed the impact without responding. When Jeremiah spat in his face, Nick didn't flinch.

Jeremiah turned and raised his arms in victory. Nick drew the hook from his boot, standing. With a brutal leap, he jumped on Jeremiah's back and buried the hook in his throat. The sharp tool cut deep into his carotid artery.

Jeremiah made a strange gurgling sound and shook Nick loose. Nick went sprawling in the dirt as Jeremiah yanked the hook free. That was a fatal error, but he was already a goner. Blood sprayed from the wound, gushing down his shirtfront like a river. He clapped a hand over his neck, but he couldn't stanch the flow.

He fell forward, dead before he hit the ground.

Nick studied his lifeless body, feeling numb. He'd done what he'd come to do. He'd achieved his vengeance in the most gruesome way imaginable. But now he didn't want it anymore. He only wanted Avery, and he'd already lost her. Even if they both survived, she'd never forgive him.

The physical exertion took its toll. Nick didn't have the strength to rise. When Jonah reached him, gun in hand, Nick held up his palms. Then his stomach rebelled, so he rolled over and dry-heaved in the grass again.

"You killed my brother."

Nick shuddered and wiped his face, leaving a smear of blood. "He had it coming."

"I'm not like him. I'm not like my father."

Nick didn't argue, because Jonah had a gun trained on him.

"I'm not like them," he insisted. "I knew violence would be their downfall. I vowed to rise above it."

Nick just stared at him. Jonah didn't appear to be rising above it, at the moment.

"I finally realized that it didn't matter if I was the better man. People don't follow my father because he's good. They follow him because he's magnetic. It has nothing to do with purity of the soul, or lightness of the spirit. The words of his sermons don't matter. They respond to the performance."

Nick wondered if he could take the gun from Jonah without getting shot. He really didn't want to grapple with him. He was exhausted. "Where's Ellen?"

"Do you mean Hannah?"

"Yes."

"She told me you have a team coming. Is that true?"

"Yes."

The first light of dawn glowed at the edge of the horizon. Nick could hear a helicopter approaching.

"That's them."

"I guess I should get on with it."

"You can testify against your father, Jonah. It's not too late. You can still be a better man. You can rise above this."

Jonah's green eyes filled with tears. He lifted the gun and pulled the trigger.

Chapter 22

Three weeks later

Avery entered her apartment and locked the door behind her.

She tossed aside her purse before collapsing on the couch. It had been an emotional roller coaster of a day. She'd visited Grace and her baby at the hospital. Avery had held the tiny, downy-haired newborn and cried her eyes out. She'd cried for her mother, and for her little sister, who'd never had the chance to live. Finally, she'd cried for Nick.

Grace had patted Avery's shoulder in sympathy. New motherhood had softened her sharp edges a little. Either that, or they were giving her some good painkillers. Before Avery left, she promised to stay in touch.

In the aftermath of the chaos at The Haven, Grace had become the state's leading witness against Jeff

Silva. She'd overheard him ordering Jeremiah to kill Caleb, the baby's father. She'd watched the guards beat Caleb to a pulp. Although she hadn't seen the actual execution, his dead body told the tale well enough. Jeremiah's Ruger SR-9 had delivered the fatal bullet.

Father Jeff had been arrested for a litany of crimes, including marijuana cultivation without a permit, and several charges of conspiracy to commit murder. Three other bodies had been found in the woods near the commune. They all belonged to former members, young males who'd disappeared under the guise of holy service.

The fact that Father Jeff hadn't killed them with his own hands didn't matter. He was a Manson-like figure with total control over the cult and everyone in it. The man who'd confessed to shooting Special Agent Chris Davidson retracted his statement. He'd admitted to witnessing the murder, which had been directed by Jeff Silva and carried out by Jeremiah.

Without Father Jeff, the entire community fell apart. He'd been proved a false prophet. Avery heard that Nadine and Brent ran away together. Isobel was devastated by Jeremiah's death, but free of his abuse.

Imogen had been inconsolable. She'd refused to believe that Jonah had shot himself. She blamed herself for his downfall. She'd recognized Avery as Hannah, and run straight to Jonah with her suspicions, setting the awful events into motion.

Avery bore her no ill will, but Imogen's hysteria had caused Avery a lot of suffering in the hours of the raid. She'd been locked in the dark cellar all morning while law enforcement searched the commune. Nick, who'd been beaten within an inch of his life, refused medical treatment until she was found. Imogen hadn't told anyone where Avery was. She'd been too busy weeping over Jonah's dead body.

When Nick finally found Avery, she'd been in a state of acute shock. She'd assumed that Nick had been killed, and that she would be next. She'd cowered in the dark, musty space, imagining awful things. At one point she'd broken a glass bottle to use as a weapon. She'd clutched a shard so tight, she'd cut her hand to the bone. She'd completely lost her grip on reality, and seeing Nick alive didn't help. His face had been mis-shapen and bloody. Instead of hugging him in relief, she'd screamed in horror.

Needless to say, their reunion hadn't been romantic.

They'd spoken only once in the days that followed. The conversation had been brief and stilted. He was under investigation for the steps he'd taken to recruit her. They weren't supposed to be in contact, but he'd called to apologize, and to encourage her to tell the truth.

She hadn't. Not the whole truth, anyway. When two agents came to her apartment to interview her, she'd explained that Nick had tricked her into believing Grace was her sister. They'd told her that Nick had confessed to the deception, and the misuse of depart-ment resources. She'd just corroborated his story. The lies she'd told were ones of omission. She'd withheld the intimate details of their relationship. Perhaps he'd done the same, because the agents hadn't grilled her about it.

Aunt Ruth *had* grilled her about it, and so had her best friend, Corrine. Avery had spent the previous weekend at Chuck and Laura's house, for the birth-day party of their youngest son. Avery couldn't escape Ruth's questions, so she'd answered them honestly. She'd embraced the family time with open arms.

Something had changed inside her. She'd faced the
demons of her past, and she was stronger for it. She
might not have seemed strong, after that stint in the cellar, but she'd survived. Nightmares from her childhood
no longer haunted her. She didn't sleep easily, however.
She was plagued by dreams of Nick.

She couldn't help it. She still wanted him. She admitted this to Corinne, who'd squealed with delight
and congratulated her on having a red-hot affair with a
sexy undercover agent. She'd admitted it to Ruth, who'd
hugged her tight. Neither woman suggested the relationship would work out. They were happy she'd taken the
risk, and they believed she was a survivor. She would
survive the heartache.

Avery wasn't so sure. Holding Grace's baby had shat-
tered her into pieces. There were too many feelings to
process. Her chest ached from the weight of them. She
hated Nick for putting her through this. She hated herself for loving him.

She knew she should forget him. He wouldn't call
while the investigation was ongoing. He might not call
after. Then she would know he'd lied about everything,
and she could move on with her life.

Until then, she was in limbo. She wouldn't go back
to work until August. She'd signed up for a school psychology conference next week. The weather was beautiful, but she didn't feel like going out. She felt like
wallowing in misery.

While she burrowed into the couch, hugging a pillow to her chest, she thought of the kitten she'd meant
to adopt. It had probably gone to another home. Tears
pricked her eyes. She swiped them away, dragging in
a rough breath.

A knock at her door brought her out of her sad reverie. Her pulse skyrocketed, because she knew that knock.

It was Nick.

He was standing on her doorstep, as he'd done twice before. His face was no longer grotesquely swollen, as it had been the last time she'd seen him. He'd healed completely. She almost couldn't tell he'd sustained any injuries. There was a faint hint of a bruise under his left eye, and his nose wasn't quite as straight as it had been. His hair looked like it had been touched up by a barber. He was wearing a basic T-shirt and dark jeans. He was so handsome, her breath caught in her throat.

"Can I come in?" he asked, tentative.

She stepped aside to allow him entrance. After she closed the door behind him, they stared at each other for a long moment. His eyes never left her face.

"You look good," he said.

"So do you."

His gaze trailed down her body, taking in her tank top and flowy skirt. Her mascara was probably smudged from crying over the baby, but he'd seen her without makeup. He'd seen her *naked* and without makeup.

"You…take my breath away."

Although he sounded sincere, the flattery didn't affect her. There was so much more between them than surface attraction, and she was feeling bleak. She'd been crying over a kitten she'd never met two minutes ago. If he thought he could come in here and make everything better with a few compliments, he was wrong.

"I'm sorry," he said in a low voice. "I'm already screwing this up."

"Why don't we sit down? I have iced tea."

"That would be great."

She poured two glasses and brought them to the coffee table. He sat down across from her, just as he had the night they'd met. He drank in nervous gulps. His forehead was damp with perspiration, which struck her as endearing. She was glad this wasn't easy for him. She sipped her tea coolly, waiting for him to speak.

"There's no excuse for what I did," he said. "It was unprofessional, and unethical. Immoral. It was the worst thing I've ever done, basically. I prioritized my revenge over your safety, and I hate myself for it. I thought I could protect you from danger, but I didn't. I failed on every level."

Avery had been wondering about a few specific details. "Did you enhance the photo of Grace to make her look like my mother?"

"I enhanced it to make her look like you. Power of suggestion did the rest."

"Did Ellen really have an accident?"

His brows rose in surprise. "Yes. I would never have recruited you otherwise."

"What else did you lie about?"

"I withheld information more than I lied."

"What did you withhold information about?"

"The watch," he said, holding her gaze. "It wasn't recording us."

"And?"

"I was there to investigate Jeff Silva, but I suspected Jeremiah of shooting my colleague. He became my main target."

"You got what you wanted, then."

"No," he said softly. "I wanted you. If I could do it all over again—"

"That's the thing, Nick. You can't."

He went silent for a moment, studying her face. "You were right about my motivations. I was obsessed with completing the mission because I felt responsible for Chris's death. The guilt was eating me up inside. Eventually, I realized that avenging him wouldn't make any difference."

"Then why did you come back that night?"

"What do you mean?"

"You were outside the gate. You'd discovered Caleb's grave. You could have gone to the road and been safe. Instead, you came back to kill Jeremiah."

"No," he said quietly. "I came back for you."

She rose from the couch, troubled by his announcement. "That doesn't make sense. There were guards everywhere. They were looking for you."

He stood with her. "The guards were amateurs."

"They were heavily armed amateurs. You could have waited until your team arrived. Why didn't you?"

"Because I promised to protect you with my life."

She paced the living room, her arms crossed over her chest. "You thought you could protect me by walking into a situation where you were sure to be killed on the spot?"

"That's kind of the deal, isn't it? I said I'd risk my life, and I did."

"You had nothing to gain."

"I had everything to gain," he said, his voice rising with agitation. "I couldn't just walk away and leave you. I couldn't wait hours for backup. Jonah had you in the cellar." He closed the distance between them, cupping her face. His thumb swept over her cheek. "I know he hit you. What else did he do?"

"Nothing."

"He didn't get the chance to do more, because I came back."

She pulled away from him. "You shouldn't have left!"

"You're right," he said. "I shouldn't have taken you there, and I shouldn't have left you alone. I knew Jonah was getting suspicious. Time was running out for me to collect evidence. I should have escaped with you."

She arched a brow. "Instead of sleeping with me?"

He inclined his head, guilty as charged. "I was reckless and impulsive in more ways than one. I shouldn't have touched you."

She swallowed past the lump in her throat, because this part hurt the most. "You used me."

"No. Not in the sense you mean."

"You used sex to keep me quiet and docile," she exploded. "You screwed me into oblivion so you could get away!"

He had the grace to look embarrassed. "That wasn't planned."

"Wasn't it?"

"I didn't seduce you, Avery. If memory serves, you begged me to touch you. Perhaps you remember whispering in my ear? 'Please, more, yes, right there'?"

It was her turn to flush.

"I took you to bed because I couldn't control myself. I wasn't thinking about the case. I wasn't thinking about anything beyond having you, as many times as possible."

Some of her anger drained away, and warmth crept in. His eyes blazed with passionate sincerity. "Mission accomplished," she said lightly.

"Not even close," he replied.

She shivered at the implication that he wasn't done with her. He hadn't come here just to apologize. Desire thrummed between them, stronger than ever.

"I've replayed that night over and over again in my

mind," he said. "It seems like a fantasy now. Something I invented, too good to be real."

"It was real," she murmured. She'd also spent more than a few evenings reexamining every moment. "Did you get in trouble for that?"

"I wasn't interrogated about it. I would have told the truth, if they asked. The internal investigation focused on your recruitment."

Avery was glad the investigators hadn't learned about their sexual relationship. For all Nick's faults, she couldn't blame him for that weakness. She had begged him to touch her, and she believed him when he said it wasn't a planned seduction. They'd both been out of control, unable to resist each other. "What was the result?"

"I admitted to misconduct and tendered my resignation."

Her jaw dropped. "You didn't."

"I did, but my SAC wouldn't accept it. He wanted to take down Jeff Silva just as much as I did, so he was willing to overlook the ethics violations. Everyone in the department was clapping me on the back. McDonald cared more about the outcome than my tactics. A misconduct demotion would smear his reputation and ruin mine. He couldn't promote me, either. We worked something else out."

"What?"

"A lateral transfer. It will keep my record clean. I requested placement in the Portland field office, under Richards. I won't be doing any more undercover work. She needs an experienced homicide investigator."

She gaped at him in disbelief. "Why would you transfer to Portland?"

"To be near you."

She was speechless.

Nick grasped her upper arms, imploring her to listen. "I don't expect you to forgive me, but I have to tell you how I feel. I love you, Avery. I want to spend the rest of my life with you. I will never lie to you again, and I'll do anything to regain your trust."

She stared at his mouth, unsure she'd heard him correctly.

He released her arms with a frown. "It's too soon. Of course it's too soon. I shouldn't have said all that. I just wanted to let you know that I'll be here, if you ever decide to give me another chance."

She moistened her trembling lips.

"If you don't, I'll be here anyway," he said, nodding. "I'm not going anywhere. I'll wait forever."

She had to be clear. "You…love me?"

"I love you."

"Since when?"

"Since…before that night."

"Really?"

"Yes. I was in love with you before we slept together. After, there was no question."

"You'll do anything for me."

"Anything." He proved it by falling to his knees before her and twining his arms around her waist. "Please, let me make it up to you."

She stroked her fingers through his short hair. "I love you, too."

He glanced up at her in awe. "You do?"

"Since before that night."

"You're kidding."

"No. I've spent the past three weeks in agony, wondering how to get over you."

He rose to his feet again. "You want to get over me?"

"I don't think I can. You've ruined me for other men."

He offered a wolfish smile. "I guess that's only fair, because I can't live without you."

She wrapped her arms around him. "I'm glad."

He crushed his mouth over hers, kissing her breathless.

"Tell me," she murmured against his lips. "How were you planning to make it up to me?"

With a low groan, he swept her off her feet and carried her to the bedroom to show her. They spent the entire afternoon tangled in each other. He demonstrated his love and devotion until they were both dizzy with exhaustion.

There were no nightmares after she fell asleep. No memories of the commune plagued her in the wee hours of the morning. She stayed in the safe haven of Nick's arms for the remainder of the weekend.

By the end of it, they were planning the rest of their lives together.

* * * * *

*Don't miss these other exciting titles
from Susan Cliff!*

Stranded with the Navy SEAL
Navy SEAL Rescue
Witness on the Run

WE HOPE YOU ENJOYED
THIS BOOK FROM

HARLEQUIN
ROMANTIC SUSPENSE

Danger. Passion. Drama.

These heart-racing page-turners will keep you guessing to the very end. Experience the thrill of unexpected plot twists and irresistible chemistry.

4 NEW BOOKS AVAILABLE EVERY MONTH!

COMING NEXT MONTH FROM

HARLEQUIN
ROMANTIC SUSPENSE

Available June 2, 2020

#2091 HUNTING THE COLTON FUGITIVE
The Coltons of Mustang Valley
by Colleen Thompson

Sparks—and bullets—fly when Sierra Madden, a bounty hunter with loan sharks on her tail, and framed fugitive Ace Colton team up to find out who really shot his father. The Colton family holds tremendous power, which puts them in mortal danger...

#2092 COLTON'S LAST STAND
The Coltons of Mustang Valley • by Karen Whiddon

FBI agent Fiona Evans has been sent undercover to investigate a cult. When the cult leader's supposed son, rancher Jake Anderson, appears on the scene, they both have a hard time focusing on stopping his mother's machinations as their attraction burns brighter.

#2093 DANGEROUS REUNION
by Marilyn Pappano

A family goes missing, throwing Cedar Creek in turmoil. Former ADA Yashi Baker destroyed Detective Ben Little Bear and their relationship with one cross-examination on the witness stand years ago. But the kidnapping draws them together, forcing them to revisit a love lost.

#2094 SHIELDED IN THE SHADOWS
Where Secrets are Safe • by Tara Taylor Quinn

A probation officer and a prosecutor team up to protect a woman in danger from an unknown abuser. As they work through a treacherous case, love never enters the equation... until their attraction becomes too hard—and lethal—to ignore.

———————

HRSCNM0520

Shots rang out. At first, Jayden Powell thought a car
had backfired. Ducking behind a tree by instinct, he
identified the source as gunfire seconds before the sound
came again and he fell backward with the force to his
chest. Upper right. The only part not shielded by the
trunk he'd been using for cover.

Lying still, in agony, his head turned to the side on
the unevenly cut lawn, Jayden played dead, figuring that
was what the perp wanted: him dead. Praying that it was
enough. That the guy wouldn't shoot again, just for spite.
Or kicks.

A blade of grass stuck up his nose. Tickling. Irritating.
Damn. If he sneezed, he'd be dead. Killed again—by a
sneeze. Did his breathing show? Should he try to hold
his breath?

Why wasn't he hearing sirens?

They were in Santa Raquel, California. It was an oceanside town with full police protection—not some burg where they had to wait on County, like some of the other places he served.

His nose twitched. Had to be two blades of grass. One up inside trying to crawl back into his throat. One poking at the edge of his nostril. Maybe if his chest burned a little more, he wouldn't notice.

Where the hell was Jasper? His sometime partner and fellow probation officer, Leon Jasper, had waited in the car on this one, just as Jayden, the senior of the two, had insisted. Luke Wallace was Jayden's offender. His newest client. He preferred first meetings to be one-on-one.

Good thing, too, or Leon would be lying right next to him—and the guy had a wife with a kid on the way. A boy. No…maybe a girl. Had he actually heard yet?

Jayden was going to sneeze. If he took another breath, he'd be dead for sure. Maybe just a small inhale through the mouth. Slow and long and easy, just like he'd been doing. Right?

Shouldn't have let his mouth fall open. Now he had grass there, too. It tasted like sour bugs and…

Sirens blared in the distance. An unmistakable sound. Thank God.

ᴸ84ᴼ

Get 4 FREE REWARDS!

We'll send you 2 FREE Books
<u>plus</u> 2 FREE Mystery Gifts.

Harlequin Romantic Suspense books are heart-racing page-turners with unexpected plot twists and irresistible chemistry that will keep you guessing to the very end.

FREE
Value Over
$20

YES! Please send me 2 FREE Harlequin Romantic Suspense novels and my 2 FREE gifts (gifts are worth about $10 retail). After receiving them, if I don't wish to receive any more books, I can return the shipping statement marked "cancel." If I don't cancel, I will receive 4 brand-new novels every month and be billed just $4.99 per book in the U.S. or $5.74 per book in Canada. That's a savings of at least 13% off the cover price! It's quite a bargain! Shipping and handling is just 50¢ per book in the U.S. and $1.25 per book in Canada.* I understand that accepting the 2 free books and gifts places me under no obligation to buy anything. I can always return a shipment and cancel at any time. The free books and gifts are mine to keep no matter what I decide.

240/340 HDN GNMZ

Name (please print)

Address   Apt. #

City   State/Province   Zip/Postal Code

Mail to the **Reader Service:**
IN U.S.A.: P.O. Box 1341, Buffalo, NY 14240-8531
IN CANADA: P.O. Box 603, Fort Erie, Ontario L2A 5X3

Want to try 2 free books from another series! Call 1-800-873-8635 or visit www.ReaderService.com.

*Terms and prices subject to change without notice. Prices do not include sales taxes, which will be charged (if applicable) based on your state or country of residence. Canadian residents will be charged applicable taxes. Offer not valid in Quebec. This offer is limited to one order per household. Books received may not be as shown. Not valid for current subscribers to Harlequin Romantic Suspense books. All orders subject to approval. Credit or debit balances in a customer's account(s) may be offset by any other outstanding balance owed by or to the customer. Please allow 4 to 6 weeks for delivery. Offer available while quantities last.

Your Privacy—The Reader Service is committed to protecting your privacy. Our Privacy Policy is available online at www.ReaderService.com or upon request from the Reader Service. We make a portion of our mailing list available to reputable third parties that offer products we believe may interest you. If you prefer that we not exchange your name with third parties, or if you wish to clarify or modify your communication preferences, please visit us at www.ReaderService.com/consumerschoice or write to us at Reader Service Preference Service, P.O. Box 9062, Buffalo, NY 14240-9062. Include your complete name and address.

HRS20R

"You're wrong on several counts, Annabelle." He leaned forward, the noise of his movement drawing her attention, the proximity of his body making her pulse spark to life with renewed fervor. "I intend for our marriage to be real in every way—meaning for as long as we both shall live. As for pretending we're something we're not, we don't need to do that."

Her heart had started to beat faster. Her breath was thin. "What exactly does a 'real' marriage mean?"

"That we become a family. We live together. We share a bedroom, a bed. We raise our son as parents. It means you have my full support in every way."

It was too much. Too much kindness and too much expectation. She'd thought he would be angry with her when he learned the truth, and that she could have handled. If he'd wanted to fight, she could have fought, but this was impossible to combat. The idea of sharing his bed...

"Sharing a home is one thing, but as for the rest—"

"You object to being a family?"

He was being deliberately obtuse.

She forced herself to be brave and say what was on her mind. "You think I'm going to fall back into bed with you after this many years, just because we have a son together?"

His smile was mocking, his eyes teasing. "No, Annabelle. I think you're going to fall back into bed with me because you still want me as much as you did then. You don't need to pretend sleeping with me will be a hardship."

Her jaw dropped and she sucked in a harsh gulp of air. "You are so arrogant."

His laugh was soft, his shoulders lifting in a broad shrug. "Yes." His eyes narrowed. "But am I wrong?"

Don't miss
An Heir Claimed by Christmas,
available December 2020 wherever
Harlequin Presents books and ebooks are sold.

Harlequin.com

Get 4 FREE REWARDS!

We'll send you 2 FREE Books plus 2 FREE Mystery Gifts.

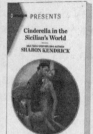

Harlequin Presents books feature the glamorous lives of royals and billionaires in a world of exotic locations, where passion knows no bounds.

FREE Value Over $20
